Cold
Blood V

Cold Blood V

Edited by Peter Seller and John North

Sundial

an imprint of

Mosaic Press
Oakville - Buffalo - London

Canadian Cataloguing in Publication Data

Main entry under title:

Cold Blood V

ISBN 0-88962-570-0

1. Detective and myustery stories, Canadian (English).*
I. Sellers, Peter, 1956

PS8323.D4C642 1994   C813'.087208   C94-931767-5
PR9197.35.D48C642 1994

Published by MOSAIC PRESS, P.O. Box 1032, Oakville, Ontario, L6J 5E9, Canada. Offices and warehouse at 1252 Speers Road, Units #1&2, Oakville, Ontario, L6L 5N9, Canada and Mosaic Press, 85 River Rock Drive, Suite 202, Buffalo, N.Y., 14207, USA.

Mosaic Press acknowledges the assistance of the Canada Council, the Ontario Arts Council, the Ontario Ministry of Culture, Tourism and Recreation and the Dept. of Communications, Government of Canada, for their support of our publishing programme.

$\mathcal{S}$undial an imprint of Mosaic Press
Copyright © Peter Sellers, 1994

Cover and book design by Susan Parker
Printed and bound in Canada
ISBN 0-88962-578-6 PB

In Canada:
MOSAIC PRESS, 1252 Speers Road, Units #1&2, Oakville, Ontario, L6L 5N9, Canada. P.O. Box 1032, Oakville, Ontario, L6J 5E9
In the United States:
Mosaic Press, 85 River Rock Drive, Suite 202, Buffalo, N.Y., 14207

TABLE OF CONTENTS

INTRODUCTION

Back in 1986, nobody wanted to publish the first volume of Cold Blood. One of the biggest obstacles seemed to be the concern that there wouldn't be enough original material of sufficiently high quality to warrant one book, let alone a series. Well, use the W.P. Kinsella line that has now become a cliche, "If you build it, they will come."

The first Cold Blood book, released in February, 1987, received virtually no unsolicited submissions. Instead, it was pulled together from available original material by the prominent likes of Ted Wood, Eric Wright and Tony Aspler along with reprints including two stories by non-Canadian authors (American Edward D. Hoch and Britain's Tim Heald). The reviews were very good.

By the time Cold Blood II was in the works, unsolicited manuscripts had begun arriving. The number received has gone up every volume since, to the point where Cold Blood V received over 150 unsolicited manuscripts. Each book has been critically praised. Each book has sold increasingly well. And stories from the first four volumes have been nominated for a total of 11 Arthur Ellis Awards, winning twice.

Number V boasts the tried and true Cold Blood formulas: a mix of new voices along with the reliable veterans. So Ted Wood and Eric Wright and William Bankier stand alongside Sue Pike and Maureen Jennings and Mary Jane Maffini. They are united between the covers by a talent for a very difficult craft.

Cold Blood V also boasts a new co-editor. Arthur Ellis Award nominated short story writer and Toronto Star crime fiction reviewer John North shared the enormous task of dealing with the overwhelming volume of stories submitted. He has been a Cold Blood fixture since his first published story appeared in volume II. Now, his presence will be even more greatly felt.

Stories originally published in the books have been reprinted in magazines, in other anthologies, in school textbooks and been recorded on audio tape.

Over seven years, and now five volumes, Cold Blood has provided Canadian authors with an ongoing market for short crime fiction. It's also provided readers with the opportunity to relish the finest such stories available.

Special thanks goes to Howard Aster at Mosaic Press who saw the potential of the series and has supported it every step of the way. We've built it. Now come on in and enjoy.

Peter Sellers
Toronto, June, 1994

Murder In The Green

TED WOOD

Ted Wood, a.k.a. Jack Barnao is the creator of two series of successful novels featuring the characters of Reid Bennett and John Locke. He is one of the only two authors with a story in every volume of the Cold Blood series.

The soggy lawn squelched under their feet and Cassidy looked down distastefully. "Why'd anybody bother to murder the guy? He'd've caught his death of cold in a couple more days camped out here, dumb bastard."

Wall sniffed. "Show some respect for his civil liberties. He was making a statement, picketing Queen's Park. Ask any of these other cold, wet dimwits."

They reached the tent where the uniformed officer was standing. A gaggle of protesters, the men all with beards, the women all without make-up, had formed around the tent. They were hectoring the officer who was enduring them, as he was enduring the thin November rain.

One of the bearded men shoved his "Stop raping the planet." placard in front of the detectives. "We demand justice." he shouted.

"Right on, brother." Cassidy said. "Let me through and the process starts."

"Let them through" a woman shouted. "They have to start burying the truth."

"Thank you for your cooperation, madam." Wall said.

"I'm not a madam. I'm Ms." she snarled.

"Whatever." Wall nodded to the uniformed officer. "In here is it?"

"It?" the same woman screeched. "He referred to Jonathon as 'it'."

The young policeman said "The body's inside, detective, but the scene's messy. Before they called the Parliament security guy down off of the steps, half this crowd had gone in to take a peek. I've secured the scene since I've been here but it'd already been disturbed."

"Great." Cassidy said disgustedly and ducked to enter the tent. It was dim inside, what light there was in the November morning filtered even further by the canvas of the tent. Wall pulled a little penlight out of his raincoat pocket and checked the still figure in the sleeping bag which lay on top of a piece of foam rubber.

The dead man had been in his forties, Cassidy judged. He had a beard, of course, the nifty Che Guevera model. His eyes were open and there was a black thread of dried blood from the corner of his mouth down to his ear. His sleeping bag had a crusted dark stain around the heart.

"Somebody snuck in while he was sawing it off and stuck a knife in his heart." Wall said.

"Pity." Cassidy said.

Wall glanced at him oddly. "I didn't know you were a treehugger."

"No more'n anybody else. Cassidy said. "But I've got Leaf tickets tonight. They're playing the L.A. Gretzkys."

"Scratch that one." Wall told him.

Cassidy didn't answer. He was looking around the tent. "I figure the best way to preserve the scene is to slash the canvas let the M.E. take his looksee without tramping in here any more. That way we'll be able to make a better examination of the scene after."

"Wrecking the tent. That's gonna go over big with the locals." Wall said. "Who's gonna break it to them."

"You, of course." Cassidy ducked to leave the tent. "You're a touchy-feely nineties kind of guy. Me, I'm the old-fashioned storm trooper type, they'd riot if I told them."

They wriggled out and stood up. Two more police cars had arrived and uniformed officers were quietly trying to ease the protesters back from the tent. Naturally they were protesting.

"You want to go call the coroner while I get on with this?" Cassidy asked.

"Sure. And I'll get a wagon. We can strike the tent and take it downtown for a closer look."

"Indoors, out of the rain? Not just a pretty face, are you?" Cassidy said.

Wall walked off and Cassidy turned his attention to the protesters. "Why are we being excluded? What's your agenda?" A young woman was shouting into the face of an equally young policeman. She'd be pretty if she gave herself the chance, Cassidy thought. He took out his little rosewood snuff box, stooping slightly to keep the precious tobacco shielded from the rain and took a pinch.

The same young woman shouted. "This pig's doing drugs." "Snuff." Cassidy said, and sneezed on cue. "Want some?"

She recoiled in horror.

Cassidy sneezed again, happily, blew his nose and asked the woman "Who's in charge here?" He shut the lid of his snuffbox with a satisfying little click and slipped it back into his pocket. His ploy had worked. She had stopped shouting and was staring at him like an entomologist with a new kind of bug.

By now, the protesters had all fallen silent, not sure what kind of reaction was called for. Most of them had lowered their placards, inverting them and resting the message on their feet to keep the cards off the wet ground, like soldiers at a cenotaph, reversing arms. "Well?" Cassidy asked again. "Is anybody in charge."

A short man with a grey, bushy beard stepped forward, trailing his placard in one hand. He spoke in a booming voice. "We don't subscribe to conventions such as being in charge. I am, however, the secretary of Greenworld."

"And your name is?" Cassidy smiled with scrupulous politeness.

"George Steiner," the man boomed. He probably practiced booming in the shower, Cassidy thought. Not that he spent a lot of time in showers.

"Well Mr. Steiner, can you tell me what the sequence of events was last night?"

"It's Dr. Steiner." the little man corrected. "If you mean what time did we go to bed, I can't answer for everybody but I retired at midnight."

"And was the gentleman in this tent, Jonathon Mallory, is it? Was he already in his tent?"

"I think so. Just the watchperson stayed up after that, tending the fire."

"And who was that?"

"Sister Estelle." Steiner turned and nodded at the woman who had done all the screeching earlier.

"Thank you, sir. I'll have to speak to you at greater length later on. Will you still be here?"

"Not even murder can keep us from our mission." He said grimly.

"Good for you." Cassidy said. "But in case you change your mind, can I have your name and address, please?" He expected an argument, remembering the horror stories older men had told him of the sixties when protesters had been trained to refuse to give names and to exchange clothes with one another in the paddy wagon. Steiner was not so difficult. He gave an address and Cassidy wrote it down, along with the notation 5 ft. 4. 160, beard.' in case the good doctor was playing games.

Cassidy excused himself and spoke to the young woman who had lowered her placard and was weeping softly. "I'm sorry to have to ask you questions, but it's essential." He said.

She looked up at him, rain and tears mixed on her bleak face. "Go on." Most of the other people in the group had gathered around, listening warily.

"First off, could I have your name, please? Dr. Steiner called you Sister Estelle but I can't be that familiar.

He thought she would argue but her grief was genuine.

"Stella Lenchak." she said. "What's your question."

One of the men said. "You don't have to tell him anything. Estelle. You've got rights."

Cassidy looked at him mildly. "So did your fearless leader. Now I'd like to help find out who cancelled his. Could we have a little space here, please?"

The woman turned to the other people. "I'm okay. This is important."

The same man repeated. "You don't have to," but she just nodded and turned back to Cassidy.

He said. "Thank you, Ms. Lenchak. I'm told you stayed up after the others had retired for the night. Is that right?"

"I had the first watch." she said.

"You were a sentry, what?"

"We had no need of sentries, or so we thought. I tended the fire."

"I see. Kinda like a vestal virgin." Cassidy said easily.

"Are you being funny?" she snapped.

"I didn't think so." Cassidy said mildly. He craved a pinch of his comforting snuff but didn't want to send her off on a tangent. "You what? Stood, sat, watching the fire?"

"I sat. On a groundsheet with another over my head and shoulders."

"Where? Could you show me, please?" He tilted his hand, like an usher towards the circle of ash where the remains of the campfire stood. A few logs lay there, steaming in the rain.

She walked with him to the side of the circle and pointed to the ground. "I was sitting there.

"Facing the fire?" She nodded. Her back had been to the murder scene, he saw. "Was it raining hard at the time?"

"Poured down, the whole four hours." she said. "But I kept the fire going. Not like this." she dismissed the steaming mess with a flick of her hand.

"Was anybody else moving around?"

"Everyone had retired." she said.

"Yes, in your own group. But were there any other people around?" He found the correct cueword. "Any homeless persons, for example."

"I saw nobody." she said.

She had nothing more for him and he wrote down her name and address and went back to the group. Most of them volunteered names and addresses, although they insisted it was not necessary, they would be camped in front of Queen's Park until the government promised to stop all logging in Algonquin Park. One man refused to give his name. "I don't have to tell you a thing." he said proudly.

"No sir, you don't. If you want to obstruct the quest for justice for your leader, that's your democratic right." Cassidy told him loudly. "If you think trees are more important than the life of a man, go to it. But if you had any respect for him, you'd help. You decide. I'll be back."

He turned away, leaving them to chew that over as he watched Wall returning with the coroner in tow.

The coroner was an aging dandy. Today he was wearing a trenchcoat along with his usual homburg hat and cigarette. He shook hands with Cassidy. "Couldn't you have found a nice warm indoor murder, Jack?"

"We don't pick 'em Doc. Just pick 'em up." He led the way to the tent where Dr. Steiner was talking to the uniformed man. Cassidy introduced the coroner and then Wall sprang his request on Steiner. "We're going to have to impound the tent and its contents, anyway, Dr. It would help our investigation if we cut the tent up along one side. Is that all right with you?"

"I don't own this tent. I'll have to ask the others." Steiner said fussily.

"Be a leader." Wall told him. "We've got to do it anyway, why not give us permission?"

Steiner thought about that for a second then nodded his head. "Right. Do what you have to, officers."

Wall brought out his Swiss Army knife and dug it into the rain-tightened canvas of the tent wall. It went through with a satisfying little pop and he ran it down the height of the wall, then went back to the top and cut horizontally, opening a gaping inverted L.

"Thank you, I hate tents." The coroner tossed his cigarette aside and stooped to look in. He reached for the throat and then straightened up and checked his own watch. "Can't be certain but I'd think he's been dead since around two a.m.."

"Great. All this crowd was curled in their own tents, they say." Cassidy told him.

"Well somebody was moving. Somebody with a knife. Stuck it right in his heart by the look of it. I'll know better when I get him to the morgue."

Wall took out a piece of chalk and ran it around the body, making an outline on the foam rubber. "Okay then, I'll get the guys to move him to the morgue," he said. "Then we'll pull the tent down and send it in for the crime scene guys."

"He's about number six on my hit parade." the coroner said. "I won't get to him until late today at the earliest."

"That's okay. We've got a bunch of things to do first " Wall said gloomily. "Thanks for turning out."

"No choice." the coroner said. He brought out an old silver cigarette case and offered it to them. They shook their heads and he lit up and stomped away, waving over his shoulder.

Steiner was standing a little way off, nervously. He came back now. "What did he say?"

"Said your man was stabbed in the heart." Cassidy dumped the news on him roughly, checking his reactions. The short man put his right hand over his own heart defensively. "Poor Jonathon."

Wall said, "Tell me about him, sir. What was he like?"

Steiner took a deep breath, gathering himself like a singer, then he started speaking in a low, deliberate voice. "A wonderful, caring man. Concerned for the planet, for the human race, for world peace."

"What did he do?" Cassidy asked. "Like for a living, when he wasn't saving the world."

"Don't you dare mock him." Steiner breathed. You weren't fit to tie his laces."

"Pardon me." Cassidy said, "I'm not being flippant. It's just we don't come across good guys much in our line of work. It's a shock to my system."

Steiner looked at him sternly but went on. "He is, or rather was, a publisher. He published Greenworld ."

"Must admit I've never seen a copy." Wall said. "Was it a subscription only kinda magazine?"

"An alternative publication." Steiner agreed. "Not in large circulation."

"Where would we get a copy?" Wall asked.

Steiner frowned.   "Is that important?"

"I don't know until I've seen it. Could be useful." Wall said.

"What was his full name and address, do you know, sir?" Cassidy asked. He took that down and then asked the big question. "Who were his enemies?"

Steiner shook his head. "Until this happened, I didn't think he had any."

"He must have made enemies." Wall said softly. "All this picketing. He must've teed people off, company owners, like that."

"Multinationals." Steiner said and his eyes widened. "Of course. That's where to start looking, officers. The environmental criminals he confronted. One of them took their revenge on him."

"It's been my experience that those guys use lawyers, not violence." Cassidy said. "Fate worse than death, whole flock o' lawyers after you. Like being pecked to death by parrots."

Steiner looked at him suspiciously. "Do you always conduct yourselves with such levity?"

Wall pulled a sober face. "Death is a fact of life, doctor. We work with it all the time. We have to ventilate."

Steiner frowned. "I don't like it."

"I don't like murder." Wall said. "But we deal with it every goddamn' day, doctor. And we deal with it our way."

"Right." Cassidy said. "Our uniformed officer tells us that a number of the people here went into the tent to view the deceased before security was called. Can we find out which of them did?"

"Of course, if it will help." Steiner gave them a last quick look to check if they were grinning and then led them back to the gaggle of protesters who had gathered around the remains of the fire. As they walked over Cassidy looked at Wall and mouthed "ventilated?"

"Right." Wall mouthed back. "You'd know the word if you read anything outside the sports pages."

Steiner was talking earnestly to his troops. All of them were listening carefully except for one lean man who was trying to breathe life into the fire, using a pile of tiny wood shavings he had cut from the edge of the pole that held his "spare our forests" placard. He had piled them on top of one dull red spot on a wet log and was crouching to blow on it, ignoring the rest of them as smoke rose from his pile of chips.

"It's important to the job of finding out who killed Jonathon that these men know who went into his tent this morning." Steiner said. "It does not jeopardize our agenda to help them. I trust everyone will do what they ask."

"Who found him, and when?" Wall asked.

"I did." It was another woman, young and plain. With her hair and cheeks soaked with rain she looked forlorn.

"And you are Ms...?" Cassidy asked.

"Hunter. Debbie Hunter. I had made a pot of coffee and I took a mug in to him."

"That happened at what time?"

"Seven-thirty." She stifled a sob. "He hated getting up early."

"Who else was up at that time, besides you?"

"Just Douglas." She nodded at one of the beards. We were making coffee together."

"And you went in and found him. Then what?"

"I screamed." she said. "I just screamed and Douglas came running up and I told him and he went in."

"Was the tent flap sealed when you went in?" Wall asked her. She nodded and he short-circuited her story. "And then everybody got up and came over to see what was going on, right?"

"Most of us did," she nodded.

"Could I have the names, please, of everyone who went into the tent?" Cassidy asked and then wrote as a dozen or so of the people volunteered their names and addresses.

"I'm not being personal here," Wall began, "But if this were a hotel, instead of an encampment, we would need to know who was in which room. Can you tell us please, who was in which tent?"

Like Noah's Ark. Cassidy thought as he sketched the scene and wrote down the details. Here they were saving the world while they shacked up in couples, two to a tent. Male-female in most of them, male-male in one, female-female in another. The two men sharing the tent were standing close together, intimately. The two women, Stella Lenchak and Debbie Hunter, the vestal virgins, did not seem to have anything going between them.

The man at the fire had finally coaxed a small blaze from his chips and was busily splitting another placard pole into kindling with a heavy clasp knife.

Cassidy looked at it and the strength the man was using to split his wood. No sweat for him to go through a man's chest, he thought. "I see this gentleman has a very practical knife here," he said. "Are all of you carrying camping gear like this?"

It seemed all the men were. They sneered at him for sneaking around to the question of who had a knife, but they all produced knives on cue, plus matches. Always matches, Cassidy noticed. This bunch would have fried in hell rather than carry an ecologically unfriendly lighter.

"We hear that Jonathon was stabbed." One of the men said as he showed his knife.

"Looks that way. The M.E. has to check." Wall said. "Lots of weapons here." The same man said grimly. "How will you ever know who did it."

"We'll find out." Cassidy told him. "That's a cop's way of making the world a better place."

A blue paddy wagon pulled up at the edge of the park and then a car. Two plainclothesmen got out of the car and walked toward them. "Who's the wagon for?" one of the man asked roughly. "Are you arresting us?"

The detectives ignored the question, walking over to meet the crime-scene men. "I like the sound of this job." one of them said in greeting. "Wrap the crime-scene up and take it back to the office. It should happen more often."

"Listen. I want it checked real clean." Cassidy told them. "As soon as the ambulance has taken the body, strike the tent and lay it out as flat as possible in the wagon. Then go through that thing like you were chasing microbes."

"Plenty of 'em in there if that hairy bunch has been in it." one of the crime scene men said. "The ambulance on its way?"

On cue the ambulance pulled in at the curb, behind the police car. "There. All modern conveniences." Wall said.

The two detectives watched while the body was removed. The protesters all came over to watch as well, standing back, behind the orange crime-scene tape silently as the body was lifted out. Then the crime-scene men struck the tent, leaving all the pegs and poles attached, folding it flat and getting two uniformed men to help them carry it by the corners and place in the wagon. It lay inside almost flat.

"Nice work." Cassidy. said. "Give it a good going over. We'll be back later. We've got to go check out the deceased's pad."

"Don't get any on you." the plainclothesman warned.

The dead man's apartment was a surprise. Instead of the squalid basement they had expected, they found a penthouse in a forty-year old apartment block in a treed section of the city. It was spacious and well-furnished, with a mixture of antiques and comfortable modern items. There were landscape paintings on the wall and one lacquered screen with mountains and cranes flying.

"Looks Japanese." Wall said.

"Looks like money." Cassidy said. " Judy dragged me out to the antique show in Yorkdale last spring. They had a screen like that there. Price was nine thousand bucks. I've bought cars for less."

"This guy didn't own a car. Cars pollute. Screens don't." Wall reminded him.

They went further into the apartment, to the bedroom with a queen-sized bed, covered with a beautiful handworked quilt. "This guy, Jonathon Mallory, he was divorced, right?" Cassidy queried.

"For years." Wall said. "So how come he's got all the good furniture and the lady-like linen, right?"

"Girlfriend?" Cassidy said. "Somebody must've thought he was cute, nifty little beard an' all."

"But nobody at the rally, love-in, whatever the hell it was, was anxious to own up to sleeping with him."

"Maybe he didn't screw disciples." Cassidy said. "Anyway, he must've had money. Let's see if we can find where it came from."

The next room they went into was Mallory's office. It had a big computer setup, a large worktable covered with files, and a pile of magazines with the title "Greenworld" on the cover.

Wall picked a copy up and flicked through it. "It's got ads in it. I didn't expect that. Figured with his politics he'd stay away from the running dogs of capitalism."

Cassidy took a copy and checked. "Yeah. I figured that too, all this holier than thou crap and yet he's taken somebody's bucks for a page."

"Dull ad." Wall said. "Look at this one. "Hackman's Paints, coloring your world, safely" and some crap about not polluting."

"No big companies in here." Cassidy said. "No Esso, or Ford or Dupont or anybody big. All small places."

"Maybe that was how he kept his conscience clear." Wall said. "The little guys don't pollute, whatever."

"Or maybe the big guys wouldn't touch a book like this." Cassidy frowned. "I don't know who would've read it anyway, but look around. This thing was most likely printed right here, on his computer. So he wasn't paying big printing bills. Must've brought it out for pretty much the cost of the paper it was printed on."

"Too small for the big advertisers? That what you're saying?" Wall wondered.

"I don't know. Anyway, Let's check, see what all he's got here."

Their search uncovered Mallory's personal papers, including his bankbook and a set of books for his magazine, printouts from the computer. Wall frowned over these. "Advertising revenue. Would you believe it, these Mickey Mouse outfits were paying as much as two grand for one of his ads." He pointed out an entry. "This is last month. Hackman's Paints. Two thousand."

"Ads are expensive, aren't they?" Cassidy shrugged. "Hell, it costs a fortune to get an ad on the Superbowl."

"I don't think this guy Hackman sells enough paint to advertise on the Superbowl." Wall said. "I've never heard of Hackman's Paints. Have you?"

"No." Cassidy said carefully. "Let's go talk to them."

They made a list of companies who had advertised in Greenworld and checked the addresses. Four were in Calgary, three in Montreal, one in Vancouver, but the others were all in southern Ontario, largely Toronto. They started their inquiries at Hackman's Paints.

They found themselves at a low, shabby factory building in the east end of the city. There was a heavy smell of oil in the air and the place had a grubby, Victorian feel. They flashed their ID to the receptionist and a worried-looking young man came out to meet them. "I'm Rod Hackman. What can I do for you gentlemen?" He seemed nervous.

"I'm Detective Sergeant Cassidy, this is Detective Wall, Homicide Squad. We'd like a word, in private, please. Mr. Hackman."

Cassidy saw the receptionist's eyebrows go clear up to her hairline as Hackman led them back through the big, open manufacturing floor.

It was hot and noisy and the workers were wearing paint-smeared coveralls. Hackman led the way to his office. It was small and cramped and had not been painted in a long time. There was a low window overlooking the floor and Hackman's desk was against it, where he could keep his eye on the work.

He sat down heavily. His face was the color of lead. "You said you were from the homicide squad? How does that affect me?"

"Maybe it doesn't." Wall said easily. "We're making inquiries into the death of one Jonathon Mallory. He's an environmental activist, published a magazine called Greenworld."

The news did not make Hackman any calmer. "How can I help your inquiries?" he asked.

"Well, we notice that you're a regular advertiser in his book, magazine, whatever. We wondered if you could tell us anything about him." Cassidy said. "Like you must have met him, on business and so on."

"I have met him." Hackman said slowly. He cleared his throat and Wall and Cassidy exchanged glances. He was guilty as hell. But of what?

"When was that, sir?" Wall asked.

"Every month. He would come around to discuss our advertisement."

"Don't companies usually have an agency to do that kind of thing for them?" Cassidy asked. "Like, my wife's cousin is in the business."

It was the first time Wall had ever heard that but he said nothing, just looked at Hackman, his face radiating interest.

"The big companies, yes." Hackman said. "We're not in that league."

"Don't do much advertising, sir? That what you mean?"

Hackman cleared his throat again. "Not much, no. A little in the trade publications. you know, Canadian Paints and Finishes, Colorworld, things that go out to the wholesale buyers."

"How much would a business need to spend, to have an agency working for them?" Cassidy asked.

Hackman frowned. "Look, officer. I'm trying to run a business here. You come in and tell me that some guy I do business with is dead. Okay. I'm sorry to hear that. If I can help, I will. But where the hell is this leading, all this advertising talk?"

The phone rang before Cassidy could answer and Hackman swept it up. At once his face changed, taking on a soft, salesman's expression, friendly, relaxed. "Rog. Nice to hear from you. How's everything?" He swung his chair so he was facing out of his window and waited before saying. "Ten thousand? Hey, no problem. I can get it to you by the fifteenth, no sweat. But come on, I give it you at that price, I'm nothing but a busy fool."

It took five minutes to complete the call, then he hung up and turned back to the detectives, his face set like stone again. "This business about advertising. I don't have time to instruct you in the science of marketing, officers. With all respect. If you've got some questions that make sense, please ask them. Otherwise, I'm too busy for this.''

"Fine. How about this one?" Wall asked. "How come you never even asked how or when he died?" He paused. "Like did you know already, sir?"

"If you must know, it was on the radio news at noon. I was out at the coffee truck when it came on and I heard it then."

Hackman said. "I felt sorry for the guy, for anybody who gets himself killed, but I've got eighty-seven people depending on me to keep this place running, to keep them working, keep their families fed. Mallory's not around, too bad for him."

"How many magazines, outside of, what did you call them, trade publications? do you advertise in?" Cassidy asked. "And don't waste time looking in file folders for answers because you know the answer, don't you?" He paused and added "Sir." after the fact.

Hackman looked at him and worked his mouth nervously. "You can't come in here shouting at me." he whispered.

"Who's shouting?" Wall asked. "I was here, I didn't hear my partner shout. He asked you politely for an answer. What is it, Mr. Hackman?"

Hackman's mouth worked again and the word that came out was barely audible. "None." he said.

"There." Cassidy beamed. "Didn't hurt a bit, did it?"

"What are you getting at?" Hackman asked, in a raspy voice.

"I'm asking why a man who's stretched to the limit for a buck would blow around twenty-five grand in a year to run ads in a magazine nobody but a bunch of hairy activists and maybe some left-wing politicians ever reads." Cassidy said.

"Right." Wall nodded agreeably. "Like it seems to a couple of policemen that perhaps the late lamented Jonathon Mallory had found out something bad about Hackman's Paints. Like maybe you dump solvents down the public sewer system, whatever. And he gave you a choice. Like what's it to be? A regular ad for x number of months, or a bunch of picketers outside your front door killing off any goodwill you have left in this business."

Hackman reached into his desk drawer and came out with a pill bottle. He shook out a couple into his hand and swallowed them. "I didn't kill the sonofabitch." he said. "But I'm sure glad he's dead." He picked up a coffee mug and drank down whatever was in it, pulling a face as he did so. "And that's all I'm going to say."

Cassidy stood up. "Thank you for your help, Mr. Hackman. We'll be in touch." He and Wall nodded and left the office. Hackman watched them through the window as they crossed the paint-splattered factory floor and then picked up the telephone and dialled an internal number.

When the other person answered Hackman said. "This is Rod. Stop payment on the cheque to Greenworld and don't write any more." He listened, nodding impatiently and then said. "That's right. We're not advertising there any more."

The detectives made two more calls on Greenworld advertisers before returning to headquarters. The executives at both companies were better poker players than Hackman would have been but from both they came away with the same certainty that they were right.

"Great." Wall said as they walked into their office. "So we've got, what, twenty-some people with a motive but we're no closer to finding out who stuck a knife in the bastard. They're all glad, that's all."

"So let's talk to the crime scene guys. Maybe the guy who did it dropped his business card." Cassidy said. "We're due a little luck."

They stopped off at the eighth floor and went into the crime scene office. A clerk was working on a computer on a desk pushed so close to the door that it would hardly open. Beyond her the crime-scene tent was standing with one side slashed completely out.

"You here for the jamboree?" the clerk asked sourly.

"Cheer up. We'll have a campfire later, roast weinies." Wall promised.

She looked at him and rolled her eyes. "Doug. It's the brains." she called over her shoulder.

Douglas Findlay, the senior crime scene man was kneeling in the tent. His partner was standing beside him, taking notes. They both turned to the detectives and the senior man stood up, brushing at his knees.

"So." Cassidy said. "What news of fresh disasters?"

"Lots of staining." Findlay said.

"What kind?" Wall had his own notebook out.

"What would you expect from a heart wound?"

"Blood." Wall said. "Any sense to it?'

"Not a whole lot. Couple of smears, like handprints."

"They must have been made at the time of the stabbing. The blood looked pretty crusted when we got there." Cassidy said.

"The prints are unreadable." Findlay said. "Just smears. I'd say you're right. Someone made them at the time of the killing. That means it's the perp. We'll do our best to read them. Think you can get palm prints from all the people there?''

"I can try." Cassidy said. "But the natives are not friendly. They'll probably tell me to crap in my hat."

"The knife had been wiped on the sleeping bag." Findlay went on. "Hard to say how long the blade was but it looks like a broad blade, a sheath knife, hunting knife."

"The coroner will have an idea on that." Wall said. "But they're all carrying jeezly great camping knives. We'll never get a match."

"Found something else." Findlay said lightly. "Saved the best for last. Look at this." He turned and picked up a plastic evidence bag off the desk. It contained a little plastic applicator with a piece of paper in it.

"Okay. I give in." Cassidy said. "What is it."

Findlay grinned. "It's a pregnancy test. And yes, I've checked it out with my friendly neighbourhood drugstore and it's from the Instachek company. It turns green like this when it's positive."

"So the rabbit died first." Cassidy said. "Thanks Doug. Can we borrow that?"

"For sure." Findlay said. "Got a femme to cherchez, have you?"

"Got a couple." Cassidy said. "But before we go, let me have a look at the tent, can I?"

"Oh ye of little faith." Findlay said. He was peeved but trying not to let it show. He stood back while Cassidy lifted the flap of the tent and peered in.

Cassidy nodded. "Thanks Doug. You done good, like always. Now there's one other thing I'd like you to arrange for me."

"Shoot." Findlay said.

"Can you get somebody to take a look down all the drains in the roadway around Queen's Park. Start at the crime scene but head each way. I think you'll find a knife down one of them within a hundred yards."

"Will do. You go get 'em" Findlay said and the two detectives picked their way out of the tight door.

"Back to the scene?" Wall asked as they got into the car.

"Not yet. I'd like a minute at the morgue first." Wall said.

"You're the boss." Wall said. "But what the hell for? Like it's one of the broads, right? One of them must've been playing kissy-face with fearless leader. It got serious when she got pregnant. She shows him the evidence. He talks about the importance of his work and how he can't be tied down with a wife and kid, she cancels his check. Right?"

"Right." Cassidy said. "No argument. Only which woman was it?"

"You're gonna find out at the morgue?" Wall asked. "I think so." Cassidy said. He dug out his snuffbox and took a mammoth pinch, sighing with pleasure. "Don't disturb my train of thought. I'm making like Sherlock Holmes here." He blew his nose and Wall sighed and drove.

They were still too early at the morgue. The coroner was sorting out the human debris from a multi-car pileup on the 401 and his assistant told them that he would not be examining Mallory's body until the following morning.

"That's okay." Cassidy said cheerfully. "Can I take a quick layman's look at the dear departed?"

"Of course." The assistant led them down to the storage room and rolled out the drawer with Mallory's name on it. The body was as it had been in the tent, still wrapped in its light blue sleeping bag.

Cassidy looked at it for about a minute, not touching anything then said "Thank you. That's fine. Let's go."

Wall said nothing as they drove on up to Queen's Park. By now there was a crowd of curious onlookers gathered around the fringe of the campsite. The demonstrators were huddled together, talking among themselves. Their placards were stuck in the ground around their camp like flags around a fort, but the heart had gone out of the protest.

The two detectives walked over to the encampment and nodded to the uniformed sergeant in charge of the scene. He nodded back and kept out of the way.

Steiner was in the middle of a group discussion and he looked up angrily when he saw the detectives.

"We've been told we have to strike camp. It's not fair. We won't do it."

"I'm not here about that, Dr. Steiner." Cassidy said.

Steiner ignored him. "It's the ultimate insult. We've had one of our number murdered and now the cause he gave his life for is being spurned."

"Yeah." Cassidy said. "I'd like to speak to Ms. Lenchak and Ms. Hunter please."

The two women were on opposite sides of the ring of people around Steiner. They both looked anxious.

One of the men said "What's this about?"

"It's private, sir. If you're an attorney and the group has retained you, you're free to accompany the women. Otherwise, I would ask you to stay out of it."

"I'm a friend. We've got to stick together." he said angrily.

The two women had come forward, nervously, not speaking. Cassidy gave them a big smile. "Thank you, ladies. Can we have a little privacy, please?"

One of the other women shrilled. "Chauvinist. The word is women, not ladies."

"I stand corrected." Cassidy said with the same huge smile. "Ms. Lenchak, Ms. Hunter. If you please."

He led them away from the crowd, out under the shelter of a bare tree. From the steps of the parliament buildings a photographer with an enormous lens was taking their picture. Cassidy turned his back to him. So did Wall. Without making an issue of it they had sheltered both women from the camera.

Cassidy said. "The investigators who went through the tent made a couple of discoveries. One positive, if you'll excuse the pun, one negative."

He paused but neither woman spoke and he continued. "The positive find was this." He produced the plastic bag and held it up. Both of them peered at it, neither one spoke.

"This is a pregnancy tester, tradename Instachek. He waved the bag. "When it goes this shade of green it means that the person using it is pregnant."

He lowered the bag. "Now, all of the other women in your group seem to be teamed up with men. You two aren't."

"Stereotyping." Stella Lenchak said bitterly. "Everyone has to be in pairs. My mother thinks so, you think so. The whole bigoted world thinks so."

Cassidy said. "I submit to the pair of you that, whichever one of you is pregnant felt the same way. You went into Mr. Mallory's tent with the news. He refused to take it seriously. No agreement to marriage or to a," he paused and used the words as if they were in italics "'serious commitment.' So, you stabbed him through his cold hard heart."

"This is ridiculous." Debbie Hunter snapped. "We're women, not monsters. We're not capable of such a thing."

"Heaven has no rage like love to hatred turned," Wall said. "Nor hell a fury like a woman scorned."

The women stared at him in astonishment and Cassidy said, "You have to excuse my partner. He read a book once."

"Congreve." Wall said happily. "The Mourning Bride."

"Yeah. Well." Cassidy said. "This little bag narrows it down to one of you two. You both had the opportunity, while you were on watch and the rest of the campers were asleep. The question was, which one?"

Wall took over now, with the practiced ease of a longtime partner. "We could have asked you to take a pregnancy test, but you'd have refused, which is your right. And we could have watched you until you had an abortion. But that would have been a shabby way of doing things."

The women were looking at one another. Both had the same expression of horror on their faces and Cassidy realised that both of them had been sleeping with Mallory, but that the other had not realised.

"So." He slipped the bag back into his pocket. "All of that watching and fussing was out of the question. But, like I said, the crime scene lads found something else. Something negative."

"What was that?" Stella Lenchak asked, through tight lips.

"That was the absence of stains." Cassidy said. He saw a man walking towards them and recognized Findlay, dangling something in a plastic bag. He'd found the knife, obviously. Good, that would have fingerprints and blood on it, probably.

"Ms. Hunter." he said softly. "You told me you took Mr. Mallory a cup of coffee at seven thirty. He was dead. You were beside yourself with horror. People came running. But you never spilled a drop in the tent, did you?"

Suddenly both women burst into tears. Stella Lenchak put her arms around Ms. Hunter and held her, rocking her gently. "No jury will convict you." she said. "He was a lousy chauvinist sonofabitch. He deserved what he got."

Naked Truths

MARY JANE MAFFINI

Mary Jane Maffini won the Ottawa Citizen 1994 WRITE NOW! short story contest with an entry entitled Death Before Doughnuts. She works for the Canada Institute for Scientific and Technical Information and lives in Aylmer, Quebec.

Myself, I like to be the observer. I mostly hang back and watch what's going on and note the details and the reactions of people. That's what I'm best at. As a rule, Verona does all the talking.

This works pretty well when everyone keeps their clothes on but the minute they come off, the observer encounters a bit more trouble. And trouble's exactly the sort of thing that comes of following Verona. I should know. I've been following her since we were girls in St. Malachi's Home.

Prospecting, Verona calls these excursions of ours. Mining for gold in the hills of the unsuspecting. And it was prospecting that brought us to Whispering Pines in the first place.

"This time," she said, "opportunity's knocked, walked through the door and dropped its drawers."

"I can't believe I'm doing this," I said, as we lined up for the registration desk in what they call the Main House. Even though the four-colour brochures left no doubt in our minds about the theme of Whispering Pines, the naked, chattering people surrounding us took a bit of getting used to. Already, I needed a smoke, but Whispering Pines was a non-smoking environment according to the brochure. Verona made sure my Players Light were safely back in Toronto.

"Stop whining," Verona said, "do you want to make a living or not?"

I wasn't so sure.

Eye contact, I told myself as we waited to sign in. And not much of that. It was too late to turn around and leave. The shuttle was already parked and Carlyle, our driver, was busy carrying stacks of small suitcases into the reception area.

We stood there with our fellow passengers from the shuttle, and gave new meaning to overdressed. Of course, Verona didn't seem to mind at all.

In the brochure they call the foyer the Grand Hall. They go in for capital letters a lot at Whispering Pines. I admired the acres of hardwood floor, the lush terra cotta and turquoise area rugs, the jade leather sofas and the ten-foot wide stone fireplace running from the floor to the vaulted ceiling. Mind you, it wasn't easy to concentrate with the number of bare backsides and frontsides that crossed my vision.

I turned my attention back to the line of people checking in and still wearing clothes.

The couple in front of us were tall, slender and thirtyish, the kind who might look all right in the altogether. In front of them stood two people who just might have been retired nuns. I tried to imagine their motivation for being at Whispering Pines. Verona said people come to Whispering Pines to experience freedom, wildness and risk in a comfortable facility without the slightest bit of real danger. Fat chance with Verona around.

A big guy about forty-five in Reeboks and nothing else zeroed in on the people waiting to register, his hand outstretched. Verona reached out to shake it.

"I'm Bob. Welcome to Whispering Pines." Bob didn't need to be dressed for success to let you know he was in charge. "I know you ladies are going to like it here just fine."

Bob had more teeth than a piano and I figured it took him a good half-hour to get his hair styled in the morning. My hand crunched when he shook it.

"We're glad to have you," Bob said.

"And we'll be glad to have you too," Verona said under her breath.

I admire that in Verona, her ability to say something behind your back right to your face without letting her smile slip. She reminds me of a cat, always looking like she knows all the answers and she's not planning to let you in on any of them.

"Go ahead and look around. Get acquainted. You'll find folks real friendly here," Bob said, sliding his hand on Verona's shoulder as he oozed toward the next lump of newcomers, shuffling self-consciously in their clothes.

"Make sure you get settled in time for the barbecue," Bob said, loudly enough to be heard all the way up and down the line.

The scent of hickory smoke drifted around the Grand Hall. Through a long line of french doors you could see pink bodies holding plates and laughing as they clustered around the row of massive black barbecues set up on the brick patio.

Behind us in the line, a bulky woman and her much smaller husband chattered.

"I already find folks friendly, don't you?" she said. "I just love to get out and meet people, don't you?"

I didn't. I just loved to curl up at home in front of a Jays' game with a brew in my hand and not one single other person within shouting distance. That's what I love. I was only there because Verona kept carping about cash flow. She gets kind of twitchy whenever her personal reserves start to dip. That's when we have to go prospecting. I guess it's just natural insecurity when you think about her background. Me, though, I don't want too much and I'm content to sit on that sofa until the bank balance drops near four figures. I suppose it's a good thing that Verona is the brains in our business and I'm the operations side.

"My name's Marg," said the woman behind us. "And this is Hedley. Say hi, honey." She pointed to a man who looked remarkably like a balding ferret.

Marg was into the size twenty plus range with a new-smelling perm and a shy smile. Her peach jogging suit probably cost her three hundred bucks but it only accentuated her bulk.

"Honey?"

Hedley didn't answer. He gawked at every woman in the room. I was pretty sure Hedley wasn't what the Whispering Pines brochure meant by mature, sophisticated people.

Hedley's eyes tracked a willowy blonde in red spike heels. She was headed towards us, smiling, when she caught her heel in the fringe of the area rug in front of the fire place. You could hear the ripping sound from where we stood. Hedley grinned as she bent over to yank her heel from the fringe.

"Hello everybody and welcome," the blonde inhaled as she reached us. "I'm Sherise, your recreational director. We're so glad you're all here."

Hedley pivoted on his small feet and stared at her breasts, conveniently at his eye level. I wondered how Marg could resist bopping Hedley a good one.

The willowy blonde's smile dimmed for a second as she observed Hedley. It's hard to know what Miss Manners would recommend in dealing with a ferret-man who has his pointed nose one inch away from your nipples. The subtleties of modern etiquette may be even further obscured when you're the recreational director in a nudist colony. But Sherise was a trooper and a resourceful one at that. I'm sure that Hedley never realized that the elbow he got in his ribs when Sherise turned to Verona was anything but an accident.

I flicked a glance at Verona to see how she reacted to Hedley. But she wasn't paying any attention to the little creep. She was watching Sherise. From Verona's narrowed eyes and pursed lips, I figured she hadn't taken a shine to Sherise. Verona's used to being the most attractive woman in any room and this Sherise gave her a real run for her money.

Sherise's curvy coral smile stayed bright. Sherise's outstretched hand hung in the air. Verona just looked at her. I broke the stand-off by reaching out to shake Sherise's hand.

"Welcome," she said, "we'll do everything we can to make your stay a real adventure."

"It already is," I said.

Sherise laughed. "You'll get used to Whispering Pines and then you'll really start to enjoy yourself."

"Really?" I said.

"Really. Well, we'll see you at the dance tonight."

"Dance?" The expression on my face was probably the same as if she'd said "We hope you'll join us for the public flogging."

"Don't miss it," she said, "buffet dinner, a great Irish band, good dance floor, the works. Now you two should hurry up and put those suitcases away and get back out here. People are dying to meet you."

She glided off to the next group of newcomers, clumsy in their clothes.

Before she got far, Bob grabbed her arm and jabbered on about her tearing the carpet that was now going to cost a frigging fortune to get fixed. It's my job to observe, so I observed. That means listening in too. Sherise yanked herself out of Bob's grip and stomped over to Carlyle. Carlyle appeared to be stuck with the carpet problem because Bob and Sherise swanned off to meet and greet.

I took the opportunity to stroll over and say hi to Carlyle as he rolled up the carpet. I wondered how it felt to work at a place like Whispering Pines and I thought I'd ask him while I still had my clothes on.

"No way," said Carlyle, as he rolled up the carpet, "this ol' uniform's ever coming off. I make that a condition. They didn't like it much at first but they don't got a lot a choice. I'm the one who knows everything goddam thing that goes on here and does everything that needs to be done. I'm the one who handles all the driving and maintenance here. Like this here carpet, eh, nothing to fixin' it, and here's that tightwad Bob carrying on like it's gonna break the bank."

He slung the carpet over his shoulder and started for the back door. "See ya," he said.

"I'll save you a burger," I said. I figured Carlyle would be a good friend to have at Whispering Pines.

***

"For Christ's sake, unbend a little," Verona said to me, as we headed towards our cottage. "You'd think nobody'd ever been to a nudist camp before. Everyone else feels perfectly at home."

It seemed that way. There must have been a hundred people seeming perfectly at home in the altogether and considering their general appearance I don't know why they weren't all beet red with embarrassment.

"Eye contact," I muttered. "Eye contact." I repeated it like a mantra as we strolled through the open air recreation area.

"Great location," Verona said, pointing toward the lake shimmering beyond the black pines. Miles of unspoiled, evergreen forest surrounded the water.

And acres of flesh, I thought, keeping my eyes on the cottages ahead instead of on the residents of Whispering Pines.

"Hi there," Verona said, with a frisky little wave, every time we passed another person.

Don't look down, I said to myself.

Whispering Pines was not in the least what I'd expected. For one thing, the bodies I tried not to stare at were not the kind that would ever find their way into a centrefold. Still they strolled and smiled and waved as though they felt pretty good about themselves. Go figure.

"This will be good for you," Verona said, as we passed a group of energetic folks playing tennis.

"Don't stare at any bouncing bits," I told myself.

We stopped momentarily to observe what looked like a croquet game when Marg and Hedley puffed up behind us.

"Looks like we're in the next cottage to you," Marg said. "Isn't that great? That's great, isn't it, hon?"

"I guess we'll be seeing a lot of each other." Hedley smirked.

The cottages were log with small shutters and clay pots of flowers flanking each front door. The flowers in the pots were the same as the name of each cottage.

Marg and Hedley had Marigold Cottage. We had Geranium.

The moment of truth came as we unpacked inside the pine-lined cottage with the red and green accents.

"Don't put it off," Verona said, referring to the shedding of my clothes.

"I'm not putting it off."

She smiled as she snapped open her suitcase.

"What do you have in that case?" I asked. "Why do you have a big case like that if all we need is our deodorant?"

"Nail polish," she said, pointing to what must have been twenty bottles of the stuff laid out in a nice little tray.

"Nail polish?"

"Exactly."

"What for?"

"Did you notice anything on our walk?"

I flashed her a look. I had noticed plenty and we both knew it. Even though I'd spent my walk from the main house to the cottages looking at the trees, the grass and the pathways, it's my business to pick up on everything.

"What did you notice?" she asked.

"That people here are extremely well groomed. Perfect make-up, tans, and nails. That everyone is wearing scent." I'd sniffed Stetson and Obsession and Red so far.

"That's right. It's important when you don't have clothes to help you out," Verona said. "Every little bit counts. Did you notice everybody's hair was perfect?"

Of course I noticed. Everyone's hair was flawlessly casually airy and sprayed to keep it that way. I let the comment slide. My hair would never be perfect and I couldn't have cared less. I have other strengths.

"I thought people came to these places to be perfectly natural, away from the status of clothes and away from all the crappy artifice like nail polish. This is the real me, without my thousand dollar suit. What you sees is what you gets, that kind of thing."

Verona shook her head. "You're being silly," she said, lining up her collection of lipsticks next to the nail polish on the little pine vanity.

"Well," I said, "I hope you know what you're doing, dragging us here."

"Are you kidding. This is quite a little money-making operation." Verona said, as she put on her lipstick. "Figure the amount of money we invested in our one-week stay in this cottage, and this is the cheapest of Whispering Pines' accommodations. Now multiply that by the number of guests who were there for the week. And then multiply that by 52 weeks per year."

"Fifty two ...?"

"That's right, they keep the Main House open all winter. This place is like a license to print money for that Bob guy," she said, checking her face carefully in the mirror. "Let's make that pay off for us."

Twenty minutes later I stood clothesless in the cottage. I rejected Verona's offer of eyeliner, lipstick and a quick squirt of Miss Dior. As ready as I ever could be to leave Geranium Cottage and meet our new friends. I didn't mention to Verona that I was still estimating my chances of slipping away from her, hopping into my clothes and thumbing a ride back to Toronto.

"A bit of red polish on those toes would help," she said.

"Forget it," I said, striding out the door, au naturel from one end to the other.

"Would you reconsider wearing a bit of blush?" she asked, slipping up behind me.

But I'd already forced myself outside.

A youngish, blondish man carrying a large purple towel over his arm and smelling of Drakkar emerged from Petunia, the cabin on the left. He looked a lot more like the people in the brochures than Marg and Hedley did. I would have ducked back in but Verona cut off my escape route.

I could hear her chuckling.

"You're new here, I guess," the youngish, blondish man said, extending his hand. "I'm Kevin."

Although he extended his hand in my direction, Verona shook it. I stood rooted to the ground. I didn't need Verona's offer of blush. I had my own.

"Yes," Verona said, "we just got in."

"You'll really like it here. There's a lot to do. Great people. Hope to see you at the dance tonight."

I began to develop a crop of excuses for missing the dance. Dysentery, halitosis, osteoporosis, quadriplegia.

"Hi there, neighbours," Marg boomed behind me. "Isn't this great?" She beamed at Kevin. "I'm Marg and this is Hedley."

But Hedley stared with admiration at Verona's backside.

"Nice to meet you," Kevin said fragrantly as he backed away faster than most people can move when they're going frontwards. "Sorry, got to head off now. Meeting someone for a swim. See you all later."

***

Marg was much improved by removing her clothes. Her three-hundred dollar jogging suit made her look dumpy, matronly and as far as you can get from stylish. But once liberated from it she billowed about, a complex blend of pink curves topping slender ankles and connecting to tiny hands with long perfectly manicured pearl-pink nails. She smelled quite nicely of White Linen and she wore make-up which I hadn't noticed before. Even her cork- screw perm had loosened up. A makeover from lumpy to lavish. Marg was exactly the kind of girl who would have turned Rubens' head.

Hedley on the other hand managed to look smaller, meaner and more on the make without the civilizing restraints of his wardrobe. Hedley led the charge back toward where the crowd was chowing down.

Verona took to the less is more situation like she'd spent her life in public without clothes. She strolled along, trim and perky from hours spent in the health club, the hair stylist and the esthetician. As we trotted across the grass common area toward the action at the barbecue, the croquet players waved to her.

"Stop shivering," she said to me, "It's not cold."

"There's a wind."

"There's no wind, it's just a warm little breeze."

Maybe so, but I was unaccustomed to having warm little breezes tickle my bum.

"You look like you have a steel rod instead of a spine. Relax. Nobody's going to talk to you if you look so tense."

Of course, that's precisely what I hoped.

***

The barbecue was worth the wait. The crop of new arrivals milled around with plates and frosty beer steins and hungry expressions.

"Isn't this great?" Marg said, nudging up to us at the condiment table with two hamburgers on her plate. "I love seeing all these new faces, don't you, hon?"

But hon was not focusing on faces. His head jerked this way and that as each new set of breasts bobbed by.

"...isn't it, hon?" Marg repeated. Expecting a reply.

"Oh yeah," Hedley chuckled, taking a bite of his hamburger. "And not just new ones."

"What does that mean?" Marg said, with a small furrow between her perfectly plucked brows.

"It means," Hedley said, with his mouth full, "that I saw someone I met before when the someone was someone else. That's all." His mean little eyes flickered with amusement, making me think of a rat in an alleyway.

"Oh Hedley," Marg said, giving a vicious squirt with the ketchup dispenser, "talk sense."

Verona and I exchanged looks. She shook her curls. Emphatically. No way Hedley could have ever met us when we were someone else.

Hedley slid toward Verona like a kid heading for a dessert table. She edged passed him, leaving the same distance between them. I had to admire the way she managed to get a mustard smear across his belly as she passed him. Verona bit into her hamburger like she tasted success.

Around us Bob and Sherise worked the crowd, shaking hands, smiling, nudging shoulders, patting arms, throwing back their heads and laughing at the same tired little jokes. They looked good together, perfectly maintained, flawless skin and teeth, hair sprayed to casual perfection.

"So what did you get so far?" Verona whispered when I caught up to her later.

"A few good prospects. I think I have a line on at least one man of the cloth, although it's not on him now. Excellent representation from the banks too, unless I'm losing my touch, but I don't see anyone political so far. I think Carlyle will prove quite useful."

"Yummy," she said, "keep at it. I smell money already."

The wind picked up and giggling guests held onto the paper napkins on the table. I brushed my hair out of my eyes. "I told you to use a little hairspray," Verona hissed. None of the other women had to brush their hair out of their eyes. Bob's locks stayed put even when the wind began to seem more like a gale. Trust that oversized phoney to wear a toupee even in a nudist colony. Probably glued on too. Only Hedley's sparse strands fluttered in the wind as he stood back and watched the crowd, his eyes glistening.

As I sashayed off to deliver Carlyle his burger, all I could hope was that Verona was right and this little gold mine would top up the coffers for the next six months.

***

The August air had a fall nip in it as we walked through the dusk to the Main House for the dance. Kevin joined us as we left Geranium Cottage. We wore the all-weather coats the brochure recommended you have on hand at Whispering Pines for the occasional cool weather challenge. I found the coat distracting, the feel of silky lining unfamiliar against my skin. The outdoor recreation area was full of giggling, chatting people heading towards the dance, every hair in place. I could smell their fresh deodorant and toothpaste and hairspray, not to mention the perfume and aftershave.

I much preferred the scent of wood smoke from the large stone fireplace in the Main House. It promised warmth although I was hoping I could keep my raincoat on. But I didn't get away with that. A naked girl in a little cap collected all the coats and jackets at the door.

We shared a table with Marg and Hedley and Verona pressured Kevin into joining us. Carlyle had converted the Grand Hall to a festive dance theme. There were round tables with green cloths and flickering candles, a raised stage for the band, coloured ceiling lights and even one of those suspended glittering glass balls. The room was full of noise and laughter but I was busy trying to get used to the feel of the vinyl seats. The band provided an excellent distraction. I would have bet the week's revenue at Whispering Pines that this was their first gig in the altogether.

They shared self-conscious grins although most of the guys had guitars or drums or a keyboard to hide behind. Except for the fiddle player. The fiddle player's blush still hadn't died down half an hour after the guys started to set up on the stage.

I nursed my Blue and watched them. Misery loves company. The red-headed fiddle player's sharp-boned face and lean body complemented an endearing lack of muscle development. His brown eyes said I'm only doing this because I need the money. You could tell by the blush. And he wasn't a talker. In the entire half an hour, he didn't say one word to the other guys in the band. Just a nod or a half- grin when necessary. He struck me as the kind of guy you could sit on the sofa with, each with your own beer, watching the game and not yammering at each other. He looked like he needed a smoke too.

So when I accidentally bumped into him at the bar during intermission, I was surprised when he looked into my eyes and grinned. By the time I got back I had an extra stein of Blue, a smile on my face and a telephone number written on my hand, just like a teenager.

All around our table people were restless, waiting to clap and dance and hop around without their clothes, impatient for the band to play again. Not me. As the band started to play You've Lost that Loving Feeling the crowd surged to the front, laughing and swaying in time. Marg and Hedley were there. Verona too dragging Kevin behind her. I could see Bob and Sherise encouraging the foolishness, calling out to stragglers at the tables.

I clutched my Blue and stayed in my chair. Ahead of me a sea of bums moved to the music. I was having dirty thoughts about the fiddle player when all hell broke loose.

It started with Marg's scream, high, bubbling, drifting above the gyrating crowd. The first reaction was confusion. The gang on the dance floor took nearly a full minute to spot Hedley writhing on the floor. From my spot at the table I could see Verona's face. I pushed my way up through the crowd. Easier said than done since people started to panic. Some pushed to get closer, most pushed to get away. In the tangle of bodies, chairs were knocked over, people tripped and shrieked.

By the time I reached the centre of the floor, Hedley's eyes stared without blinking at the glittering glass ball in the ceiling. A festive ribbon of red trickled from the puncture in his chest down his rib cage and onto a widening puddle on the parquetry. What kind of weapon would inflict such a tiny wound and still lead to death?

Marg's wail still rose high and steady over the crowd.

***

With the speed the Ontario Provincial Police got there, I figured they'd been just waiting for the opportunity to drop in on the folks at Whispering Pines.

And as if the stress of checking out a murder scene wasn't bad enough, there was the awkwardness of where to look. I caught the cute young constable's eye a couple of times. I thought he was probably telling himself to maintain eye contact and to not look down. I understood.

"I think he likes you," Verona said. "Better be careful. Don't want to get too close."

I knew what she meant and there was no danger. I was very, very correct in my discussions with Constable Duffy, never mind if he was as tempting as a triple fudge sundae.

During the investigation, Verona was the only cheerful person left at Whispering Pines.

"Murder," she whispered in my ear, "who would have thought that would happen? What a stroke of luck."

Fine for Verona to feel so chipper, but I didn't care for the riskiness in a situation where one naked person could skewer another naked person in front of a hundred other naked people and hide the evidence right under every other naked person's nose. Also I'm never all that comfortable around the police.

The rest of the people hung around in dejected pink lumps. Some were clutching the styrofoam cups of hot coffee that Sherise and Carlyle handed out. Others, like Marg, had blankets slung over them to fight off shock. Marg was in bad shape. I didn't think a blanket would do the trick.

"I don't know what she's howling about," Verona said, "she's better off without the slimy little creep."

I was inclined to agree but I could still see Marg's point of view. Sure he'd been a slimy little creep but he'd been her slimy little creep.

The wicked, fun-filled atmosphere in the Grand Hall got bleaker and colder as the night stretched on. The scent of blood and death goes badly with sweat, spilt beer and stale perfume, perhaps that's why my stomach was heaving. We huddled as far as we could get from the yellow tape that surrounded the scene. The conversations were furtive and low, the people deflated, the freedom and laughter doused. People exchanged shifty, embarrassed glances whenever someone's bare bum squeaked on the vinyl chairs.

"This has certainly taken the fun out of the Whispering Pines experience for me," a red-haired woman wearing an acre of cubic zirconium said as her husband covered her bony shoulders with a Hudson's Bay blanket.

"No kidding," the guy next to her said. He sounded cool but he kept rubbing the side of his bald head until it was red.

Conversations buzzed and fizzled as the OPP IDENT team bagged and vacuumed every scrap of fuzz and dust in area surrounding Hedley. Plain clothes investigators came for the men, one at a time.

"What do they want?" the cubic zirconium woman asked.

"They just need to sort out what happened," her husband said. "Nothing to worry about."

"They're looking for the murder weapon," I said.

The bald guy stood up, shook his body and giggled. "Well, I got nowhere to hide it."

Everyone looked at him, ugly thoughts written on their faces.

"No way," squeaked the bald guy, interpreting the looks, "whatever killed that guy was sharp, sharp, sharp."

He had a point. Something portable yes, small and easy to slide into Hedley and then back out again without being seen. And the police didn't seem to have found it on the dance floor.

I looked off to the farthest corner of the room where the band was. Nervous and naked, trapped after the gig from hell, they were lighting up under one of the No Smoking signs. It was all I could do not to join them.

Instead, I sidled up to Kevin by the stone fireplace.

"I hope this doesn't make the papers," he said.

His forehead was rumpled and the goose bumps on his arm were visible from where I stood. I didn't have the heart to tell him that this sort of thing is what newspapers exist for.

Together we watched as a woman officer joined the team. Acid burning in my throat replaced the heaving in my stomach.

It was time for us girls to go through our paces.

**

"You'd think the police'd never seen a murder before," Verona said as she sat on the red and green checked quilt in Geranium Cottage and touched up the silver polish on her toe nails.

"It could be a first for them, murder in this setting."

"Don't be provincial," Verona said, leaning back to admire her work.

"Well, that body search was a first for me. And I can't say I ever want another one."

Verona grinned.

"I wish you wouldn't keep grinning," I snapped. "This murder is not amusing, it's very inconvenient. How are we going to top up our revenues with the law crawling all over the place?"

Verona looked up and grinned. "You know, I've seen Sherise somewhere before too. I think you better follow up on it. And you're the one who notices everything and since we want to get out of here quick and with a bit of income, let's put those two things together and give the law a hand.''

***

In the morning, I dropped in for a little chat with Carlyle. After all, he was the man who knew everything and did everything at Whispering Pines. Sure enough, he was able to confirm my idea about what was long and sharp and extremely portable and where it would be. That took care of the how of Hedley's death. The why seemed straightforward. Hedley had spotted someone who didn't want to be spotted. Someone who apparently had a powerful reason for not being spotted. High stakes of some kind. But Hedley had arrived when we did and walked over to the barbecue with us. He hadn't had a chance to meet many of the other guests. Just the staff, ourselves and Kevin.

Which was bringing us to the who. A handful of people interested me too. Kevin, for instance. Why did he back away from Hedley so fast when they met? Why was Kevin so worried about the papers? Was he somebody? Was he somebody's son? Was he the person Hedley said he'd seen somewhere else as someone else?

On the other hand, could the murder have been provoked by Hedley, himself? He seemed to bring out the worst in people. What about some jealous husband? Maybe Sherise after Hedley came one inch too close once too often? And what about Marg? If ever a woman had a husband worth killing, it was Marg.

Well, whoever it was, the killer had planned it, brought the weapon to the dance and used the music and action as a cover.

But the police had not turned up the weapon in the room or in any of the body searches. I thought about that as I shlepped back to Geranium Cottage, nodding to the tennis players bravely swinging despite the murder. The smiles were dampened a tad, the waves less carefree, but every perfect hair was still in place. Halfway to the cottage, I jerked to a stop. The final piece popped into the puzzle.

***

''Did you get it taken care of?'' Verona asked, after Carlyle drove me into the nearest village and back. Carlyle and I reeked of Players Light and I was enjoying wearing my clothes again, even if I picked up few disappointed looks walking back to Geranium Cottage. It was one positive thing I'd take away with me from Whispering Pines, a true pleasure in the feel of my jeans.

"It's gone," I said, "Special Delivery."

"Did you make your calls?"

"Yep."

"And?"

"Jackpot. It was her all right. Him too. A lot of people were able to confirm the connection."

Verona, of course, wore only a grin. She gave one of her catlike stretches. "I almost hate to leave this place," she said, "there's something about going around naked that frees you up emotionally." She glanced at her watch. "Good. I checked the office and he should be there now. Slip out of your duds and we're ready to roll."

***

"Let me tell you how you did it." Verona sat across the desk from Bob, her eyes glittering, looking like she owned the knotty pine office. But then she always enjoys the part where you trap the guilty party and toy with him. That's the cat in her, I guess.

"I don't know what you ..."

But Verona didn't give Bob the satisfaction of listening.

"Hedley recognized you, didn't he?"

Bob shook his head. Deep red blotches surfaced on his chest and neck. "He certainly didn't ...."

"I think he did, Bob." Verona's little cat smile spread over her face. "I think he recognized you from a different place when you were using a different name."

She looked at me. "Don't you agree?"

I rearranged my facial expression so that Bob and Verona could interpret it in any way they wanted. I hate the part where she toys with the guilty party.

"I think he recognized you in your former occupation as a small time porno flick maker and distributor. That really wouldn't have gone down well with your clients, would it, Bob? Might have made them a bit skittish. They might have been a bit reluctant to socialize with Sherise if they fully understood her career path. And they might have wondered if you have cameras scattered around here recording things that could come back to haunt them. They might even have slipped into their clothes and headed home, wanting their piles of money back. Word would get around pretty quickly. That would definitely cause a nasty blip in your cash flow."

No answer from Bob on this one.

"And, of course, the police might have been interested in talking to you. Something tacky about an outstanding warrant related to the age of some of the girls in your films."

Behind the gleam in Verona's eye, you could see the chill.

"What did he ask for his silence, Bob? Money? Women? Or did he want to torment you?"

"I don't know what you're talking about," Bob said. The muscle twitching on his upper lip said otherwise.

"I think you do," Verona said. "I think you do and I think it worried you. I think it worried you enough to get rid of Hedley."

Bob crossed his arms over his chest and stared out the window. Two OPP cruisers were idling in the parking spaces in front of the Whispering Pines office. Constable Duffy and his colleagues were winding down their on-site investigation.

"It was the carpet needle, wasn't it, Bob? Long and sharp and available. You gave him a quick jab in the heart and that was it. Easy to do with the crowd around dancing. Nobody would see you do it and nobody would even figure out what happened to Hedley until he was actually on the floor for a while. Simple and elegant. Allow me to compliment you."

The look on Bob's face, I was glad he didn't have that carpet needle with him.

"And then," Verona said, "slipping the needle under your hairpiece while you were bent over Hedley. I gotta hand it to you, Bob. Unfortunately for you, my colleague, unlike the rest of the gang at the dance, makes her living from being a good observer. And she noticed your hair was too good to be true."

Bob flashed me a look. He puffed out his chest, which probably worked well for him in the world of business. It was less effective without a suit and useless with two women who had him by the short and curlies, so to speak.

"This is a ridiculous allegation," he said. "You couldn't possibly have any proof of such nonsense. Where's the weapon then?"

Constable Duffy climbed out of the car and started toward us.

Verona chuckled. "We know exactly where the weapon is. Back with Carlyle's repair kit."

Bob shot a look through the window where Officer Duffy was strolling toward the office. Bob turned the colour of natural yogurt. He opened his mouth but no sound came out.

"I'm sure Officer Duffy would find it amusing," Verona smiled. "It would save him a lot of work. Especially since my colleague managed to retrieve the hairpiece you disposed of. Hardly singed. I imagine it has traces of Hedley's blood on it. Doesn't take much I hear with the magic of DNA analysis. And it won't be hard to trace the hairpiece to you." She smiled at me, fondly. "My colleague doesn't miss much."

I nodded my head at Bob. After all, I take a certain professional pride in my work.

Constable Duffy's footsteps crunched on the steps outside.

I could hear Bob's quick intake of air. There was no way out of the office without knocking over Constable Duffy.

"I think this Duffy likes you," Verona said to me, "he probably sits around imagining you with your clothes on."

"Not my type," I snapped as the door opened.

Bob squirmed in his chair. Sweat trickled down the sides of his face.

"Well," Constable Duffy said to Bob, "we'll be leaving now. But the investigation will continue. Afternoon, ladies. You'll all be available if we have other inquiries?"

Bob nodded without a sound.

"Of course," Verona said.

I smiled.

"Okay, Bob," Verona said as the pine door closed behind Constable Duffy, "let's get down to business."

Bob sat there, his back rigid, his skin grey as putty. His mouth opened twice without sound. On the third try he managed to ask, "What business are you in?"

I watched Constable Duffy's blue uniform as he ambled to the cruiser. He opened the driver's door and climbed in. He must have seen me watching because he raised his hand in a little wave.

I waved back.

"We're in the discretion business, Bob, and we see you as a major client," Her lips curved like a shiny pink scimitar. "I guess you can look on it as a sort of insurance against being arrested. We don't come cheap, but I think you'll be pleased with our service."

Bob watched the cruisers pull slowly out of the parking spot. His confidence seeped back in from some offsite storage. As the second cruiser pulled out of sight, his old smile slid back into place.

Verona chuckled.

"Don't get that look in your eye," she said, "there's no use at all trying to use that carpet needle on us. My colleague has already sent the evidence to our legal advisors. Just in case, you understand. A bit of a cliche, I realize, but what can you do? So you can see it's in your interest to have nothing happen to us at all."

She smiled compassionately at Bob.

"We only deal in cash," she added. "One time payment only. Absolutely no gouging."

I smiled myself. The price would be a bit higher than usual because Carlyle would be getting an appropriately hefty tip. I like it when things turn out well for everyone. And once again, they had. Our little cash flow problem was taken care of, we were on our way out of Whispering Pines and I still had the fiddle player's number written on my hand.

Louisville Slugger

JAS. R. PETRIN

Jas. Petrin's stories have appeared frequently in Alfred Hitchcock's Mystery Magazine and the Cold Blood series. He lives in Winnipeg and has been nominated for, and won, several writing awards. His story Man on the Roof from Cold Blood II is available on a Durkin-Hayes audiotape with the same title.

Going in, Larry's lawyer told him, "Think positive."

That was easy for him to say.

What happened that night, Larry Brown heard the creepy-sneaky-type noises coming up the stairwell, and slipped out of bed and down the stairs in time to let the shadowy figure in the kitchen have it good with the "Genuine Powerized Louisville Slugger" that he kept stowed behind the dining room door for exactly this type of situation.

The intruder -- his first arrest -- drew six months probation.

Larry Brown wasn't so lucky.

The way it was explained to him, and it was his own lawyer doing the talking, Larry could have killed the guy cracking him in the head like that. Assault with a deadly weapon. As for the intruder -- a man with the unlikely name of Moon Hoyte, if you could believe it -- the guy claimed he had wandered into the wrong house by mistake. He claimed he was looking for some girl he used to know, and his subconscious mind had played a trick on him. He said he'd had no intention of pulling a robbery. He swore he'd already been backing out of Larry's place, and therefore he hadn't been a threat to anybody.

"But that's not how it was," Larry said.

His lawyer gave him a patient look. "Larry, I'm quoting from his sworn statement. I'm repeating what he said on the stand, under oath."

"He lied."

His lawyer shrugged. "If you're going to get hung up on the truth, you'll never understand what happened here. Where there is little factual evidence, the thrust of justice proceedings is argument. Argument determines outcome. Truth -- absolute truth -- doesn't count as much as most people think it does. The guy wasn't a threat."

"Yeah? How was I to know that?" Larry was off-balance right then, still not understanding how anybody could say with assurance what the precise intentions had been of an intruder who claimed he was operating under the direction of his subconscious mind. Larry also felt stunned, the six-month probationary sentence the judge had slapped him with still ringing in his ears.

"Remember, Hoyte didn't have a weapon on him," his lawyer said, sounding more like the mouth who'd represented the intruder than a man whose fees were coming out of a lien against Larry's meager retirement savings. "There was no sign of a struggle, and you really whacked him. The court had no option but to conclude that you used excessive force. You whacked a defenceless man."

"A defenceless man who broke into my home."

"It doesn't matter that he broke into your home. He didn't break into your skull, that's the point." His lawyer swung his dour face slowly from side to side. "Look, I'm not siding with Hoyte on this. Nothing could be farther from the truth -- "

There was that word "truth" again.

" -- but, Larry, I want you to understand what happened here. You can't use unreasonable force. Not at any time, not for any reason. So sayeth the law. It's specific on that point."

"But I had no way of knowing how much force was required."

"Granted. Which explains why the judge went easy on you, why you're free on your own recognizance, and why you ought to have thanked the judge as I advised you to do."

Thanked him. Jesus.

"The judge leaned in your favour."

In his favour.

"I think he was impressed by the fact that you're retired armed forces. -- What was your job in the army again?"

"Medical orderly."

"Yes, but what did you do?"

"I moved dead guys around."

"Yes. Well. Not exactly armed combat, but it helped, that's the thing."

Larry said, "And this other guy, Hoyte, who broke into my house, is he free on his own recognizance too? No, don't answer that. He is, isn't he? Free on his own recognizance?"

The lawyer, sitting there, nodded.

"And is he ex-army?"

His lawyer shook his head.

Larry didn't understand any of this. It was one lousy deal as far as he was concerned. He pulled a hand down his face and said, mystified: "The cops that showed up that night said they knew about the guy. Said they'd suspected him for months of break-and-entering in the area, only they couldn't get nothing on him. They told me I ought to be given a medal. Then in court they show up and make me sound like an axe-murderer."

"You used a bat."

"A bat-murderer, then."

"The officers were simply responding to the questions that were put to them. It was my job to bring out your side of it, and I did so. You heard me make those arguments, Larry, but..." His lawyer glanced up. "Where are you going, Larry? Larry -- ?"

Larry didn't want to hear anymore. A sudden indignation was beginning to well up in him. Not only was he indignant but he was bewildered. Free on his own recognizance! He headed for the door.

His lawyer trotted after him with a few more patronizing thoughts. "Okay, so a couple of cops sympathized with you in the heat of the moment that night. But cops simply enforce social policy. They aren't the law, Larry, any more than soldiers are. You ought to know that."

Oh, but he did know it. He knew it now, all right.

"Oh and Larry..." His lawyer leaned into the corridor after him with a very stern fatherly frown on his face. "I did my best for you, but you are on probation. Please remember that. You can't get involved in something like this again for the next little while."

Sure. Like it was something Larry did a lot of. Sitting at home with a bat, just itching to whack someone.

The elevator doors rolled shut.

***

You felt stunned. Let down and betrayed. You felt as though you'd been through a major disaster of some kind, and you knew it would be a while before the full impact of all that had happened sank into your numb brain. There you had been, asleep in your bed, as law-abiding a citizen as anyone could be; and then you woke up. Why? Because you sensed a stirring in the house. Coming awake, you were already beginning to think "intruder!", mindful of the media reports every day of people stabbed, robbed, shot -- even cut up into pieces and devoured, for God's sake. That guy Dahmer? You couldn't just lie there, so you got out of bed, snuck downstairs and whacked the guy. Maybe you went a little heavy, but hey, what if you had erred on the light side? Would you be here today? Who could say? Hell, the guy could have been packing a Swede saw, for all you knew, along with his salt shaker, steak sauce, his knife and his fork.

There had been no intent on your part. You had simply reacted, protecting yourself. So go figure. Civilian life was just like the army, that was pretty clear -- a party-mix of plain folks and idiots. And the really scary thing was that the idiots seemed to be winning.

***

Larry phoned his son Roger. Roger had moved to Toronto to live with his mother and study law. When Roger's voice came on the line -- it sounded very tight, very superior -- Larry asked him flat out what was the logic behind a law like the one they had slapped him with. A man protecting himself and his home, in the middle of the night. Roger listened, letting Larry get it out of his system. Then, while admitting he wasn't an expert on this particular facet of law, 'being more into the corporate side of things, you understand,' he ventured a cautious statement:

"Wrong-doers have rights, too, you know, Dad."

"Jeez. Tell me about it," Larry said.

"And laws like that also prevent household calamities. Like people shooting meter-readers. Believe it or not, things like that do happen. Some shift-worker gets up groggy, finds a meter- reader in the house, and aggresses against him." Aggresses against! Roger was picking up some nifty new courtroom expressions lately. "It's a well-meaning attempt by society to prevent tragedy, Dad. Terrible mistakes people have to live with for the rest of their lives."

Larry wasn't impressed. "Right. But how often did tragedies like that happen? I mean, before they changed the law? How many meter-readers got aggressed against? Hundreds? Thousands?"

"I don't know -- "

"Were there, like, shift workers shooting meter-readers to death on a regular basis? Were we running out of meter-readers, is that what the problem was?"

"You're being ridiculous, dad."

"I don't even have a meter-reader. I got outdoor meters because I like my privacy."

"And don't we know that, me and mom."

Roger's voice had cinched up tight and superior again with that last comment.

He sounded an awful lot like that damn judge.

***

A little later that same day, Larry took a drive down to the Food Fare to get milk, eggs and bacon, planning to treat himself to a breakfast that didn't come out of a Styrofoam box. While he drove he mulled things over, wondering what had gone wrong with the system. Surely laws were originally meant to protect peacable citizens, not to benefit intruders. How had it come about that they now protected the bad guys? People who waltzed into houses in the middle of the night where there might well be babies, old ladies, any sort of innocent person they could "aggress against", and all the time mindful of the fact that if things went too badly wrong, they had a briefcase full of laws on their side.

No wonder cops freaked or took early retirement.

At the Food Fare he parked the car, dutifully shunning the empty handicapped stalls, and went inside, finding the big store practically deserted this time of day. He rounded up the items he needed and carried them in his arms toward the till. It was pure chance that made him glance up a connecting aisle and spot Moon Hoyte. Hoyte was in the pharmacy section. Hard to miss him with that big patch of plaster stuck to his head. He was helping himself to the non-prescription drugs big-time, scooping fistfuls of them into the half-opened front of his Chicago Bulls jacket.

Their eyes met.

Hoyte winked.

He finished boosting capsules into his jacket and sauntered calmly away.

***

Larry rang his lawyer. His lawyer listened politely. When Larry was finished his lawyer said, "Okay, so what exactly are you proposing we do about this?"

Larry looked at the phone.

"God damn it, the guy's on probation. He was there in my face, ripping off a pharmacy -- "

"That's the key word, Larry. Was. He isn't ripping off a pharmacy at the present moment, so far as we know, so if you report this incident to the police, you will be called upon to substantiate your allegation. Was there a witness?"

"I was a witness. I seen him. Stuffing pharmaceuticals into his coat -- "

"Pharmaceuticals. That's not surprising. He must suffer some king-size headaches, considering how hard you belted him."

They were back to that again.

"What's that got to with it? He's on probation. And there he was, ripping off a store. That's the plain and simple tru -- "

There. He had almost said it. That word truth again.

His lawyer said, "And did you alert the store manager, Larry? Did you take steps to apprehend the thief?"

How could a lawyer be this stupid.

"God damn it, after what I went through last time, you got to be kidding me. You are kidding me, right?"

"You claim he was there in your face."

"He was. I could of reached out and -- "

"And what, Larry?"

Larry didn't answer.

"Whacked him?"

Larry couldn't think of anything to say.

His lawyer said, "One thing I am happy about, Larry. I'm glad the Food Fare doesn't have a sporting goods section. One that sells bats."

He hung up.

Now Larry thought of it, the Food Fare did sell bats. Nice Little Leaguers, "made with pride", that he could have took and knocked that smart punk's socks off. He went on thinking about that while he dialed again and got the police.

***

A couple of uniforms showed up. They took down Larry's statement, then looked at their watches, and said they'd drop by and have a talk with Mr. Hoyte real soon.

"Soon?" Larry looked at them. "I think you better go see him right now. And take along a couple of ball-peen hammers and a wrecking bar so you can do a proper job of searching."

The officers glanced at one another, and one of them said, "Mr. Brown, we know where you're coming from. But we can't simply storm in and take people's houses apart over what you've told us here."

Larry watched them go and he realized that they were right. They were absolutely, one-hundred percent right.

Nobody was going to take seriously anything Larry said, a law-breaker himself, now. A man who was free on his own recognizance.

**

A couple of days later Larry's phone rang at ten in the morning. Ten a.m. was a time, he'd learned in the army, that you normally heard from the upper ranks, those guys who didn't knuckle down to work until nine but liked to clear their in- baskets well before lunch.

It was his lawyer.

"Larry? Listen. I've got something here. A little chit-chat. You know that guy you whacked?"

Could he forget him?

"This fellow Hoyte, Larry, I'm afraid someone must have been talking to him. I doubt this would ever have occurred to him all on his own."

"What?"

"The Hoytes of my experience are usually glad to see the last of a courtroom."

"What are you telling me?"

"They aren't, as a rule, all that comfortable with the legal process."

"What is it?"

"The thing is, Larry, Hoyte is apparently preparing an action against you."

"Against me?"

"That's right. For damages. He's going to sue you, Larry, is what it is."

"What for?"

"Unlawful assault causing bodily harm and mental anguish. Half a million dollars is what he's asking for, but don't worry about it. We're going to fight it like hell."

"Half a million?"

"That's right."

"Dollars?"

"Uh-huh."

"Don't worry about it?"

"I told you. We're going to fight it." There was a pause. "You will be retaining this office to argue your case, won't you? It'll cost something, of course." He gave a chuckle. "I hope we didn't quite clean out the old war chest last time."

"Half a million dollars?"

"That's right. But think positive. We're going to fight this one, Larry. We're going to fight it like hell."

***

They fought it like hell and Hoyte won. True, the judge reduced the claim from five-hundred thousand to ten grand, but Hoyte had won his case as far as Larry was concerned. Ten grand was about all he had left, consisting of his retirement fund, and his share from the sale of the house after he and Althea broke up.

His lawyer was pleased as punch with the outcome:

"I told you we'd fight it, Larry, and we did. Five hundred thousand down to ten grand? Listen, that's a hell of a victory, don't ever doubt that for a minute." He looked at Larry, trying to keep the professional satisfaction out of his voice, and losing that particular battle on all fronts. "What's the matter?"

Larry looked at him sombrely. "I'm just sort of wondering," Larry said, "how does Hoyte pay his own legal fees?"

"Legal Aid." His lawyer gave a cheerful laugh. "I have to admit it's ironic. As a taxpayer, you're helping to pay his fees, Larry."

Larry was silent a moment while he attempted to digest this piece of unpalatable information.

"I'm paying his fees, and I'm having trouble paying my own fees?"

"That's the system."

"Man," Larry said.

"The argument is that you can afford to purchase legal advice, and he can't."

"Jesus," Larry said. "They should look at my bank account."

"How is your bank account?"

"Ten grand's about all I have left,"

"All that's left of your savings, you mean?"

"All that's left, period."

"You mean you can't appeal?"

"It's worse than that," Larry said. "If I have to pay Hoyte, I don't think I can pay you."

His lawyer fell silent. When he spoke again, the irrepressible glee had gone out of his voice.

"Larry, you've been through hell. But don't joke about this. I sure as heck don't want to sue you on top of everything else." He forced a thin smile. "We'll work something out. You must still have some assets. You really ought to try and think positive..."

Think positive.

Well, sure.

If you looked at it logically and philosophically, you could see that, once again, your lawyer was right. You truly did have a lot to be thankful for. Consider the burglary, the guy busting in on you, with that judge you'd of probably got ten or fifteen years, if, say, Moon Hoyte had died. But he hadn't. And you were free on your own recognizance.

And as for this latest skirmish, well, hell. Look at it from the positive side and you were four-hundred and eighty grand to the good. You were practically rich.

***

They worked out a settlement.

Larry scraped up some extra dough by selling off a few things: his entertainment center, his VCR, his television. Also a leather, reclining, TV-watching chair he wouldn't be needing anymore, and a microwave he'd used for making TV dinners in when he sat in the chair to watch the television.

He was trying hard to think positive, but something was stirring deep down inside him. A sense that he didn't need that stuff anyway, that he wouldn't have time for TVs or anything else for the next little while. He had a feeling that he was going to be otherwise occupied.

***

He started with Hoyte's old address off the legal documents, the place the guy had been living before he lucked into the criminal justice lottery. It was one of those flop-houses, you look at it you think you must have taken a dive through a time warp, a place with the lingering smell of the unwashed guys who'd pushed the CPR. railroad through here a hundred years ago.

The place had three floors. Six rooms to a floor. Larry knocked on all the doors and looked at all the faces over all the chain locks. People growling that they didn't know Hoyte and didn't want to know him. Hoyte's neighbours. Just plain folks.

Striking out there, Larry went on a walking tour of the neighbourhood, asking at grocery stores, gas stations, arcades, and TV repair
shops. Also second-hand stores, auction houses, pawn shops, the sort
of places he figured a guy like Hoyte, considering the type of business
he was in, would probably have developed something better than a
nodding acquaintance with.

But all he got was blank stares. It was late in the day when he
stopped at Angelica's Uni-Sex Beauty Emporium.

It didn't look like an emporium. It looked more like a made-over
cow shed with a joblot of rolledroofing tacked onto it, and the woman
who came out of the back room didn't seem very angelic, unless you
liked your angels on the chunky side with freeze-dried blue hair and a
hard-bitten look around the edges.

But that was okay. Larry thought she was beautiful. She knew
Moon Hoyte and admitted it.

"I bet you're a cop," she told him. "You got that look." She lit
a cigarette and tipped back her head to blow a plume of smoke straight
up. "I want old Moon to get everything that's coming to him. Which
is a lot. I oughta know."

"Can you tell me where he lives now?"

"Three years that bum sponged offa me, borrowing money, stiffing
me with phone bills, disappearing weeks at a time and then showing up
out of nowhere to flop here whenever he damn well felt like it. I hope
you find him and put him away for the rest of his no-good life."

"You know where he lives?"

"You wanna know what that schmuck did to me one time? Pawned
one of my hair dryers. Can you feature it? I come home from the Bingo,
take one look in the salon, and I go, "Moon, Jesus H! What did you go
and do now? I'm running a business here, for crying in the sink!" He
goes on watching Top Cops. He says, 'Hi there, sweetie. How was the
Bingo? Did you win some money I could borrow?'"

"Where does he live?" Larry asked.

She squinched her eyes tight.

"That's important to you, huh?"

"That's right."

She was trying to read him. Sizing him up. Finally, she stubbed out
her cigarette, observing:

"You know, you're a guy who could stand to have his hair styled."

"What would it cost?" Larry asked, getting his wallet out.

It was hard information he got from the Blue Angel. Not that he needed the sixty-seven dollar style and trim, considering what little hair, and cash, he had left. But in return the Angel poured out her heart to him, a spurned woman wanting to talk.

She rummaged in some papers by her phone and gave Larry the address of the new town-house Moon Hoyte had recently moved into. And something else. A bonus. Intriguing particulars about some guy who was Hoyte's former business associate.

Larry was surprised.

Hoyte had a business associate?

The Angel said that the business associate had been Hoyte's best buddy for a time, but had been dumped, same as her, on the day that Hoyte "came into money".

"After all we done for him, soon as he gets some dough, he's gone. Like a sock in a laundromat, you don't see him for looking. Was I mad. I says to Nucky -- "

"Nucky?"

"Moon's best bud."

"Oh."

"I says to Nucky, 'That's what we get,' I says, 'for bending over backward for that man.' Nucky gives me a look and says he feels like he's been bending over frontward for him, but I says, 'Nucky,' I says, 'listen, all this bitterness won't get us nowheres. We got to keep open minds, and open hearts. This'll get taken care of in God's own way.' Nucky says, 'God's own way, huh?' 'Yes, I says. You don't know. Maybe there'll be a truck, I says, run him over in the street. Something heavy, right? With a lot of wheels on it.' "

The Angel turned away for a drag on her cigarette, came back and breathed tobacco breath down Larry's neck. The scissors snipped and clicked.

"What did Nucky say?"

"Oh, he's a philosopher, that Nucky. He said that Moon was kind of a beer fart under the blanket of life. And he said what goes around comes around, that being Nucky's favorite philosophy."

"Have you got Nucky's phone number, too?"

She had to think about that. She put down the clippers and held a mirror to the back of Larry's head. "You know, hon, there's men your age...well...I dunno. What would you think about a flat-top with maybe a bit of a rat-tail down here at the back?"

***

Larry dialed the number the Blue Angel had given him. The number of Moon Hoyte's ex-buddy and business associate, the Philosopher King, Nucky.

Nucky could have been Jamaican. He could have been a guy from Barbados. He sounded like some laid-back individual in a rugby shirt that had sail boats on it. He was unresponsive at first, and very suspicious, but he was also intensely curious about how Larry had gotten his number.

Larry mentioned the Angel.

"Her! Well, that explain it. That wooman, mon, she like to toke, you know?"

Larry said he wouldn't disagree, thinking the guy meant she liked to spark a roach once in a while. But Nucky straightened him out on that.

"Her big mouth! She goin' to toke herself into one serious diffeeculty, one of these times, know what I'm sayin', mon?"

"Oh. She likes to talk. Yeah, that's certainly true," Larry said, trying to sound agreeable. Then he added, "But her heart's in the right place. She told me to put my bitterness behind me, and not to let this thing Moon did to me prey on my mind."

"That soun' like her, all right." Nucky said. Then he asked, "What thing Moon did?"

"Well, it has to do with the way Moon doesn't play square with a guy. I mean, when you have a business arrangement with somebody you expect it to mean something."

"Mon, what you toking? You did business with Moon?"

"Didn't everybody?"

Puzzlement on the line. Larry hurried on:

"All I'm saying is, when you've been through a lot with someone, through all the scrapes, all the tough times, well, when the big one finally comes along, you got a right to figure you deserve a fair share of the pie."

Nucky grunted.

"Moon's money. You know somethin' 'bout that?"

"I know lots about it. I think I can say I know more about it than he does."

"No kidding?" Nucky was hooked. "And is there more where that came from?"

"Sure, there's more." Larry fingered his small change.

"What you say your name was?"

"My name is Larry."

"Larry, huh? You listen to me, Larry. How 'bout we get together, and toke about old friends. And then maybe we see what way the wind is goin' to blow, okay?"

He rattled off a time and a place, and then hung up. Larry showered, changed his clothes, and was about to go out the door to the meeting when the telephone rang. He lifted the receiver and a sarcastic voice said, "Is this, uh... I mean, am I speaking to the Slugger?"

It was Moon Hoyte.

***

Hoyte came across on the phone like a guy working hard to make you believe he was seriously bored with you. He chewed gum with slow, loud, smacking sounds.

"You been to my old neighbourhood asking around about me?"

"That's right. I thought we could talk."

"Well, I don't know," Hoyte said, "it might not be convenient."

Like he was all tied up with the demands of his work, this guy who crawled through bathroom windows for a living.

"It's important."

"What for?"

"For business."

"I don't see we got any business."

"I believe we do," Larry said. "At least, that's what a buddy of yours told me today."

"What buddy of mine?"

The gum-smacking had stopped, and Larry could just about hear Hoyte's ears prickling. He knew had to play this just right.

"A pal of yours named Nucky."

Hoyte said nothing.

"See, we were talking, Nucky and me, and we discovered we had a common acquaintance. You. Your name just seemed to pop up."

"What'd he tell you about me?"

"Not a lot. But I'm pretty sure he's going to. See, we're getting together. Nucky sounded a little bit put out with you over something, and he wants to fill me in on a few things. Now, what do you suppose that's all about, Mr. Hoyte? Hello? Are you still there, Mr. Hoyte?"

But Mr. Hoyte had hung up. Some sudden new demand on the busy man's time.

Okay, Larry thought, that's done.
Put two cats in a bag and then shake it.

***

Nucky wasn't at the parkade. Larry tramped up and down the concrete stairwells looking between the rows of parked vehicles for fifteen minutes, but couldn't find him. So he got back in his car and drove down the ramp. He would go looking for Nucky at the address the Angel had given him.

When he pulled up out front of a single-detached house close to the Uni-Sex Beauty Emporium, he noticed an odd thing. The front door of the place was standing open. He went up the walk, knocked, and when nobody answered, he stepped inside.

"Nucky?"

There was no answer.

Larry looked down the basement stairs. He walked through the kitchen. He checked the bathroom, the small back bedroom, but there was nothing, no sign of Nucky, and nothing to explain where he might have gone.

Larry went back out to his car, thinking, and drove slowly home. He parked in the driveway, found his house key on the ring and let himself in. Then he stopped in his tracks.

His living-room was a disaster. It looked as if two very angry antagonists had rampaged there, battling one another ferociously and demolishing the place. His sparse few sticks of remaining furniture were tossed every which way, lamps lay smashed on the floor, end tables were overturned.

If there had not been a bloody-minded battle here, then someone had made a darn good attempt to make it look as though there had.

Keeping his cool, he went through the rest of the house carefully. All seemed in order, the other rooms were untouched. Then, finally, because he was a man of a methodical nature, he went out to his garage and threw up the big door.

And that's where he found Nucky.

At least, he guessed it was him. Nucky the business associate. Burglar. Philosopher-King to blue-haired chain-smoking ladies, a man who wouldn't be "tokin" ever again about old friends or anything else, now sprawled on some old cardboard under one corner of Larry's work bench, as if in his last moments he had been attempting vainly to find a small private place in which to hide himself.

What goes around comes around, Nucky had maintained, and something or someone had definitely come around for Nucky, all right. With a vengeance.

And, with a bat.

Yes, a bat. The bat was lying next to the body. It was a Louisville Slugger.

Larry peered at the body. It seemed to have bled very little. Some blood had trickled out onto the cardboard, suggesting that maybe Nucky had still been alive when the bat had gone to work on him, but Larry couldn't tell for sure.

I believe I'm being framed, Larry thought.

He scratched his chin. There had been two cats in the bag, and now there was one. What should he do now? Call the police in and try to explain how the body of Larry's second intruder in a matter of months just happened to be lying dead in Larry's garage, beaten to death with a bat? Should he take his chances with the system again, and think positive?

Or should he handle this his own way? Think standing up and adapt?

***

Larry was waiting in the darkened apartment when the headlights swung into the parking stall below. He moved over into position at the end of the new green velour sofa, and waited at parade-rest with the bat cradled in his arms. When Hoyte came through the apartment door, Larry switched on the lights.

Hoyte went rigid.

The first thing Larry noted was that the head-plaster was gone. Then he noticed how natty a dresser Hoyte had become, this sharp-faced little man who had worn nothing but grubby clothes and chin stubble throughout the trial. Now he sported a soft tan leather jacket over a brown silk shirt, beige trousers with a crease you could draw blood with, and burgundy Gucci loafers, a good two-hundred dollars down there on each foot. Larry took in the full picture, wondering why he hadn't dressed this well when the money had been his.

Hoyte recovered a little and slipped his jacket off, but he didn't try to hang it in the closet. He stood there, looking back at Larry, holding onto it.

Larry hefted the Powerized Louisville Slugger in his gloved hand, poked the club end of it at Hoyte and began to explain the situation.

"I busted your patio window getting in off the deck, and then I made a slight mess of the place fumbling for the lights."

Hoyte was gripping his jacket by the lapels and keeping it low in front of him like a bull-fighter's cape, a toreador wondering whether to drop the damned thing and run for it, or keep standing his ground until the bull ran over him.

"I came here to talk to you about your old friend Nucky. I was wondering if there was anything you wanted to tell me about him. You know. Anything at all."

Hoyte didn't move.

"I'm listening," Larry said agreeably, "if you want to go for it."

Hoyte's gaze roamed carefully over the half-opened cupboards, the tumbled seat cushions, the drawers jutting wide with their contents strewn over the rug, and the big plush rocker heeled around backwards, facing the wall. He took it all in slowly, the way people do when it's dawned on them that strange hands have been poking among their private things.

Larry knew just how he felt.

Hoyte continued to stand there. The jacket's sateen lining threw back the light. Then Hoyte's foxy face turned suddenly clever, triggering Larry's built-in alarms.

"Hello, Slugger. Say. You mind if I put my jacket away?"

"Go ahead."

Hoyte nodded and lifted the jacket. As he did so his right hand slipped under the lining.

Larry dropped the bat. He wouldn't need it for this. With one quick step he was on top of Hoyte, taking a handful of silk shirt up near the throat and dragging the skinny guy into the room, while kicking the apartment door shut with his foot. Keeping Hoyte's forward inertia going, he quick-marched the guy across the room and slammed him down face-first on the bar, making the bottles jump. Then he turned Hoyte around and gave him a quick jab, keeping a stiff wrist and leaning into it, sending the guy butt-first through the smoked glass panel of his new brass and wicker coffee table.

The place was really getting messed up.

"Don't do that again," Larry said.

He scooped up the jacket and out tumbled a gun, a nice little Luger 92S; he'd seen similar ones when he was stationed in Europe. He snapped the magazine out and ejected the chambered round. Then he put down the gun and picked up the Louisville Slugger again.

"Ready to talk?" Larry asked.

Hoyte grunted.

"I'm curious," Larry said, "what really would have happened if I hadn't whacked you the way I did that night. Say if I had done what they said I ought to, turned on the light and tried to reason with you."

Hoyte was coughing down there in the broken glass. Maybe he smoked too much.

"How the hell do I know," he said. "Maybe got the bat away and give you a whack."

"Yeah?"

"Or took you out some other way."

"Without a weapon?"

"Weapon? Hell. There was all kinds of weapons." Hoyte got slowly to his feet. "Go in a kitchen, there's knives all over the place. That's what I might of done. I had the most to lose."

Larry wasn't so sure who'd had the most to lose, the way things had turned out.

He took down a bottle of rye, poured a shot into a glass and slid it towards Hoyte along the counter, feeling generous. After all, it was Larry's own money that had paid for the stuff. Unless Hoyte had ripped it off from a liquor store, which was certainly far from impossible.

"I guess," he said, "you're pretty happy about the way the system worked for you."

Hoyte was gingerly pinching glass splinters from the seat of his pants. "I don't know nothin' about the system, man. An' I don't wanna know."

"I believe you."

"But I'm no dummy. I could of been a lawyer. I could of been a judge." He leered. "How would that be, huh? A guy like me up there under those robes."

"Might be an improvement," Larry said.

Hoyte brushed the rest of the powdered glass off his butt. He was gradually reasserting himself. The lord of his castle.

"So what you going to do?"

"Well," Larry said, "I'll tell you. In a couple of minutes I'm going to walk out of here."

Hoyte blinked.

"You mean you ain't gonna hit me with that thing?"

"Uh-uh. I'd probably be nailed for harassment. It wouldn't surprise me, the way things have been going."

"Harassment? That's what you call it, batting a guy?"

"What would you call it? I saw Nucky."

Hoyte looked insulted. Then an evil grin darted to his lips. "Hey, I didn't touch him. You did. He broke onto your place, and you walked in and whacked him. You do that to people. The law knows that. They got a sheet on you now."

Larry was slipping into his coat, shifting the bat from his right hand to his left. "I'm going to go home and wait for the cops to stop by. They'll do that, I guess, soon as they get through talking to you."

Moon Hoyte frowned.

"Why would they talk to me?"

"To investigate this break-in."

"Hell, man, you walk outta here, no way I'll call this in."

"I know it. So I'm going to do it for you. I'll say I'm a neighbour and that I heard a lot of hollering."

Sweat shone on Hoyte's narrow face. His little animal brain was working overtime behind his small, dark, flickering eyes.

"Go ahead then, if you want to. Won't do you no good. I'm clean. I'll tell 'em Nucky's at your place. Murdered with a bat."

Larry shrugged.

"That's your story, and you're stuck with it. Myself, I think they'll have other ideas when they find Nucky's body."

Larry stretched out one foot and turned the velour rocker to face Hoyte, giving Hoyte a good look at his old partner-in-crime. Nucky slumped there in the big chair squinting at them. On the way over here with Nucky tucked in the trunk of the car, Larry hadn't been sure what exactly he was going to do with the little guy; but he had been determined that Hoyte wasn't going to weasel out of this with some phony alibi, some smart lawyer, some twist. He could have just dumped Nucky in Hoyte's parking stall and let the cops make what they could of it. But this was better.

Larry went to the door.

"You should be thankful. I helped you out a bit by tossing the place. You can tell them old Nucky broke in to rob you and you had to whack him one. Defending your home. They ought to go easy on a guy defending his home. That's only natural, don't you think, Mr. Hoyte?"

Larry tossed the bat into the centre of the room. If any prints were found on it, they wouldn't be his. The last he saw of Hoyte, he was standing among the ruins of his trashed apartment, staring uncomprehendingly at his ex-business associate and best bud Nucky, who had his pockets stuffed to bursting with all the Hoyte jewelry and small personal items that Larry could jam into them.

Larry went home to tidy his house.

***

His lawyer, on the phone, said, "So you heard what happened?"

Larry waited for it. "You know the guy that's been giving you a rough time? That Hoyte?"

Larry said that if he thought real hard, he probably could remember Hoyte -- yeah.

"They pulled him in last night on a homicide."

"No kidding."

"You won't believe this, but the way it appears, Hoyte walked smack into a B and E going on in his very own place."

"What goes around comes around," Larry said.

"There's more. The intruder turns out to be one of Hoyte's old accomplices. They must have had a falling out. Anyway, apparently they tangled over this and Hoyte killed the guy."

"Killed him, huh?"

"Yeah. Whacked him with a bat, then pitched the poor dope off the balcony, a thirty foot drop to the parking lot. Massive head injuries. They can't tell where the bat injuries stop and the parking lot injuries begin." Larry's lawyer seemed almost to gloat. "The cops were pulling up to the place when the victim came over the railing, Larry. They actually witnessed it! When they went upstairs, Hoyte was blundering around yelling it was your doing, but of course, that didn't wash." His lawyer sounded very pleased. "I said to think positive, didn't I? Hoyte won't walk this time. He'll draw ten years at least. Larry? You still there, Larry?"

"I'm here."

"You're awful quiet."

"I was just thinking."

"Yeah? What about?"

"I was thinking," Larry said, "that maybe Hoyte should have just batted him. What do you think?"

Meloncholy

MARGARET HAFFNER

Margaret Haffner is an agricultural biotechnologist who has published three mystery novels and two children's books. She lives in rural Ontario with her husband and two sons. Her most recent novel Killing Frost was published in the summer of 1994.

Maureen Quesnel cringed as the nerve-grating tones of her neighbour, Annie Dransford, wafted over the fence on the humid August breeze.

"Oooh, oooh, Maureen! Isn't it a lovely day?" she tittered inanely.

Robert Frost may have thought that good fences made good neighbours, but that premise assumed both parties understood the purpose and symbolism of the fence itself. According to the Concise Oxford Dictionary, a fence was a hedge, railing or bank, etc., PREVENTING ENTRY or exit from a field or such like. Annie Dransford clearly had little use for dictionaries.

Maureen always made it a point to keep her gate closed and latched but despite its formidable construction of wood and metal, it was apparently invisible to Annie. Maureen involuntarily clenched her small fists and held her breath as her nosy, garrulous acquaintance swung it wide open and sashayed through as if Maureen's small garden was merely an extension of her own large lot.

"My, aren't your roses magnificent today, Darling," Mrs. Dransford cooed as she buried her plump, garishly rouged face into the delicate blooms and breathed deeply.

"Hello, Annie," Maureen answered through thin lips. "I'm afraid I don't have much time to talk this afternoon. I have a lot of chores to do before I leave for work."

"Not to worry, Dear, I can talk while you work. It's so nice to have a little chat with one's friends, don't you think? It makes the job go ever so much faster!"

Annie plunked her fat body down in a white wicker lawn chair which creaked alarmingly under the assault.

"Got anything to drink, Luv? I need something to wash down my doughnut." She stuffed the last of her pastry into her generous mouth. "Besides, it's awfully hot!"

Maureen had been working indoors since early that morning, painting her kitchen in the stifling heat. Annie's sole activity to this hour, Maureen knew, had been to lounge in front of the television in her airconditioned bedroom.

"No, I don't," she replied shortly but then, against her will, found herself offering to make some lemonade.

"Great. Make it with lots of sugar - I like it sweet. A sprig of mint would be nice too. And ice cubes...!" she called after her hostess as the screen door banged shut. Annie settled back in her chair shifting impatiently to get comfortable. She'd have to tell Maureen to put some soft cushions on these oldfashioned chairs.

Inside the kitchen, redolent with paint fumes, Maureen gripped the counter edge for a moment, her knuckles white with tension. Sighing, she made her way around painting paraphernalia to the freezer for a can of lemonade concentrate. It was the unsweetened kind, and didn't have that unnatural pink colour which seemed inexplicably popular. No doubt Annie Dransford liked it that way Maureen thought savagely as she pulled off the lid and started scooping the pale yellow slush into a pitcher whose cornflower blue pattern matched the decor.

The entire room was a delicate combination of white and blue; pale blue walls with a darker blue border, gleaming white appliances and white enamel trim. It was on this trim Maureen had been working that morning. The counter top was marbled blue and white and the curtains on the window over the sink were fluffy white pricillas with dark blue ties.

Maureen paused as she waited for the water to run colder and stared out the window over her beloved garden which received the bulk of Maureen's energies. The yard was small - only thirty feet wide and forty feet deep, but in it grew a profusion of lush plants. In the eight years since she had bought the house after her husband's untimely death, she had judiciously located selected shrubs, ornamental trees and climbing vines so that now the neighbouring houses and even the dividing fences were invisible. It was her secret garden, or at least it was supposed to be.

In the foreground, cunningly designed flower beds, brimming with the paint box hues of perennials, provided an illusion of riotous, untrammeled growth. A crescent-shaped bed of annuals, the zinnias and asters just coming into bloom between the lobelia and alyssum, balanced the foreground, and an arch of lilac bushes led the eye through to the herb and vegetable gardens beyond.

The sound of a slap and a muttered "dratted flies" jerked Maureen back to the present. Annie was not in view from the window and for a moment Maureen had forgotten about this blot on the horticultural perfection.

Maureen's hand hovered over the sugar canister irresolutely but in the end she replaced the lid without taking a scoop. Darned it she were going to ruin an entire pitcher of lemonade to suit that woman! Perhaps it if were sour enough Annie would waddle back to her own home for her sugar fix.

Annie stretched out her hand lazily to accept the glass.

"No mint!" she exclaimed in annoyance. "Now Maureen, I know you grow some lovely mint in your herb garden, so don't try to tell me you don't have any!"

"I'll get some," her hostess murmured, pushing her lank, greying hair off her forehead. A halo of untamed wisps framed her colourless face as more and more hair escaped from her lopsided bun. Anything to avoid an argument - she'd had too many of those while her husband was alive.

Ducking through the lilac arbor, Maureen fled, temporarily, from the demon who plagued her otherwise carefully ordered existence. For the first two years after Maureen had relocated to this small town she knew she'd chosen the perfect home. Anxious to obliterate all trace of her unlamented husband, she had dived into decorating and gardening, two pursuits Arthur had disallowed as extravagant of both time and money. Feminine frills and pastels brought airiness and soothing lines into the interior atmosphere and hard work and a flare for landscaping began to transform the dusty yard into a refuge. Her neighbours had been perfect - she almost never saw them, and they exchanged only polite nods on their chance meetings. But then old Mr. Elliot had died, the Dransfords had moved in next door, and a crack formed in the walls of paradise.

Six years later, Annie Dransford, now a widow enjoying the fruits of a large life insurance policy, made Maureen's business her business, and Maureen's home her own. There was no respite. In her darker moments, Maureen was certain mousy Mr. Dransford had been literally pestered to death by his shrill and lazy wife and Maureen feared that she would soon follow him into oblivion. If only she could be more assertive and forbid Annie's incessant visits! But even as a child she'd been a doormat... Oh, she knew what words she itched to say to her neighbour, but she also knew she would never utter them.

"What on earth are you doing back there, Maureen? My ice cubes will be melted before you ever return with that mint!"

Turning, Maureen saw to her dismay that Annie had made the effort to penetrate to the back garden. Instead of ordering her home, Maureen merely bent and snipped a sprig of mint, proffering it wordlessly.

"Ta," Annie grated, dropping the leaves into her glass and stirring the contents with a stubby finger before taking a big gulp.

"Yuck! This is sour! Are you sure you put sugar in it?"

"Lots," Maureen answered. "It should be very sweet."

"Well it isn't," Annie complained, but nonetheless proceeded to empty the tall glass.

"Shall we go back to the house?" Maureen suggested, trying to steer her visitor away from the vegetable garden, but it was too late.

"Your tomatoes are gorgeous today, Luv," Annie exclaimed catching sight of the crimson globes hanging like bright Christmas balls from the burdened plants.

"They've come along just lovely. I do so love tomatoes, Dear, you won't mind my taking a few," she continued, hurrying over to where the vegetable plants stood in regimented rows, no weeds or yellowing leaves marring the perfection.

Without waiting for a reply, Annie dropped her glass onto the raked earth and grabbed for the tomatoes with greedy fingers. Maureen raised a hand in protest as her prize tomatoes changed ownership. Annie had an unerring eye for the best.

"I was planning to enter them in the fair...," Maureen objected weakly.

"There will be more; don't be selfish. Anyway, you always win. It would be Christian to give someone else a chance," Annie commented absently as she approached the peppers which were hanging luxuriously from shiny plants. The best of these followed the tomatoes and Annie's arms received them hungrily.

"Get me a basket, will you Maureen? I can't carry all these."

"I don't have one."

"Oh, there's a box over there, just by the carrots. That will do."

"It has grass clippings in it," Maureen protested.

"That's all right," Annie shrilled as she kicked over the box to empty it.

"There," she wheezed with satisfaction as she deposited her load. "Now I can carry some carrots and onions too."

Mrs. Dransford proceeded to tug at several carrot tops and succeeded in extracting three carrots from the rich soil. She had broken the stems off some dozen plants in so doing. The same fate befell the onions a moment later before Annie finally straightened with a groan and surveyed the rest of the garden.

Maureen watched impotently, furious inside but unable to bring the pillage to an end. Even if she did protest now, Maureen knew Mrs. Dransford would be back to cause even more havoc as soon as she had left for work. All too often prize flowers and vegetables disappeared overnight while Maureen was at the hospital and she knew where they went. After all, the flowers frequently wound up in the front window where all the world, including their rightful owner, could see them. When Maureen had diffidently objected, Annie had pointed out that Maureen had way more produce than she could use by herself and she, Annie, was merely ensuring that it didn't go to waste.

"Whatever are those?" Annie demanded, pointing to some pale golden spheres nestled under wide, dark green leaves in the far corner.

"Don't touch them!" Maureen shrieked, galvanized at last to protest.

Annie regarded her in astonishment. "Why? What are they?"

"Melons. A new variety," Maureen gulped, red filling her pasty complexion. "I had to send all the way to Holland for the seeds and they were very expensive. Besides," she continued more confidently, "they're not ripe yet."

"How can you tell?" Annie demanded suspiciously.

"The variety description says they get a faint blush of pink near the stem when they're ready to harvest and you can see there is no sign of pink yet," Maureen explained in a rush, interposing her body between her precious melons and her neighbour.

"I'm the only person in the county growing these and I'm going to enter them in the fair next week. The biggest two should be perfect by then so I'll show them both: one for appearance and one for tasting. Rosy Dawn melon is said to be magnificent with tuna salad."

Annie tried to get a closer look but Maureen found the strength to deftly block Annie's moves.

"Here, take your vegetables home and put them in the 'fridge," Maureen urged, thrusting the box of loot at her adversary. "You don't want them to wilt!"

Stymied, Annie retreated but not without casting one last avaricious glance at the forbidden fruit.

For the rest of the week Annie was even more ubiquitous than usual and more than once Maureen came into her garden to find her neighbour's fat form looming over the melon patch as she carefully examined the fruit for hints of colour change. Maureen was beginning to panic. On one hand she desperately wanted her Rosy Dawn melons to be ripe for the fair, now just days away, but she feared for their safely. Maureen was sure she'd seen Annie licking her lips as she stroked them possessively.

Two days before the fair the two largest melons were ripe. They nestled, luscious and alluring in their leafy bed, promising an ecstasy of flavour to whoever ate them. Maureen knew the coveted award for 'Overall Best Produce of the Year' would be hers. So the day before the fair she screwed up her courage and telephoned Annie to remind her not to touch the melons. And before she left for the hospital that afternoon, Maureen visited her charges one more time. All was well.

Although it was midnight when she returned, and she was very tired, Maureen took a flashlight and hurried down to her vegetable garden. A brief sweep of the light told her what she wanted to know so she retired quickly and slept well.

By noon the next day Annie Dransford had still not been over to invade Maureen's peace. Maureen smiled in relief. By four o'clock (it was Maureen's day off) she still hadn't appeared and Maureen became anxious. At eight p.m. Maureen picked a basket of her perfect produce and headed next door to investigate this unique state of affairs. A timid tap on the back door elicited no response so she tested the door and, on finding it unlocked, she went in, calling Annie's name as she did.

Maureen had searched the kitchen, living room, dining room and family room before she finally found her neighbour lying on the bedroom floor. Her knees were drawn up underneath her as if she'd been having stomach cramps. One fist clenched the dirty bedspread which trailed onto the floor and then tangled around her. The other hand was clutching the telephone receiver. The blue eyes popped unattractively and a trickle of dried vomit dribbled down her chin. Annie Dransford was very dead.

Maureen returned to the kitchen where the remains of a meal of Rosy Dawn melon and tuna salad lay in disarray on the table. Swiftly she cut open a new melon from her basket and ate a few mouthfuls. She sighed in quiet ecstasy. It delivered even more than it promised! Deftly

Maureen removed the melon Annie had been eating and replaced it with her own, tipping the tuna salad into the cavity and mixing it around with a few drops of liquid bacterial culture from a glass vial. The original melon she wrapped neatly in foil and dropped into her bag. She didn't really think anyone would notice the mark of a hypodermic syringe at the base of the stem but Maureen was the careful type. It had been a brainstorm to mention the tuna salad. Canned fish was famous for carrying Clostridium botulinum, the bacteria responsible for the most deadly form of food poisoning - botulism.

With a tiny smile hovering on her thin lips, Maureen calmly returned home, momentarily replaced the receiver of her telephone (she hadn't hung up after calling Annie the afternoon before), and then began to dial 911.

Duty Free

ERIC WRIGHT

Eric Wright is one of Canada's most successful crimewriters. He has published ten Charlie Salter novels and a number of short stories. His awards include several Arthur Ellis awards from the Crime Writers of Canada. At present Salter is enjoying a "sabbatical" while Wright tries to think of something else to write about.

It was impossible for an observer to mistake what was going on. The couple in the corner of the airport lounge were involved in a marital fight, all the more savage for being conducted in near whispers. It was evidently the end of the holiday; their nerves were raw, and they were tired. Probably, in their late fifties, they had under-estimated the amount of energy their trip needed, and now they just wanted to get home. But the plane was delayed, a delay which, when added to the requirement to arrive early for security reasons and to the long journey to the airport, would mean they had spent six or seven hours preparing for the flight, and there was still the flight itself, another seven or eight hours.

"I don't think a bottle of duty-free will make the slightest difference," she said. "They've got scotches here you don't ever see at home. I think it's bloody ridiculous." She spoke to the air in front of her.

"Bloody ridiculous or not," he said, addressing himself to the window, "When we get there I want to go home and go to bed. I want to walk out of the gate at the other end and go home. I don't want them asking me if that's the only duty-free I've got, and turning out my bags to prove it."

"Everybody buys duty-free," she said, lifting up her foot and addressing the heel of her shoe. "Everybody. They're more likely to wonder why you haven't got one, and make us turn everything out."

"Will you shut up!" It was still only a whisper, but his voice was filled with fury. "It's bad enough that you have to use that great sodding bag which you thought they'd let you carry on. I told you once, I'll tell you again, I want to get out, get home. I've had enough. Besides, George will be waiting for us. I'll ask him buy you a bleeding bottle of scotch, shall I? Now shut it!"

He lifted his small carry-on bag off his lap and tried to sort out his clothing. He was wearing a shirt, tie and pullover under a heavy tweed jacket, and he was carrying a raincoat in case the weather in London was bad. He changed his paper-back over from his raincoat to his jacket pocket, then left it out entirely as he tried to think through the garments he would stow in the overhead locker.

"Sit still," she said. "You're driving me crackers." He put the raincoat, the book and his bag on his chair, touched her elbow and pointed to them as an instruction for her to guard his possessions, and went in search of a place where he could have a last cigarette; but before he had gone five steps their flight was called and he had to scurry back and load up to get in line. She watched him drop his paperback twice, shaking her head. "I was wrong," she said. "If you had duty-free to carry, too, we'd never get on that plane."

The first three hours of the flight passed in the usual routine of drinks, food, and more drinks, then the film came on and the plane settled down. It was not full, but she had booked them in non-smoking seats, so once the trays were removed he went back to look for an empty seat in the smoking section. Watching him come down the aisle was a man in a check shirt with the air of someone looking for a chat. As he drew level with the row, the man nodded to him and indicated the empty seat beside him and he sat down.

"Give me five," the man said, as soon as he had lit up.

"Do what?"

"Give me five." the man repeated holding out his hand at a forty-five degree angle, face up.

Gingerly he placed his own palm on the outstretched hand and slid it across.

"Wayne." the man said.

"Henry."

"How ya doin', Henry?"

"Very well, thanks."

They smoked in silence for a while, then the stewardess announced that the duty-free shop was open. Wayne said, "I already got my share.

You?'' When Henry did not respond, he said, ''I noticed in the lounge. You don't have any duty-free. You buying any?''

''No.''

Wayne twisted in his seat. ''Not even your allowance?''

''No.''

''Would you do me a favour? Would you walk a bottle of cognac through for me? I don't want to declare it and pay thirty bucks or whatever, but if you don't have any you could carry it through for me.''

''No. Sorry. I'm in a hurry. I don't want to chance being stopped. I've had a very tiring day and I want to get home.''

''Why would they stop you? One bottle of booze?''

Henry waved his hand to push the suggestion away. ''It's too much to carry. Sorry.'' He got up from his seat quickly, nearly forgetting he was smoking, stubbed out his cigarette and went back to his wife.

''That was quick,'' she said.

''Man back there wanted me to carry through a bottle of duty free. He's got a bottle over his allowance.''

''And I suppose you said yes.''

''No, I didn't.''

After a minute, she said,''How did he know you don't already have your allowance?''

''He's been watching us. In the lounge and here.''

''Watching us? Why?''

He thought about it. ''Not so much us as everybody, looking to see who might not have duty-free.''

''You sure?''

''Why would he pick me out?''

After that he tried to sleep, but an hour later he was still thinking about Wayne and his duty-free. As the breakfast appeared he said, ''I've been thinking. I'll take his bottle through for him.''

''Just like that? Why the change?''

''I've been thinking.''

''Sorry to be so...offhand last night, Wayne, '' he said. ''I was a bit on edge. I'll take the bottle through for you.''

''That's my boy. I'll get it from the locker.''

''Hang on. Give it to me when we get off the plane. Did you check any bags?''

''One.''

"We have two. So we'll both have to wait for the luggage to come down. We could wait by the carousels and go out together. Then I won't be able to run off with your bottle."

Wayne laughed. "You wouldn't get very far."

They stood together waiting for the bags to come round. "Here's the cognac," Wayne said.

"Hang on until I've got my bags."

When all the luggage was assembled, Henry gave his wife her bags to carry and organised his own. He put his raincoat on his shoulder to leave his hands free but when he bent to pick up his bag, the raincoat slid down his arm and he had to start again. He rolled the coat into a tighter bundle and put it back on his shoulder and this time bent his knees so that it wouldn't slide down.

"Here," Wayne said, handing him the duty-free bag. Henry extended his fingers under the handle of his carry-on bag so that Wayne could hook the plastic liquor bag over them, but in leaning ever-so-slightly sideways the raincoat slid down again and smothered his hand. He put his raincoat back on his shoulder and hooked the plastic bag over his wrist, but as he curled his fingers around the handle of the carry-on bag the plastic bag slipped across the back of his hand, crushing his fingers against the handle of the case.

"Bloody hell," his wife said. "I'll see you outside," and marched off through the gate.

Now Henry got himself loaded up with everything except his overnight bag. He bent to include the handle of the overnight bag within the fingers that were already curled around the liquor bag and one of the plastic handles slipped free and the bag opened and the bottle of cognac slid out on to the floor. "This isn't going to work," he said, looking appealingly at Wayne.

Most of the other passengers had gone now. Wayne looked around the baggage area, worried and impatient. "Gimme that little sucker," he said, picking up Henry's overnight bag.

Gratefully Henry let him pick it up. "Now we'll manage," Henry said.

One of the two customs officers who were watching from behind the glass, said, "That was as good as the old sticky-hand routine," and tried to explain the vaudeville act involving three men on a scaffold trying to get unstuck from each other as they were putting a poster on a wall.

"I think they're up to something. I think we should have a look at that duty-free bag," the other officer said. He was a very new recruit to the service, this was his first week on the job and he was looking for major smugglers on every plane.

"What do you think's going on?" His older colleague was amused.

"The duty-free belongs to the bloke in the check shirt, but he's very keen to have the other one carry it through for him."

"Right. He's got extra, the other one's got none, so the bloke in the check shirt is getting him to carry it through. Nothing illegal about that. Well, there is, but it's not worth bothering about."

"I don't know." The young man shook his head. "What would make a better donkey"--using the technical term he had just learned--"than some poor unsuspecting tourist, doing someone a favour."

"You're barmy, son. All right then, just to prove it, let's stop them. You take the little man with the duty-free, I'll hold the other one up. Right? Then when you find out it's just whiskey, tip me the wink and we'll let them through. Just have a look at his duty-free, all right? Nearly time for coffee." He smiled, for he had just realised what was going on.

As Henry reached the exit, the young officer took him to one side. "How much duty-free do you have, sir? May I see?" He took the box out of the bag, broke the seal and lifted out the bottle of cognac. He stared at it thoughtfully, then put it back, aware of his colleague's eyes on his neck. "Right you are, sir. Thank you."

While he was watching his young colleague, the older officer was checking Wayne's bags. He passed a hand through the big suitcase, then asked Wayne to open the carry-on bag. "It's not mine," Wayne said. He pointed to Henry, "It's his. Henry!"

Henry had already started to walk through the gate. He came back to where the customs officer was waiting with his bag.

"Would you mind opening this, sir?" the officer asked.

Reluctantly Henry produced a key and opened the leather club bag. The customs officer lifted out his toilet articles one by one until the bag was empty. Then he checked the bag itself until he was sure there were no false compartments. Finally he began to unscrew Henry's talcum powder, then changed his mind, shrugged, and put everything back and chalked the bags. He looked up at Wayne and jerked his thumb at Henry. "You know, don't you, that if this bloke walks off with that duty-free, You wouldn't be able to do much about it."

Seeing the officer was entertaining himself, Wayne smiled. "When I get my cognac," he said. "He'll get his bag."

The officer walked over to his colleague. "Did you taste it?" he asked.

The young man looked startled. "It was sealed."

"An old trick. Probably hash oil. You should have tasted it."

He grinned. "I was wrong, too. Come on, let's get a coffee."

Outside in the concourse, Wayne said, "Thanks, pal. That could have been tricky. Those guys knew it was my liquor, but they couldn't be bothered." He handed over the carry-on bag and picked up the cognac.

Henry said, "I wondered there for a minute, if you'd got me to carry the crown jewels through. Your duty-free was the only thing they were interested in."

"And your bag. They get a bit keen sometimes." Wayne winked and walked off.

George, who had been waiting some distance away with Henry's wife, came forward now and bustled them out to the waiting car. He buckled on his seat belt and started the car. "Let's have a look at it before we go," he said.

The wife lifted her bag on to her lap and opened it up to show George.

"Christ," George said. "Must be worth a quarter of a million. Easy. Let's get out of here."

When they were well on their way, Henry's wife said, "See, you could've brought a bottle of your own through. What a performance you made of carrying a couple of bags. Not exactly inconspicuous, were you, but it didn't make any difference."

Henry said, "You don't understand anything, do you?"

Current Events

VIVIENNE GORNALL

Vivienne Gornall is a free-lance writer who lives on a small farm north of Toronto where she raises sheep, chickens, trees and children. Her work has appeared in Harrowsmith *and* Cottage Life. *This is her first published mystery story.*

I heard the deep growl of a tractor's diesel at the end of the gravel driveway.

"Damn." I raced into my bedroom and quickly zipped up a track suit over my lycra riding outfit. I shoved my leather gloves inside my bicycle helmet and put it back on a shelf in the clothes closet. Damn, I wasn't going to get to ride my bike this afternoon.

The tractor eased round the long curve and through the wide band of evergreens that sheltered the house from the road. It was my brother-in-law on his John Deere, a plow attached to the three-point hitch. The blades were raised high above the damp gravel, lifted like a woman's long skirt to avoid mud puddles.

Ross threw back the tractor door and lowered himself to the ground. His left hand removed a sweat stained CO-OP cap, his right hand smoothed back his thinning hair. It gave me a jolt every time I saw him. He was so much like Ted.

I watched his stiff-legged gait to the kitchen door. He reminded me of a billy goat I had once owned whose knees creaked like a rusty gate when he walked. I opened the door, a smile on my face. Ross' forehead was the colour of mashed potatoes in contrast to his windburned cheeks.

His eyes were shy and refused to meet mine. They scoured the stoop, like a hen searching for bugs. "Found somethin' in my turnip field, Margie," he said.

"What is it?"

"Somethin' I think ya oughta see." His lips, cracked from years in the sun, pressed shut. Ross still worked all the land surrounding my bungalow.

I pulled on an old green duffel coat. We walked out to the back forty in silence. The long undulating curves of the furrows resembled velvet-black caterpillars crawling over the rolling fields. His fall plowing was almost finished.

"I's just plowin' under the stubble when ol' Jip seen it," he said as we approached a shallow valley between two curving hills. I could see a splash of colour in the depression, like a pendant nestled in a woman's cleavage.

Jip ran forward to greet us, his quivering nose thrust into the air. "Guess I dug up somethin' that was meant to lie fallow," Ross said.

I approached the thing pulled loose from the ground by the plow. The sweet heavy smell of putrefaction hung on the fall air. Blue-bottle flies rose in a hum as I walked closer.

It was the remains of a man lying face down on the ground. A bare arm, its rotted muscle grey and fibrous, poked through the remnants of a dirty yellow tee-shirt. The blackened, decomposing fingers had contracted into hooks and grasped a lump of earth. Strands of pant fabric lay splayed on the soft caterpillar ridges. The leg muscles were tunnelled with worms. A knob of bone, the colour of old Jip's eye teeth was visible at the hip through the wasted flesh.

I fell to my knees and dug the head loose from the shallow grave, the taste of bile rising in my throat. A shot of adrenalin hit my heart with the kick of a plow mule. It was my husband, Ted.

Ross pulled me away and put his arms around me. I could feel his body shivering against mine.

I crossed myself. Ashes to ashes, popped into my mind. Dust to dust.

Ross helped me home across the fields and into the house. He sat me at the kitchen table and slipped off my muddy boots then put a log in the stove to chase the cold from the room. I saw how the seams of his green work pants strained over his ample bottom as he wrestled the log into place.

The kitchen was heavy with the smell of chores that clung to Ross' clothes. He rubbed his callused hands over yesterday's whiskers, the knuckles thick and malformed from years of hard work and cold.

"Often wondered why Teddy never sent word after he left. Didn't sit well with me. We bin tuned to watch out fer each other. Twins are like that. Two peas in a pod."

He scratched his cheeks with nails as hard as horns. "I told the police Teddy had the gypsy blood. So I just figured he'd left again like he did twenty years ago. Course he comes home with you ten years later. Who'd a thought," he mused.

"I remember building this house when youse was just married, Teddy supervising, me doin' the work. We didn't ever talk much. Twins don't seem to need to."

I'll never forget when Ted disappeared, seven months ago. It was April. The air was full of the smell of dark earth and fresh spread manure. He travelled around Western Ontario stocking the stores with wrapping paper, greeting cards, stuffed animals, perfumed soaps.

Ted never said when he was coming home. He liked to surprise me by returning when I least expected it. His route usually took about five days.

I didn't have a car of my own so he made sure I had enough milk and bread and staples from Stouffville, the little town nearby. He wouldn't want me to run short and have to phone one of the neighbours scattered along the concession road. Ted wasn't one for having anyone involved in his affairs.

He had been away eight days when I phoned his Head Office to ask if they had heard from him. The receptionist said he hadn't called in but not to be concerned. She brightly reminded me that Ted was placing Mother's Day stock in the stores and since he was their best salesman "no news was good news" as far as she was concerned. "And won't his commission cheque be big next month?" she enthused.

I waited until the following weekend and when Ted still hadn't returned, I called Ross. He contacted the police.

The officer asked me if Ted was having an affair. I had to laugh at the suggestion. Ted would never do that. I was the most important thing in his life. He adored me. Didn't the cashiers at the A&P tell me and any customers willing to listen that I was lucky to have a man like Ted? He was always helping with the shopping, pushing the cart, picking items off the shelves, paying the bill. He wasn't like most men. Stepping inside a food store with their wives to shop for groceries was beneath most of them. The cashiers liked to point that out.

The police found his car at Yorkdale Centre in Toronto, thirty miles away, a few days later. There were no signs of foul play.

They checked his bank account and found he had withdrawn one thousand dollars the day he disappeared. Eventually he was listed as another runaway husband. I knew inside me they were wrong.

A few neighbours brought over tuna-noodle casseroles for my freezer and Ted's employer set up a trust fund for me. I got a job in town at a wholesale electrical supply outlet and life returned to normal.

But each morning before I left for work, I liked to sit at the kitchen table and scan the fields, looking, watching. Spring ripened into summer and the freshly tilled fields turned green with turnip leaves. Fall came and I watched the harvesting of the turnips, their skin the purple colour of a bad bruise.

The kettle whistled on the back burner. I buried my face in my hands. I heard Ross lift the boiling kettle off the element, then shuffle around the kitchen making tea. He put the pot under a quilted cozy to steep, warmed my cup and carefully poured the tea out for me. I was touched by his kindness.

All I could grasp was that Ted had been found in Ross' turnip field. I wiped my eyes and stared at my fingers, stained and rough from the gardening and housecleaning. Ted would have taken hold of them and teasingly called them housewife's hands. His had been well manicured. They looked like the paper napkins he sold, so soft and pretty.

The tea was good and stopped my shaking. I picked up the quilt I was working on and started to do a little hand stitching. Ross didn't say a word. He just stared into space.

My mind reviewed the circumstances leading up to Ted's disappearance in the spring. It was just a year ago when it all started.

Ted had always liked me at home but I found my days long. He never wanted children so for years quilting had been my passion. Last fall I asked him if I could try to convert the attic into a small studio.

When he wondered why, I fumbled for an answer. ''I need a place to lay out my fabric. I've so many ideas for quilts and I need space. I'd like to start selling them.'' Mainly I yearned for a room to call my own. It was hard to put into words.

The next morning Ted took me to the local lumberyard and told me to buy anything I needed. I bought 'Do it Yourself Wiring' and 'Renovating the Attic'. Ted joked and winked at the staff as he struggled to the car with my tools and supplies.

I gave myself a nasty shock when I installed power on the landing at the top of the stairs. That was a day to remember. I had inserted a screwdriver between a mounting screw attached to the outlet on the front of the junction box and the live wires coming into the box. The metal screwdriver must have completed the circuit between the wires and the screw. An electrical charge shot through my body. It gave me a scare and new respect for electricity. I re-read that wiring book from cover to cover until I understood it thoroughly. Later, Ted bought a floor lamp from Sears and plugged it in. It worked.

I managed to hit my fingers several times with the hammer. My aim was terrible. I went back to the books for help, adjusted my grip and changed the angle of the nail. Eventually I could sink a nail in three blows. My aim was deadly.

"What did my princess do today?" Ted would ask as soon as he walked in the door. The attic was the first thing he wanted to see. He was not a handyman and I could tell he was impressed with my carpentry skills, despite my battered fingers.

I spent the whole winter building my studio. I painted the ceiling and walls a creamy white and installed pine shelves. I covered the floor with a bright rag rug I had made years ago. Fat quilted cushions were scattered around the room.

Ted and I wrestled an old table up the open stairwell to the attic. I was glad the narrow stairs had no railing on the right side or we would never have got the table into the room but I scared myself when we did it. The stairs were steep and treacherous so I installed a wrought iron handrail into the wall a few days later.

I may as well admit it right now. I had one secret from Ted. I knew how important it was to him to have a wife with traditional values. He hated the feminist movement and declared it was the cause of family breakdown. But I still wondered what it would be like to have him help make the meals and clean the house. What would it be like to have a job in town? I actually envied the cashiers who were on their feet for hours at the A&P. At least they knew they were alive.

My secret was that I had bought myself a bicycle. Not one of those three-speed steel framed bikes from Canadian Tire, but a twenty-one speed, microshift, TIG welded, alloy frame racer.

Ted would have been terribly upset if he had known. He'd have worried about me on the road and ranted about the chance I took of being abducted or worse. He would have forbidden it.

He would also have quickly figured out that I stole the money. Bit by bit I took it from his wallet. One glorious day I hitchhiked to a town named Aurora, ten miles west and bought the bike and the riding clothes.

When I knew he would be away for several days I pulled the bike out of the root cellar, put on my stretch suit, gloves, sunglasses and helmet and rode with the wind. I liked to go out early in the morning when the neighbours were in their barns milking and return in the late afternoon when they had already started evening chores. No one ever guessed.

Every marriage has its secrets.

"This's bin a terrible blow, Margie." Ross stared out the window at the plowed fields, the darkening sky. "First snow's comin'."

I put down the quilt and finished my tea. I had been lost in thought.

Ross hesitated then walked to the phone. "Best I call the police," he said, sweating from the heat of the stove. "Sure as hens lay eggs, Teddy didn't bury hisself out there. It's a wonder I found him. Once'd I got this year's crop off I's goin' to bed 'er down in alfalfa. Wouldn't of bin plowed fer 'nother five years at least."

I dropped the needle. I couldn't stand the thought of anyone seeing Ted's decomposing body. "If you phone the police there'll be an autopsy. They'll probably cut Ted's body apart and take out pieces to probe and poke. You mustn't let them. He'd hate it."

Ross spoke softly from across the room. His eyes were impossible to read. "Teddy looked after you like a prize pig. What happened to my brother, Margie?"

I shrugged, my heart breaking.

"You can tell me," he said. "Haven't I always been here for youse? When Teddy disappeared, you didn't have nobody to turn to. Didn't I check on you? Didn't I say you should of come and lived with me? Family takes care of family. I told you that."

It was the kindness of his words that convinced me to tell. I had carried the burden of Ted's disappearance since spring. Could I possibly make Ross understand? There was so much he didn't know about his brother.

"Would you like to see this quilt I'm working on?" I said.

He cocked his head like a robin looking for worms, then nodded.

How I loved my quilts. I poured my heart into those pieces of fabric. My latest creation was almost finished. It was the size of a single bed cover. All that was left was some hand stitching and the border.

The centre was dominated by an enormous cross, a symbol of my Catholic upbringing. Rays of coloured fabric cascaded in all directions like heavenly light. They were everywhere. I had worked the upper right in an old pattern called double wedding rings. The two bands were linked together in an unending design. The upper left was another traditional pattern called log cabin. It symbolized our home together. The lower half was filled with farm scenes.

I laid it on the table in front of Ross. He gently touched the surface of the quilt with his great gnarled hands. "Looks real good," he said.

"It's about me," I said. "See the cross in the middle? That's the church. Those long beams of colour show how the church touched all parts of my life."

Ross looked closely. The rays spread over the surface, connecting with everything. It was extremely intricate.

"There's my childhood at the Catholic school, there's my marriage, there's my father giving me away to Ted. I was just a girl."

I could see Ross puzzling through the designs, trying to keep up with my story. He would look at me, then look at the quilt. All his life he had worked with animals and crops and weather, trying to figure them out. He had had his successes and failures over the years.

But women were a mystery to him and he had never married. He once told Ted that if you wrapped all your worries together with a stout piece of binder twine, they didn't come near a woman for trouble. He said that trying to understand a female was like trying to guess when a cow would freshen. She'd sneak that calf by you the one time you weren't looking and then bawl at you for not being there.

"I like that one the best," Ross said. He pointed to the farm on the lower half of the quilt, its rolling fields passing from one season to the other in shades of brown, green, gold then white. "It looks so peaceful under the snow."

I started to stitch again. My needle rose and fell, creating a long curving pattern on top of the quilt, like a line of fencing. "Ten stitches to the inch," I said proudly.

What a strange time to be discussing my quilt. My husband lay dead in a turnip field.

"Yer tellin' me 'bout Teddy."

I nodded. "The attic had been finished for less than a week and I had it nicely organized. Ted had been drinking all evening. I was upstairs quilting. He walked into the attic and started to stuff my squares and bolts of fabric and patterns into garbage bags. He didn't say a word. I didn't either. It was best to keep quiet when he was drinking. He threw the bags down the stairs and told me to take them out to the garbage. Then he moved all his things in. It was as if I didn't exist."

I stopped talking.

Ross' eyes burned into me. "Don't slack in the traces, Margie."

I didn't want to go on, but I did. "Ted forced me up to the attic and said it was his study now. I was to get undressed because the first thing he wanted to do was 'study' me. Thought he'd made a big joke."

I rubbed my hands together. "Do you understand what I'm telling you?" I was cold again.

Ross' eyes never left my face. He didn't answer.

"Ted went back downstairs. I heard him bumping around in the kitchen, pouring himself another beer. I got undressed. When I saw him stumble on the stairs I became concerned. I knew he was very drunk. I called to him, "Ted, be careful. Grab the railing.

You know how steep and narrow those open stairs are, Ross. He reached for the lamp on the landing to turn on the light. He stumbled and his beer spilled. He slid to his knees, lost his balance and fell back down the stairs. He hollered at me but there wasn't anything I could do. He was dead by the time I got to him. I couldn't save him."

I looked at Ross. "So if you go to the police, they'll probably say I pushed him down the stairs or that we had a fight." I stopped for a breath. "I swear Ross, I never touched him, except to bury him."

I began to cry.

"Stop bawlin' like a cow with milk fever," Ross said. "Everything's goin' to be all right. Yer like me, Margie. If it wasn't me savin' his hide I guess it was you doin' it. And Ted would want his passin' to be private-like. But I can't leave him lyin' out there on the ground, like an old seed bag. It's not fittin'. He needs proper buryin'. Family takes care of family."

Ross nodded as he spoke. "Course I can't think of a better place for him to be than in my turnip field. It's class one soil and it's got new tile drainage. Come home to his roots, didn't he?"

He smoothed his hair once more. "This'll just be between you and me, Margie. Don't you worry 'bout nothin'. I'll get out my backhoe and bury him proper. It's not the first time I've cleaned up after him."

He left the kitchen a few minutes later.

I sat by the fire and quilted. It calmed me. I knew that Ted could be truly laid to rest. I hand-stitched a cross on the quilt, in the farm's brown spring earth and put his name and the year of his death underneath.

I heard the sound of Ross' backhoe in the driveway a few hours later. The kitchen door banged opened and he walked in. He shuffled his feet a little on the mat, his eyes meeting mine.

"It's gettin' dark in here, Margie. Where'd mother's old fringe lamp get to?"

"I put it upstairs months ago."

A piece of hay clung to his bottom lip. He scraped his top teeth over the lip and pulled it into his mouth.

"I done the chores then buried Teddy." There was a long pause. "The way I see it, you an' me got a lot in common, Margie. We don't mind gettin' a little shit under our nails. So I thought we could help each other out now and then, know what I mean?" He knelt down and undid his work boots. The smell of fresh manure and sweat was overpowering.

"I always took care of Teddy. I left school and worked the farm so he could stay in school. He tol' me he needed a house after he came back with you and I severed off five acres fer him. I even built it for him. I saved his hide lotsa times when he got drunk and picked fights. I've hauled his ass out of more messes than I care to remember."

He smiled at me. "Course there's many the time he did the same fer me. Two peas in a pod my daddy used to say."

Ross sat heavily in the kitchen chair. "Get me a tea, would ya' Margie?" He shuffled uneasily. "Ted told me you was pregnant when youse got married."

I could barely hear his voice it was so low. I smiled to myself. One thing about farmers, they knew everything about everybody. They didn't always let on, but they knew. Except Ross didn't really know his own brother, his twin.

"Did he tell you when I lost the baby?" I said.

Ross nodded. "He was broken up about it."

I put the tea on to steep then settled into a chair across the table from him. He scratched the top of his head with his broken nails.

"Did he tell you how?"

He gave no answer, just a shake of his head.

"I didn't have his dinner ready when he came home from one of his long trips. He'd never tell me when he'd be back. I was sick and I hated the smell of food so I found it difficult to be in the kitchen. When he saw I didn't have the meal ready, he hit me."

The silence in the kitchen was terrible. I started sewing my quilt again. "He said he'd make sure the baby knew who was the boss in this house, too."

My hand went to my abdomen as if once again protecting the child from the blows. "I lost the baby that night."

Ross' face was filled with pain. "He beat you?"

"Lots of times."

"So why did ya stay?"

"Where was I going to go? I didn't finish high school. I didn't have any money. Where was I going to go?"

"He was a hard man, Margie. I admit that. He had a mean streak. I hauled his ass outa manys a mess."

Ross looked at me like he was sizing up an open heifer at a cattle auction. "Now I'm haulin' yers out," he said. "I took the backhoe out to the turnip field and dug a grave any man would be proud of. Teddy is down so deep even ol' Jip can't smell 'im. I'll seed it down to alfalfa and a nurse crop, come spring."

The heat from the stove made his forehead shine like paste. "I'll have it now, Margie."

I sat still, not comprehending.

His big hand flashed across the table and caught me square on the cheek. "My tea Margie, I'll have it now."

I jumped out of the chair, my face seared by the pain of the blow. I could feel my cheek flushing crimson.

"My daddy used to keep mother straight just like that. He'd say, "That's for nothin', wait'l you do somethin''. It made her mind him, fer sure."

I quickly poured Ross a cup of tea and placed it in front of him.

"You pour yerself one and come sit 'side me," he said.

I shook my head.

"I ast you nice, Margie. After all, family takes care of family. You'll do well by me. Now pour yerself some tea and sit here." He stood up and pulled out a chair.

I sat down on the seat, poised close to the edge. Ross stood behind me. He lowered his massive hands to my hair and then onto my shoulders. I jumped and tried to rise but he pushed me back down.

"Now you said you got nowheres to go so just settle yerself."

His hands roamed down to my breasts. "Guess we'll keep what happened to Teddy 'tween us, right Margie? Jist you and me." His voice was a croon.

His thick fingers undid the zipper on the front of my track suit. His heavy body pushed rhythmically into the back of the chair. I could feel his mouth, sour and wet in my hair, the stench of fermented haylage on his clothes, suffocating me.

"Now get yourself up to the attic 'cause I want a turn studyin' you. I'll be along soon's my tea's cooled."

It was happening all over again. I climbed to the attic and lay against the cushions hugging them close, waiting, my body so weary. I soon heard the soft squish of Ross' damp wool work socks as he approached the stairs. I watched his head and torso come into view. He had removed his workshirt. The arms and neck of his undershirt were banded with old sweat, like tree rings. His hands were feverishly undoing the belt buckle.

"Ross," I called. "Be careful. Grab the railing."

He grasped the wrought iron bar with his left hand pulling his heavy body upwards. "You like the light on or off, Margie?"

"On," I whispered. I watched his tongue wet his lips. His left hand slid farther along the railing, his right hand reached for the lamp on the landing.

His thumb pushed the switch and the lamp exploded. Ross' body lifted and arced backwards then crashed to the floor below.

I rushed down the stairs and stood near his bulk, my legs shaking. His socks smoked. The air was acrid with the smell of burning wire, flesh and wool. The Lord giveth and the Lord taketh away.

Today is memorable. I feel like going to confession. Forgive me, Father for I have sinned. Old habits die hard. Later, I'll hand-stitch the border onto the quilt - a tedious job. That would be my penance.

Earlier today I cleaned up the shattered glass on the landing. I found a small piece of scorched fringe in the attic. It must have blown into the room during the explosion last night. Luckily I found it. It could have been discovered by the wrong person. I can't afford mistakes like that. Goodness knows I made enough of them in my life. Ted was one of them.

My thoughts rushed out like water at spring break-up. He was never my husband, he was my keeper.

Ted enjoyed hurting me. Bending my fingers, hitting me very carefully so no one could see a mark. Of course he was always sorry afterward. He'd treat me so well for awhile that I'd think my mind was tricking me or I was going crazy.

I know why he didn't tell me when he was coming home, why he did all the shopping, why he chose everything in the house. Control. All I loved was the attic and he took that from me too.

Ted used to say that I was dumber than a dog. Well, I learned a few tricks. One of them was wiring. I learned that electricity followed the path of least resistance. That Saturday night last spring, after Ted tossed my quilts out of the attic and moved his things in, I knew it was time. There was no place for me to go. I had lost more than the attic.

I quickly re-wired the lamp he had bought for the landing while he was in the kitchen getting another beer. He grounded himself by grasping the wrought iron railing. The electricity passed right through his heart because he offered less resistance than the lamp. Ted made his electrocution more effective by spilling beer over his hands.

Afterwards, I manoeuvered his body into the little garden wagon attached to the lawn tractor. I drove him out the back to Ross' turnip field. It had been disced a few days before and was ready for the transplants. It was easy to dig in the soft earth. I buried Ted's business clothes, briefcase, wallet and the remains of that ugly Sears lamp in a deep hole, not far from his body. I had heard Ross tell Ted he would seed it down with alfalfa next spring.

Monday morning, I opened Ted's banking drawer. He didn't bank in Stouffville. He knew everyone there and didn't want them involved in his financial affairs. He had chosen the town of Aurora, where I bought my bike.

I filled in a withdrawal form for one thousand dollars, forged his signature and put the form in my fanny pack. I wore gloves in case the police fingerprinted the slip of paper, but I don't think they bothered.

I put the fanny pack and a track suit inside my backpack, along with my helmet and gloves, then lifted my bike into the back of Ted's car and drove to Yorkdale Centre. I didn't have a licence but over the years, fear had taught me ingenuity and given me the will to survive. I could have driven a Sherman tank if it had been necessary. I wore gloves the whole time.

There were hundreds of people pulling into the parking lot. I was invisible in the crowd. I slung my knapsack on, took my bike out of the car and rode north.

The bike ride to Aurora was one of the happiest and most carefree in my life. Outside the bank I locked my bike to a post, slipped into my track suit then stood in line trying to look as bored and depressed as the rest of the customers. It was difficult.

I made it home slightly ahead of the hard spring rain that obliterated my tracks out to the turnip field.

Ross' body was the devil to get out of the house last night. He was heavier than Ted. I rolled him out the door and into the backhoe's scoop and buried him in the valley with Ted. Two peas in a pod.

I returned the backhoe to Ross' farm and walked home as it began to snow, covering my tracks.

It stopped snowing during the night. Good. The fields are white but the roads are bare. More snow is forecast for tomorrow. I'm going riding as soon as I finish sewing on the border.

My story is right here in the quilt. The double wedding rings go on and on forever, like a Greek motif. Look closely. There's a break in the rings marked with my baby's tiny cross.

The log cabin design is intricately mismatched. It could never be a home where children laugh and play.

Throughout the quilt the great shafts of colour from the cross grasp at the images, coiling around everything like the tentacles of an octopus.

I stitched a cross for Ross in the white fields of the family farm, the place he said looked so peaceful under the snow. I put his name and the year of his death underneath. Family takes care of family.

The Big Lonely
WILLIAM BANKIER

*William Bankier, a transplanted Canadian now flourishing in Los
Angeles, has a thirty-some year record of success in the field of short
crime fiction. He is one of the two authors who has appeared in every
volume of the Cold Blood series.*

Tatum would never forget lifting the boss's wife in his arms and
carrying her up the hospital steps. Mrs. Farr had laughed, despite her
pain. "Cornell, this feels like 'Gone With The Wind'." It turned out to
be a serious ankle sprain. Seeing her take a tumble on the front steps,
Tatum had rushed her to Emergency.

That was where he first laid eyes on Sally Sheridan, behind the desk,
taking down information. Of course, she knew Louisa Farr. Everybody
in Baytown knew the Farrs. Hungerford Farr was Maple Lane Dairy.
The milk he processed and bottled ended up on most kitchen tables
across the county.

But not everybody knew Cornell Tatum at that time. He was still
just a big, square-faced man with his cap on straight, rock solid behind
the wheel of the Farr limo.

That's how it was when a stranger arrived in Baytown. People saw
the individual, but they didn't know him. They observed him running
milk to back doors as the new helper on one of the Farr delivery wagons.
And a few may have noticed when he was promoted to chauffeur. That
happened because Tatum caught old Hungerford's eye; the boss appre-
ciated his clean-cut appearance and quiet manner.

This 'speak when spoken to' tendency had been hammered into the
child Tatum by his domineering father, Bud. Nobody in Baytown knew
that, of course. Or that Cornell was still somewhat afraid of his father,

even though he had left the old man and his trashy girl friend back in Montreal.

Sally Sheridan was the first person in town to get close to Tatum, emotionally. "Would you like a cup of coffee, Cornell?" She had heard Mrs. Farr call the chauffeur by his Christian name. He was sitting now on a polished oak bench with the heels of his shiny black boots together and the leather visor of his cap dead center on his knees.

"Milk, no sugar," he said.

"Hope you don't mind me calling you Cornell." She had always felt easy around men. Her father owned Sheridan's cigar store down Front Street near the Coronet Hotel. That was where Sid, the Farr's former chauffeur, won a lot of money in a back-room poker game. The pot was rich enough, and his deal suspicious enough, that Sid took the hint in the eyes around the table and got out of town. Which led to Cornell being offered the job as driver. This coming and going of poker players had made Sally comfortable with men. "I like the name Cornell," she said as she passed him the coffee.

"Thanks, Sally," he said. He nodded at her name-plate on the desk.

The Farrs let him take the small car of an evening, as long as the occasions were not too frequent. He picked Sally up at her house on the Trent Road. "I remember you," her father said. "You stayed at the Coronet when you got here. Came into the store for newspapers and candy." Sheridan was typical. Born in Baytown, he would never dream of leaving. But it mystified him why anybody would come here. Tatum's arrival in town was as shocking as if a Spanish galleon had sailed up the Bay and landed a party of conquistadors.

"You should get yourself a decent aerial," Tatum said. He was waiting for Sally who had raced upstairs after letting him into the house. Her shiny legs were a joyful sight.

Sheridan was watching an indistinct picture on the television. Faces could be seen through a blizzard of snow. "I get clear reception on the CBC channels," he explained. "This is Buffalo, across the Lake. I like it this way. It reminds me I'm looking at something from a long ways off."

Cornell and Sally saw a movie at the Capitol and then had a meal at the Round Spot on the highway. She made a face after they ordered. "I always have this feeling I'll die here. From the food."

She came back with him to his apartment above the garage nearly half a mile from the big house. A carpet of grass with chestnut trees separated owner and servant. "Look at this gorgeous furniture," she said.

"Best I ever had," Tatum conceded. It had all been moved in years ago from the main house when Louisa Farr redecorated.

They sat close together on a velvet settee with a magazine open across their knees. She flipped the pages. When that was done, Tatum switched the lamp to low and turned on the radio to an all-night music program coming in clear as a bell through the frosty atmosphere, all the way from Toronto. They kissed a few times, getting better at it. They lay down together, heads on a soft cushion. She fell asleep in his arms while the DJ played the Artie Shaw recording of 'Frenesi'.

A week later, Tatum held open the passenger door while Mrs. Farr climbed out and limped up the broad steps. She was inside, setting her purse on a small marble table, touching the corners of her mouth with a tissue as she studied her face in the mirror. Tatum caught up. He was carrying three shopping bags he had retrieved from the trunk.

"Can I ask you something, Mrs. Farr?"

"Surely, Cornell." She always looked directly at his chest and then, smiling, glanced up to his face.

"I've been seeing Sally Sheridan."

"It's the talk of the town. Just kidding."

"Would it be okay with you and Mr. Farr if she moved into the apartment with me?"

"I think having Sally together with you over there could only enhance the value of our property." Now she was serious; she put her hand on his sleeve, gently. "Mr. Farr has his own set of values. He sometimes reads the Lesson on Sundays."

"I know."

"Can I tell him it's in your plans to get married?"

"It certainly is in my plans," Tatum said. The wedding was quick and quiet. Sally said she did not want all the rigmarole of bridal showers and matching dresses, and tossing the bouquet. The truth was, though she did not admit it even to herself, that she did not want to concede she was marrying, after all these many years, a chauffeur. There was another side to it. Here was this big, lonely man, not bad looking and totally decent from all she had been able to learn. Becoming his wife was a good step ahead from where she had been. She just didn't want the ceremony.

So they took care of it, after three day's notice, in the vestry of St. James's United Church on Ste. Catherine Street in Montreal. Witnesses were the custodian and his wife. Checked in at the Mt. Royal Hotel, they began to enjoy a honeymoon sweeter than any holiday in Sally's experience. Being a Montrealer, Cornell knew his way around. They climbed countless steps up the Mountain to the lookout. Standing at the parapet, he pointed out the location of their hotel in a maze of streets and rooftops. He showed her the green hills of Vermont, hazy on the far horizon.

They wandered down pathways to Beaver Lake and, while she rested on the grass, he walked into the pavilion and brought back hot dogs and orange drinks. It was pure fun. But she began to notice that, after each new excursion into joy, there was a subtle change in Cornell's mood. He would recede into himself, as if there was something corrosive in the atmosphere. It seemed to be an influence from which he had to escape.

She asked him about it that evening when they had finished their lobster and white wine at a restaurant in the Old Town. "What's on your mind, Cornell? Something's been troubling you since we got here."

"It shows?"

"I think it's spoiling your enjoyment."

"You're not wrong. It's my father."

"You said your parents are dead."

"My mother is." Tatum sipped from an empty glass. "My father is still in the old house on the South Shore."

"I take it you don't get along."

"There's more to it than that."

"Yes?"

He decided to tell her his secret. "I've always suspected he murdered my mother."

It was too late that evening to visit Bud Tatum over the river in St. Lambert. They went back to the hotel and sat in the lobby, watching people come and go through the inside door of the Kon-Tiki. Cornell made a telephone call, a short one, informing his father he was in town with his bride and would he like them to drop in?

"He says come over tomorrow afternoon," Cornell told Sally who was pressing the coin-return buttons on the adjoining telephones. "It's his day off from the print shop. He's setting photo-type for a living."

The couple went back to their settee. Sally was still disturbed by her husband's revelation. "I'm having trouble understanding why you never told anybody. If not the police, then a friend. The Minister. Somebody."

"There was no evidence. Only a feeling I had. I was fifteen years old, a very immature fifteen. Sally, you would not have recognized me."

"Is it possible he was telling the truth?"

"That my mother abandoned us? Ran back to Nova Scotia to be with her family? It's possible. She used to go home for visits. But she always telephoned, she wrote letters. This time - nothing."

"And you never tried to get in touch with her?"

"I can't explain it." He gave it some thought. "It was as if the ball was in her court. No, more like I was afraid my father might be right. I might contact her and she'd cut me off. Leave me alone, she'd say. You're the reason I ran away. I didn't want to hear that."

"Okay, she took off. Women do that - not as often as they should. But now you're saying he killed her."

"He moved in this other woman. Freda Belcher. She was somebody he met where he used to drink. Freda is nothing like mother." Tatum stared at the lobby carpet. "He didn't mention her just now and I didn't ask. I hope old Freda isn't around when we go there tomorrow."

The view from the Jacques Cartier Bridge was spectacular as the taxi carried Cornell and Sally across to the South Shore. There were whitecaps on the river. Tatum was astonished when they drove through residential streets on the way to his father's house. "This was all open space," he said.

There were still vacant lots on either side of Bud Tatum's frame house. He owned the land, and he was not inclined to sell at the time. The building had a home-made appearance; no architectural drawings had been followed in its construction. There was a porch on one corner, then two sets of large windows to one side. The porch had one step too many leading the visitors up to a dark blue door.

A bulky woman responded when Tatum rang the bell. She wore a tight yellow perm and high-bib overalls with a pouch of cigarettes in the breast pocket. "Look at you," she said. "All grown up."

Tatum introduced his wife to Freda Belcher. He said, "Your hair is the same," as they went on into the kitchen. His father was at the table, using sandpaper on a ghostly wooden mallard.

"What you see when you don't have a gun." The older Tatum was a round, short version of Cornell.

"Don't get that wood dust in the sugar," Freda said. Freda snatched beer bottles from a case of twenty four on the floor below the counter. She provided tumblers for the guests.

"How long are you in town?" Bud enquired.

"Just another day or so. We're on our honeymoon, as I said over the telephone."

"If you'd let us know ahead, I could have got you something." That was the last the newlyweds ever heard of that.

Sally was offended and fascinated by the response to their visit. Freda was easy, she was taking them as free entertainment that would soon be over. But the relationship between Cornell and his father was frightening in its lack of communication. They were like secret agents sent to meet in a bar. And neither one could remember the password.

"He built everything himself," Cornell was saying. "Mixed the concrete. Cut the lumber. Carried the stones from the field."

"You were no help," the father said. "Remember.the chimney? You were twenty feet up on the scaffold you'd made and when you lifted that slab of granite, the whole thing started to collapse. You ended up clinging to a window ledge."

"Until you finally opened the window."

"You could have killed yourself."

"No thanks to you I didn't."

"And then mother might still be alive."

Freda looked from face to face. "Whatever that's supposed to mean."

Bud Tatum picked up a sharp knife and began to make fierce cuts to accentuate the decoy's wings. It was getting dark. Freda said, "I'm supposed to make supper." She opened and closed cupboard doors. "There's nothing here."

"Can we take you some place to eat?" Tatum said.

"Count us out," his father said. Freda wheeled to the window and folded her arms.

They called a taxi and raced back across the bridge. In the years that followed, Sally and Cornell talked often about their honeymoon in Montreal - the unforgettable dinner at 'Mas des Oliviers'; their romantic ride in a calèche. But they almost never referred to the visit with Tatum's father and his common-law wife.

The population of Baytown increased over the years. The number of cars on the road tripled, and not all the drivers were as careful as Cornell Tatum. Old Hungerford Farr used his driver as the subject of a sermon delivered over drinks at the club. The man had the solution to traffic dangers. Total concentration.

Almost every day, however, Tatum's attention would drift onto the question of what had happened to his mother. The honeymoon visit to the old house had done nothing to quiet his suspicion. The passing reference at the kitchen table and his father's angry reaction with the knife, supported him in his belief that there had been violence.

Some day, not now, he would confront the old man with a direct accusation. He would permit no glib answer. Tatum's grip on the steering wheel would tighten until his knuckles hurt. Maybe he would beat the truth out of him.

The letter from his father arrived ten years into their marriage, and was a complete surprise to the Tatums. Bud seldom wrote letters. This one's pleading tone might have indicated that the old man was changing, had Cornell noticed it at the time. But he did not. "I don't know what to do, son. I should never have sold to this guy, Mellanby. He keeps bothering me about this and that. But I needed the money, so I deeded over that whole side of the property. He's put up this gigantic house. I wish you could have advised me. Freda is no use. I guess I have to live with it."

Tatum sent a blunt reply. He thought Bud was complaining over nothing. Too much time on his hands, he should carve more ducks.

Sally Sheridan died five years after the incident of the letter, when she was only 46 years old. She was in the wrong place at the wrong time. Daylight robbery was taking place at the Round Spot, not far from the hospital. Two scattered individuals came in off the highway from Toronto and tried to rob the cashier at gun-point. A Baytown plain-clothes officer was eating his lunch. He drew the weapon he was licensed to carry and followed the bandits out of the restaurant.

When he challenged the men, shots were exchanged in the parking lot. Sally was walking in to pick up a western sandwich, fries and a vanilla shake to go. A bullet struck her above the right ear and she died instantly.

After the funeral, which was attended by almost as many people as might show up for a week-night softball game at the CNR Recreation Grounds, Tatum tried to side-step the pain. Alone in the apartment above the garage, he kept finding a crumpled tissue in one of her coat pockets, or a scrap of paper carrying her hand-writing. The paperback, open and lying face down on the bathroom floor, shocked him as much as if it had been a tarantula. He kicked it across the room, then grabbed it up and tore it in half.

Tatum cursed the day he met Sally Sheridan. He wanted not ever to have spent a minute with her so that he could be plodding through life now, bored but free of agony. He was like a man on a beach facing a succession of giant waves, trying to remain dry.

"Will you be all right?" his employer asked him in a troubled tone of voice. It was a glorious, sunny day and the chauffeur, chamois in hand, was buffing the hood of the black limousine.

"I'll be fine." Tatum's grey face drifted back and forth in the polished surface like a fish in deep water.

And he was fine, as soon as he managed to turn his attention from what was gone forever to what was yet to be. His father was alone now, too. He had telephoned the old man to invite him to the funeral. Bud declined to come, but he did pass on some information. Freda Belcher was dead, almost two years. Cirrhosis of the liver.

It was time. Cornell was ready. With nothing to lose but the grief attached to his bereavement, Tatum could confront his father without fear. Simply tell the truth, dammit. What happened to my mother?

This time, Tatum rented a car for the Montreal journey. All those years down the road from his wedding trip, he had no interest in checking into a hotel. His destination was his father's house in St. Lambert. There would be no bottles of beer, no pretense at hospitality.

The small, light car felt risky on the road compared to his employer's limousine. The chauffeur drove slowly on the highway. Approaching Montreal along Upper Lachine Road, he stopped at a diner for coffee and a sandwich.

On the way back to the car, he dropped money in a telephone. Now was the time to announce his arrival, when he was too close for Bud to put him off. But the telephone rang ten times, and Tatum had to give up. Never mind. Arriving unannounced might be even better.

There was a lot of traffic moving in both directions over the bridge. It was late afternoon but with plenty of grey light in the sky. Parking in front of the house, Tatum saw the new dwelling occupying the lot on the right. It was a handsome ranch- style bungalow, much more to his taste than his father's tall box beside it. Here was the home his father had complained about in his letter. Typical; Bud Tatum sold the man the land, then did nothing but carp about the structure he built on it.

The doorbell rang inside without any response. Tatum stood on the porch and wondered what to do. He began to wish he had arranged the visit. What if Bud was out of town?

A man appeared on the lawn next door, coming from the rear of the new bungalow. He was in his late twenties, dressed in casual clothes. "Are you looking for Tatum?"

"I'm his son."

"Good. He's not there, I saw him leave earlier." The neighbour approached and offered his hand. "I'm Hank Mellanby. Can I ask you something?"

"Okay." Tatum felt comfortable.

"I have to show you what it is. Can you come around back?" He led the way along a grassy path beside his house. A young woman was watching television beyond a low window. "I'm going to ask you to intercede on my behalf with your father."

Hank Mellanby's garden extended behind Bud Tatum's house. A waist-high chain-link fence separated the two properties. The new resident was leading Tatum to the fence. There was a rectangular jog in the fence, several feet long. It extended at least three feet onto Mellanby's land.

"This is your father's fence. I'm young, I'm not experienced. Everything was hectic and I was confused when the deed was signed."

Tatum was staring at the narrow slot of ground that remained his father's property, that the fence had been built to contain. His flesh felt cold, the hair on the back of his neck was erect.

"Don't tell me to see a lawyer," Mellanby went on. "I've done that. This is legal. The survey was completed, then he decided he wanted that piece. So the line was changed and I didn't catch it. But it bothers me. I'd like you to speak to the old man. Persuade him to let me buy this little section. Turn the boundary back into a straight line."

Tatum managed to say, "Has he told you why he wants it this way?"

"He calls it his veggie garden. Do you see any veggies?"

Tatum declined hospitality at the Mellanby house. He waited outside in the rental car. He must have fallen asleep and dreamed because an electric tram rolled slowly down the street and stopped. Sally Sheridan got off, looking as fresh as the day he met her. She was dressed in her travelling suit. She said nothing but stood at a distance and gave him a disapproving smile. The slight movement of her head and the raised finger told him, "Don't do this."

Tatum opened his eyes, the street was empty. It was dark, there were lights turned on inside the house. He saw Bud moving around behind one of the front windows.

At the funereal blue door, Tatum ignored the bell. He used his fist to pound on the panel, three times. The door was opened quickly to reveal Bud's frightened face. When the old man saw his son standing there, he broke into a grin that was close to tears. Collapsed cheeks showed that his dentures were not in place.

"I heard the hammering, I thought it was the Mounties. Come in, my boy. Have you had supper? How about a beer? Have one with your old man."

Tatum had never experienced such effusiveness in his father. "Why should the police come here?" he asked, following Bud into the kitchen.

"I'm so effing lonely now Freda's gone. Turns out I can't hack it. Second time I'm in an empty house. Freda drank herself to death. Well, it's one way."

Tatum lifted his beer and wet his lips. "What about mother? How did she die?"

"Your mother was a saint. I could never measure up to what she expected. You're like her. You were such a good kid. Never caused any trouble, always did your work."

Tatum felt as if he had run, full speed, into a wall in pitch darkness. "You've completely altered the past in your own mind! Don't you remember what it was like?" He felt like screaming.

"Rita was a very ordinary woman. I realize that. She drank too much, she dressed like a farmer. But that's what I deserve. You were right to leave home, Cornell. Once your mother was gone, there was nothing here for you."

The old man's face was shining on him like the sun. Tatum said, "She never went to Nova Scotia, did she? You can tell the truth now. All those years ago. What really happened?"

"Can you stay the night, son? Hang around for a few days? I find it hard, being by myself. I can't stop thinking about what's coming. And there's no avoiding it. Have you thought about the loneliness when you die? We go through terrible things in life - illness, the dentist, car accidents, pinned in the wreckage. But you always have people with you." Tatum looked far beyond the walls of the bright kitchen. "The big lonely," he said. "I'm really scared."

"Mellanby, next door?" Tatum said. "He showed me the jog in the fence. You went to a lot of trouble and expense to keep that patch of ground."

"One good thing," Bud said, trying to drag his spirits back up. "All the grief, all the stains, the things you couldn't handle, they disappear when you go. Like they never existed."

"That's not true. Everything you do has an effect on others. They still have to deal with it, after you're gone."

Smiling, the old man reached across the table and covered one of Tatum's hands with both of his. He whispered the message like a secret that was his alone. "And God shall wipe away all tears from our eyes."

"Finish your beer, father. There's something we have to look at."

"I was never any kind of war hero. Did you buy those stories I used to tell about convoy duty in the North Atlantic? I was in a corvette, but I never saw any action. That one about ramming a German submarine when it surfaced? I heard that in a Halifax bar, from a guy who was on the destroyer that did it."

"Who cares?"

"I made money from my mates. I cut hair. Listen to this. We'd come into port to refuel and reprovision. I'd set up a dozen canvasses, nine by twelve, and I'd massproduce a picture of the ship. Paint all the water, all the skies, all the gun-bursts. I could do the dozen in an afternoon."

"This isn't important."

"Then I'd set up a chair and a mirror and I had my barber kit. The guys would line up. They got a haircut, a coke, and a painting of the ship - all for ten bucks." Bud looked proud. "Lot of money in '43."

Tatum set aside his half-full glass. He got up from the table. "Have you got a flashlight?"

"Okay, you want to go out there."

In the garage, they found a lantern with a 6-volt battery. it threw a powerful beam. Tatum picked up a spade with a sharp edge. He led the way across the back lawn to the rectangular patch of ground that stretched into Mellanby's property.

"Okay if I dig here?"

"Feel free."

"Won't disturb your veggies?" Tatum positioned the tip of the spade, pressed the sole of his boot on the implement's shoulder, turned the first sod. It was slow going. The earth was packed hard. His father held the light, shifting his weight from leg to leg. For a while he set the lamp between his feet, hunkered down and watched as if hypnotized, elbows on knees, chin cupped in both hands.

Tatum was working in a hole three feet deep when he struck the first bone. "Aim it down here," he said. He began to scrape away earth. It was a long bone. There was a scattered throw of knuckles. He picked up an object and held it to the light. Rusted, mud-covered, but easily identifiable, it was an elegant wristwatch.

For the first time in an hour, Tatum raised his head and stared directly at his father. Bud was on all fours, peering into the hole. His face was a pale mask, dark eyes wide, the toothless mouth working. "It's worse than I thought," he whispered. "Look. Look how lonely she is!"

Tatum showered. Opening the grave and filling it in again had left him exhausted. He stood for a long time in the ancient tub, motionless under the flow of hot water, staring at the steam collecting under the ceiling. What was the right thing to do? Living with uncertainty about his mother had caused constant distress. But he hated the new reality.

His father was well and truly gone forever. The old man was out of his mind. A trial would see him convicted, obviously. He would end up in some institution. Tatum would be expected to show up for visits on a regular basis, bringing packages, dealing with guards. He wanted none of it. Nor did he welcome the prospect of his family scandal being brought home to Baytown.

Unlike the old days, it seemed he was allowed to use all the hot water there was. Still thinking, he closed the taps, found his towel in the steamy room and gave himself a ferocious rub-down. The idea occurred to him as he was combing his hair, staring at himself in the medicine cabinet mirror. It was a fine idea.

He, Cornell Tatum, could not be positive whose bones were there in the ground. An expert could figure it out, but he had decided not to call in the experts. Because it could very well be Freda Belcher's remains buried there. He had only his father's word for it that she had died of liver disease. And his father's word was garbage. Perhaps they argued, it became physical, and Bud beat Freda to death.

That would mean - and this perception brought a lift to Tatum's spirits - that his mother was alive in Nova Scotia! She had been there all the time, was still there, enjoying the company of her family! He would not pursue this situation to confirm it, would not seek his mother out. Finding her would mean telling her about her husband's crime. Better to let the poor, dear woman rest in peace.

Bud Tatum was eating a bowl of corn flakes when his son came into the kitchen, gleaming from his shower. Cornell picked up the cereal box. "Mind if I join you?" he said. Then, as flakes cascaded into a bowl, he asked, "When are you going to plant that plot of ground back there?"

"Never been sure what to put in."

"The earth is freshly turned. Why don't we buy seeds in the morning and I'll help you plant it."

The eyes of a child stared from the old man's face. He was taking on his most difficult decision in life, so far. A single drop of milk fell from his lower lip as he said, "Radishes?"

The Midnight Boat to Palermo
ROSEMARY AUBERT

Rosemary Aubert is a Toronto writer and writing teacher, and a member of Crime Writers of Canada. Though fiction, this story is based on her personal experience as an Italian-American immigrant to Canada as well as her research into the complex geography of the heroin trade in the 1950's.

What I loved most about meeting the midnight boat was not the motion of the waves, though I often thought the movement of the sea made it easier to sleep than the stillness of my bed. Nor was it the moonlight that I loved, for I was afraid of moonlight and am to this day. Many of the women in our self-help group speak of their fear of moonlight. Sometimes they connect it to abusive fathers or to their general terror of night. I loved my father and he never abused me in the way some of these women have been abused. But, like them, talking now about my youth, I have stirred up a memory that I had buried long ago--forty years, in fact. I have suddenly understood that my father was murdered. I have suddenly remembered that I was there when he was killed. I have suddenly realized the name of his killer.

What I loved most about the midnight night boat to Palermo was the silence. For my world, both then and now, has been a very noisy one. When I first came to this country, though I could not speak the language, I knew already that I spoke too loudly. How else could it be? There were, after all, seven of us, and we lived in a tiny hut on the shore of the inlet. We didn't call it an inlet, of course. That's a word I learned much later--in a writing class sponsored by the government. But an inlet it was, a little indentation in the rocks of the shore of Sicily. And when you spoke, if you were to be heard at all, you had to shout not only above the sound of all the brothers and sisters, not only above the arguing of my parents, but above the sound of the sea. That's what we called it. Not an inlet, the sea.

Like most of the people of our village, we were not rich. But we had plenty to eat and good clothes to wear, even though the Second World War had been over for only a few years. Twice a year, my mother would go to Rome and buy me and my sisters dresses, blouses with lace, shoes to wear to church on Sunday. Rome is a long way from Sicily, and it must have cost a lot to get there. There were no planes then, so of course, she would have had to take a boat. The trip alone would have cost more than the average fisherman in the village could make in a year. Looking back on it now, it amazes me that we never questioned such prosperity. Nor did I question my mother's attitude about these trips. For weeks before, she'd be so sweet to us, so kind. Instead of her usual severity, she'd be almost gay. Though she said she hated to leave us, it was hard to ignore her happiness, just as when she returned, it was hard to ignore how angry she seemed to be for weeks. My mother, I thought then, was an unpredictable woman. But now I see, after all these years, she was far more predictable than I could have imagined.

We were told that her trips to Rome were to visit relatives. We seemed to have relatives everywhere, and to visit one--no matter how far away they might live--was another thing we never questioned. It was to visit a relative that we came to Canada. Once we got here, we never went back. But that was a very long time ago.

When my mother was home, which was most of the time, she was a good mother. She sewed, she cleaned, and she made a tomato sauce that was famous in our little village. To this day, I can see her standing at the stove preparing it. She would start by heating a huge black iron pan and carefully dripping onto its hot surface a thin dribble of the purest olive oil. ''This is our gold,'' she would say of that oil. Then she would take a bud of garlic and carefully separating out each clove, would peel it with her slow, strong hands. When the heated oil had turned the garlic as golden as itself, she would add pieces of beef, each of which she had stuffed with bits of cheese and parsley, black pepper, salt and also with raisins--which was one of her secrets. This meat, too, would soon turn a golden color, and the smell of our little house would make your mouth water. When the meat was done, she'd remove it from the pan and put it into a pot. Then, to the drippings in the pan, she would add the tomato paste. It has been more than forty years since I have seen these things, but I remember as if I were standing there now how she would go to a little panty off our kitchen, a place where the rocks outside rose up right against our house and kept the sun from ever shining on that wall. The pantry was always cold, no matter the time of year, and from one of its shelves, my mother would take an earthenware crock of tomato paste. This paste had been dried in the sun by her own grandmother from tomatoes the old woman had grown herself. It was almost black, and I used to think it looked like poison. Yet even then I understood that this was another one of my mother's secrets. For the tomato paste made the sauce rich and thick and gave it such a deep flavor that it seemed to have been cooked not for hours, but forever. However, when she added this ingredient, my mother had to be very careful. If she added too much, or if she didn't cook it until it, too, was almost golden, the sauce would be bitter--a failure. After the tomato paste, the only other ingredient she added was fresh tomatoes. And one other thing--the real secret. When the sauce had cooked for two hours, my mother would add a teaspoon of sugar. Never more. Never less. Often, she would ask me to bring her the sugar from a cupboard across the kitchen from the stove. And often, I would take a spoonful for myself before I got to her side. Once, she caught me doing this, and she laughed.

Thursday was the day she made sauce. And Thursday was the night that it was my father's turn to meet the midnight boat to Palermo. I always thought that my father died on a Friday, but now I understand that was too simple a way to look at things. He was found dead on a Friday. He was killed on Thursday--the Thursday we, he and I, like always, were supposed to meet the Palermo boat but didn't.

My father, and all the other men in the village, worked in the sugar factory. Being only eight years old, I thought the factory had been there forever, just because it had been there as long as I could remember. Now I see that was wrong. It could only have been set up after the war, when I was two or three. When I was little, though, the sugar factory was one of the centers of my life. Though my own children seemed to spend all their time in school when they were eight years old, I certainly did not. There was only one teacher, an old woman whose son had gone away and never come back and who could speak of little else, even when she was supposed to be teaching us math or the history of the rulers of Sicily. It was easy to sneak out of school without her even noticing--or not to go at all, which was what I often did. The minute I was free, I headed for the factory.

Now it is very important for me to explain that I did not go to the factory to eat the sugar. The mysterious thing about the factory was that nobody was ever allowed to eat the sugar there. Zi Antonio had forbidden it. Anyone who so much as tasted the tiniest bit would have to leave their work--forever. Zi Antonio was the mayor of our little village, though that word--mayor--is another that we never used, that I never even learned until I came here. My father told me that Zi Antonio said it was bad business to eat your own product, that that was how people lost money, that it showed a lack of respect.

I had another way of looking at it, and it was one of the reasons that I visited the sugar factory so often. In order for this to make sense, I have to describe how the sugar factory looked. Though now that I finally know what I'm really describing, I must admit that this might not at all have been how the factory was--just how it looked to me when I was eight years old.

Unlike any other building in our village, the factory was built of some clean, smooth material--concrete, I'd say. And it had no windows. The only way you could see inside was if you stood by the wide rear door, which I often did. Once in a while, someone would come out to chase me away, and I would go. Then I would come back.

The roof of the factory was covered in pipes, sticking up toward the sky like chimneys. Sometimes white smoke drifted carelessly up out of them. Sometimes black smoke made a straight high column against the blue Sicilian sky. And sometimes steam shot up like a volcano. When this happened, it scared me and I ran away. But I always came back.

The only times I ever stayed away for long were the few times that Zi Antonio, himself, chased me. He hardly ever came to the sugar factory, though he seemed to be everywhere else in town, including our house. As I recall, the first time he caught me, I was merely wandering around the factory yard. Out there were piles and piles of barrels just like the ones we got when we met the Palermo boat. The day Zi Antonio first warned me not to play around the factory, he caught me completely by surprise because I didn't see him coming. I was leaning over a row of barrels trying to figure out if they were empty. I was thumping them, the way I'd seen my mother thump an eggplant to see if it was ripe. I'd just about decided that the barrels were in fact empty, when I heard a shout close behind me. I jumped a mile. When I came to my senses, I saw Zi Antonio towering over me like the picture of the ogre in the storybook my cousin Teresa had sent me from America. I started to cry.

Now I have to say about Zi Antonio that he always treated me and my brothers and sisters very well. Come to think of it, it's unlikely that he would be mean to us, considering how he must have hoped things would turn out--did turn out. Anyway, despite his terrible scowl, when he saw my face, his own broke into a smile.

"No, no, no," he said simply and shooed me away.

The second time he caught me, I was doing the same thing. The barrels seemed empty that time, too. The third time Zi Antonio warned me about hanging around the factory, he said that if I continued to play there, my father would lose his job. Of course, that time I listened and stayed away for months.

What I was really trying to figure out was whether the sugar in the factory was poison and whether something the men, including my father, did to it made it not be poison any more, so that when it left the factory--and then only--we could eat it.

As I remember these things, its amazes me how long such silly notions remain in a person's head. Many years after we had come to this country, when my own children were teenagers, my husband and I took a vacation to Cuba. There we saw a real sugar factory. As I leaned over the open vat of brown solution that the guide explained would evaporate into white crystals, I still wondered whether the solution (which was nothing really but sugar cane and water) was poison, and whether the complicated system of heating devices they showed us was what removed the poison from the cane!

Everybody knew that Zi Antonio was the boss of the factory. We knew also that he was a special friend of the old woman who was our teacher. We knew too, that Zi Antonio was somehow in charge of the parish church, though we assumed that must only be when the priest wasn't praying or doing holy things. Zi Antonio, for instance, was in charge of charity--being a very generous man. He was also always present at funerals, consoling the mother and the widow.

Zi Antonio was also a special friend of my mother. It was because of him, I always thought, that she took such care every Thursday when she made the sauce, for he was always our dinner guest on that night. Once I asked my mother whether Zi Antonio had a wife of his own to make the sauce. She smiled then, gently, like a picture of the Blessed Virgin Mary, and she told me that Zi Antonio had a beautiful wife who was now in heaven with the angels and the holy saints.

So, I thought, that was why one night a week, he came to dinner at our house. It was regular as the clock. All afternoon my mother would cook the sauce while my father worked at the factory. Zi Antonio would arrive. My father, coming home, would wash outside by the pump, then join our guest for dinner. Being a quiet man, my father would generally say very little at the table, but Zi Antonio was funny, and his jokes had me and my sisters and brothers--and of course my mother--laughing so hard that sometimes we didn't even finish our meal.

I ate faster than the others because I had to get ready to go with my father to meet the Palermo boat. I packed us a lunch. I got our sweaters and some blankets out of the closet and put them by the door. And I filled our lantern. We needed it to signal the big boat so that it could see where we were and so the sailors could see what they were doing when they lowered the barrels off their deck into the bottom of our boat. There were usually six barrels, but they were fairly small--and so, of course, was I. I don't recall ever worrying about whether the barrels would fit into our boat.

Nor do I recall ever worrying about our safety, though once in a while, a wind would arise, or the open boat would be slashed by rain. My trust in my father was absolute. To this day, even speaking of these things, it's as though a feeling of peace settles over me and the terrible dangers of life just seem to go away for a little. I see now, to be sure, that what I was doing with my father was the most dangerous thing I've ever done, but such is the innocence of children--of anyone, really--that we can only fear what we think is dangerous.

After dinner, Zi Antonio and my mother would visit in the little parlor that she kept so spotless. She would take the bottle of Strega out from the wooden cabinet, place it with two sparkling glasses on a silver tray and carry it out to the big chair that my own father never had time to sit in on Thursdays. Not that he seemed to mind. He was all energy as we loaded up with the things we had to carry out to our boat, though sometimes, as the door closed behind us, he had a look on his face that made me think he wanted to cry.

But I guess I must have cheered him up, because as we walked down the path to the beach--not very far from the back of the sugar factory-- I would ask him to tell me his stories of the sea, and he always did. He knew about pirates, about explorers, about the sacred missionaries of the Church. He also told me about the people--some from our own village--who had crossed the ocean to get to America. We had, he said, some relatives in Toronto and New York. But when I asked him whether they were like the relatives in Rome, his face collapsed into sadness--even anger, so I stopped talking, and together we worked in silence, stowing our gear.

By this time, the sun would be low over the water. I would lie against the pile of blankets as my father pulled slowly away from the village. As we got farther and farther out, I pretended that this night, instead of meeting the Palermo boat, we would just keep going. As the last thing to fade from sight--the chimneys of the sugar factory--slipped away, the rocking of the boat would start to get to me. I would doze off. Often, the next thing I knew, I would be lying on the boat bottom staring straight up toward the stars.

Nothing in my life since has ever equalled the peace of those nights. It seemed we drifted out there for hours, sometimes seeing the lights of fishing vessels and once even seeing a ship much larger than the one we waited for. My father and I, alone, silent, drifted in the middle of the water with no land in sight, no one to see us or talk to us or ask us what we were doing out there. I, however, asked questions.

I asked my father what was in the barrels that we took from the Palermo ship into our own. He smiled and said that it was a syrup that came from far away, a syrup that was needed in order to make sugar. Of course, I have for such a long time thought he meant some sort of extract from sugar cane, that four decades later it took me hours before this piece of his tragic puzzle fell into place. I asked him why nobody at the sugar factory could eat the sugar. This was a trick question. I knew, as all children do, that sometimes if you ask a question over and over again, the answer that has always been the same answer, can slip into a different answer--the truth. But he said, as he always did, that it was bad business, that it showed a lack of respect and that all the sugar at the factory belonged to Zi Antonio.

So I decided to ask him about Zi Antonio. He said that Zi Antonio was the boss of the sugar factory but that he, too, had his own bosses. He told me that this was true of everyone and that no matter how you lived your life, there was always somebody who had the power to tell you what to do. I didn't know what he was talking about.

I also couldn't really understand why we had to wait so very long some nights, though my father explained again and again. He said that the boat to Palermo had left a far away country called Turkey. He said that when a ship was at sea, it never knew how long it would take for its journey--that the wind could speed it or slow it, that the waves could be so high out there sometimes that the boat had twice as far to go--up one side, down the other. I laughed at this joke and, huddled in my warm sweater, settled back to enjoy the sandwiches I had made for us.

Often, when the boat did come, I'd been asleep, and sometimes I only woke up when I heard the shouts and saw the barrels being lowered down. Then I would fall asleep again and not wake up until our little boat reached the shore. I would crawl out onto the sand and wait there as my father rolled the barrels up into the yard of the factory. Then, he would take my hand and lead me along the path that went to our small house. We'd tiptoe in, and he would tuck me into bed. Usually I was fast asleep before my door even closed, my sisters breathing silently beside me. Sometimes, though, I stayed awake until my father opened the door to the room where he and my mother slept and slipped in.

Now that I look back on this, it seems that we carried out this routine for years. That, however, is the view of a child. Maybe we did it only for a few months. Maybe we did it only a few times. I don't know. But my memory of it is so vivid and complete that I remember every detail of the day that was different--the day my father was killed.

For some time before that, the arguing of my parents had been often and loud. They'd always argued, but never so much or so violently. One Thursday, my father came home from work in the middle of the afternoon. He looked different--angry and even scared. He told my mother that the sugar factory was about to close. Then, he started to drink wine. Usually, he had a little wine with his supper, but this day, he started drinking in the afternoon, which I had never seen before.

As always, my mother was cooking the sauce for supper. Despite the troubles of my father and the fact that she was fighting with him, her hands were sure as she dropped the stuffed cubes of meat into the sizzling oil. When he realized that she was making Thursday dinner as if nothing had happened at the sugar factory, he started to yell at her. How could she have Zi Antonio for dinner when he was about to ruin them all? She said Zi Antonio had nothing to do with whether the factory stayed opened or closed. I had no idea what any of this meant. I was waiting for my mother to add sugar to the sauce. My father grew more and more angry. Then, he stormed out of the kitchen. I had never seen him like this and I felt sorry for him. I ran after him, but he slammed out of the house. When I went back to the kitchen, I saw that my mother had a little cup of sugar resting on the cupboard--just ready to go into her recipe. As I did every Thursday, I stepped up to the cupboard, stuck out my finger and reached up to coat it with sugar. To my amazement, my mother slapped my hand so hard that I pulled it away, hit it on the edge of the cupboard and cut it. She was so angry she didn't even offer to help me. She told me to get out, to wash it off, and to come right back. I did everything she said. A little later, my father came back and went into my parents' room, where he remained.

Zi Antonio did come for supper that night, but there were no jokes. He wasn't even hungry. All we ate was salad, cheese and bread. He and my mother whispered as we all sat at the table. I thought they were whispering to keep from waking my father who had fallen asleep from drinking all that wine. I kept waiting for my father to wake up, for us to go out to the boat. But every time I tried to get up from the table, my mother told me to sit down.

After a long time, my father did wake up, but I knew it was too late for us to go out. It was already dark. My mother now seemed a lot less angry than she'd been. She had even put aside some sauce for my father, and she cooked him macaroni and ladled the sauce onto it. He, too, must have been over his anger, because I could see how hungry he was. He ate it all. Then he went back into the room he shared with my mother, stretched out across the bed and fell back to sleep.

I was heartbroken. All day I'd thought about our trip out to the Palermo boat, and now, clearly, we weren't going. I went to bed myself.

But I had a hard time sleeping. In the middle of the night, I got up to ask my parents if I could get in bed with them until I fell asleep. I had to be very quiet, in order not to wake my brothers and sisters. I crept down the hall. The door to my parents' room was open. I looked in. I was startled to see that a broad ray of moonlight fell across their bed. They were lying side by side--as they always did, of course. The ray of moonlight fell straight across my father's face. This startled me because he had told me many times that it was bad luck to sleep in the moonlight. Here he was, sound asleep, completely unprotected from the moon. But even more disturbing was the sight of my mother. The moonlight fell on her face, too. She was not asleep. Her eyes were wide open, staring straight up and full of tears that fell down her face, sparkling like diamonds in the pale light.

I knew then, that she was sorry they had fought. I knew, too, that the room was no place for me. I went back to my own room and fell asleep.

Things happened very fast after that. The next day, my father couldn't wake up. The doctor came. Then the priest. He was dead before either got there. They said it was the shock of knowing that the sugar factory was going to close. They said he must always have had a weak heart. They said it was such a shame--a man in his thirties with five children....

Zi Antonio saved us. He told my mother that he would look after us all. He said that his bosses had decided to send him to Canada. He said he knew we had relatives there. He said we could all come with him. And we did. My mother wore black clothes all the way to Canada. We had stopped in Rome to get them.

After we got to the new country, our lives settled down. It was strange at first to have Zi Antonio be with us every day, instead of one day a week. It was strange to have a father--he and my mother soon married--who worked in an office every day instead of a factory. And it was strange to live in a real city, instead of a village. But there were so many good things--the school, the museum, the parks, the friends. Before long, I forgot about Sicily. I never, of course, forgot about my father. But it hurt to think of him dying at such a young age. He had been my friend. Now I had other friends. And after a while, I hardly thought about him at all.

Zi Antonio offered to send me to university, but I was rebellious. When I left school, I, like my father, went to work in a factory. It was clean work. If you paid attention and worked quickly, you could make good money sewing clothes. I started on the machines that sewed cotton into pajamas. I must have made hundreds of thousands of pairs in my time. It was easy. Of course, because I was fast and accurate, I soon moved up to dresses, and then, I became one of the senior women. At the time I left, six months ago, I had been making the finest wedding gowns--sewing only by hand, beading lace that cost almost five hundred dollars per metre. Once, one of the gowns I worked on was worn at the wedding of a movie star--in Rome. It made me think about the blouses and dresses my mother used to buy for us there, and I remembered her dancing excitement when she set out on those trips.

Two years ago, the orders started to fall off. The factory owner was a very good woman, and I know she tried to save our jobs, but one by one the women had to be let go. The pajamas and less expensive items had been dropped from the line years before, but we were still doing a good business in coats and nice dresses. That too, went. Finally, there were only four of us left--the senior seamstresses--the wedding women.

Every day for two years, it seemed to me, I went in thinking it would be my last day, and one day it was. The boss was crying. I know she felt bad. But she didn't even have the money to give us a settlement. The last thing she did was pay the wages she owed us. That was it.

Except for the counsellor. The counsellor was a friendly woman who talked very slowly, as if by doing so she could make us relax. She gave a little speech about how the government had provided counselling for us all and that we had several programs that we could choose from. We could learn how to write resumés. We could explore retraining, as she put it. We could even learn creative writing--to get in touch with our inner selves in these troubling times, she said.

What could my resume say? That I had been sewing for thirty years? And for what could I retrain? It would be silly to learn something new at my age, knowing, also that the likelihood of getting a job was very small. And, as I said, I had already taken a writing course from the government.

The only program left was something called "Appreciating The Immigrant Experience." So it was this workshop that I signed up for, this workshop in which I discovered the secret I had been keeping from my "inner self" all my life.

It happened so simply and so suddenly. I went to the community centre where the workshop was to be held. At first everyone was very nervous and embarrassed. And we were all mixed together, too: Italian, Chinese, Polish--it was strange. But it was all women and pretty soon we started to chat. Then, as the weeks went along, we saw that the social worker who led the group was used to getting women to talk about their problems. A lot of the women talked about their past. Some dealt with their anger and shame over the fact that they'd lost their jobs after being good workers in their adopted country for so long. These women ranged in age from a little younger than me to a little older. But one night, there were some much younger women there--all sitting together and so pretty, the way my mother was the day she left our village to come to Canada with my step-father.

These women, too, started to talk, and before long, it became clear that one of them had a more serious problem than any of the rest of us. For this was not her only group. She told us that she went to a different group every night in order never to have to spend an evening alone. The older women were quite taken with this, and the silence was absolute as she told us in a shaky voice that she had been a drug addict.

Now, of course, for women my age, to have a daughter on drugs is the ultimate terror. I had even gone to a lecture once about all the different drugs and the history of where they came from, sponsored by the Police. We all listened to the young woman with our hearts in our mouths. The girl spoke only a little, but she was quite upset--laughing and crying as she told us about herself.

Now that I think back on it, it seems she hardly said anything, really, but maybe I stopped hearing everything after she said the one thing that opened my own past to me the way a window opens and a bird flies in. What she said was that the first time she ever saw heroin, it looked just like sugar. That it sparkled like that and that she had put out her finger and taken a little and tasted it, expecting it to be sweet, but that it was bitter. And that that should have told her all she needed to know.

I saw it, then. I saw the whole thing. I saw my father lifting up his arms to receive the barrels of opium from Turkey--just like the police told us about. I saw the factory with its frightening pipes and its strange white product that noone was allowed to eat. I saw Zi Antonio with his fine suits, with the respect, the fear of everyone in our village. And I saw my mother slipping a silk blouse out of a shiny paper bag from Rome. All of this I saw, and I was frozen.

I sat without being able to speak for so long that the other women noticed me. The social worker came and stood beside and called my name as if she had known me for far longer than a few weeks. But I was crying, and I needed more than anything to be by myself. I picked up my coat and my purse and I walked out of the centre and all the way home.

But even then, I had only figured out part of it. It took me until far into the night before I realized what Zi Antonio and my mother were doing every Thursday night while my father and I were out on the water. And then, most cruelly and fearsomely of all, I remembered my mother's sharp anger the day I watched her put the secret ingredient into her famous sauce. The day I reached out my finger to taste the sugar as I had done so many times before--and since.

I was sick the next day--but what did it matter? I didn't have to go to work. My children are grown. My husband gets his own breakfast now and goes off to work by himself. All day long I dreamed about my childhood. In fact, I dreamed so much, that by the time my husband came home, I felt I could no longer tell what was dream and what was reality.

Perhaps next week, I'll return to the group. I'll tell them I'm depressed about losing my job, that I feel tired, that I'm afraid a woman my age can never find work again. And I'll listen to the sympathy that the government is paying the social worker to dole out. But I'll never speak about my mother. To whom would I tell her story and why? From the day we came to Canada, we lived a law-abiding life. We went to school, then we worked, then we married and we sent our own children to school. Zi Antonio died, and so did my mother. My children have never much wanted to know about the old country, and I can see why. Everything there is far away and very different and anything that happened happened a long time ago. They have a good life here and as far as they're concerned, they're Canadians, and that's that. As for my husband, if I told him that I had discovered this grim secret by going to a discussion group, he'd forbid me from going out at night. All these years, I've had to fight with him about taking classes and going to women's clubs. I've finally succeeded in winning the right to enjoy my free time. Why should I jeopardize that now when free time is all that I have left?

No, I am the only one remaining who knows the secret of Zi Antonio and my mother. The night I looked in and saw my father so very still that the moonlight on his face could not wake him, I took this secret to myself, without even knowing. Now, because of a few troubled words, I do know. But the secret stays with me. It floats in my mind, detached from all else, the way our little boat floated--a small speck on the waters that lapped the shore of our tiny village, spilled onward toward the bay of Palermo, crossed the Mediterranean, then slipped out to the real sea.

Life On The Edge

JOHN NORTH

John North writes a regular crime fiction review column for the Toronto Star. His crime short stories have appeared in three previous volumes of Cold Blood as well as on audiotape and in golf publications.

The two muffled figures slowly approached each other across the frozen length of the deserted parking lot. In the moonlight reflected from the snow-covered hills each examined the face of the other. After a few seconds they smiled and shook hands. One began to laugh, the other joined in, they hugged and slapped each other delightedly on the back.

Months of meticulous planning and painstaking effort had paid off and the anticipated rewards were finally within reach. The project had started as a joke over cafeteria coffee during a discussion of their respective career opportunities. Their business was cutthroat, transient and short-lived. Effort didn't necessarily translate into rewards, security was impossible and there was no pension plan.

When they met again the following day each had carefully considered the possibilities and realized the incredible and unique opportunity they had. They had one chance to give the performance of a lifetime. This was the original one shot deal.

Although neither had a theatrical background they both thought it worthwhile to follow up the possibility and sketch out a few preliminary scenarios. If all went well their collaboration would result in a victimless crime undetectable despite massive scrutiny and speculation.

Two weeks later they met discreetly on the other side of the country. One had looked into legal and political ramifications and the other had listed the various scenes and characters needed. Collaborative effort would be a new experience for both since they had previously pursued the path of solo performance rather than partnership. In their business risk was always present, careers were notoriously short and futures uncertain. After a brief discussion they agreed they had little to lose and everything to gain and they decided to go for it. Even failure and detection would inevitably be lucrative.

Their individual roles were determined from the start by their physical characteristics and personalities. In their world appearances counted for a lot, but every individual step depended on meticulous planning, impeccable presentation and careful timing. With these elements in place the unwitting supporting players could not fail to perform as expected. The very implausibility of collusion made detection inconceivable.

Their business schedules enabled them to meet several times over the next two months and they refined their plans in a series of hotel rooms. Trust was total since the potential rewards were so great and neither stood to gain by betraying the other. Although the main performance would be a one-off affair its outcome would determine the eventual payoff. Accordingly they carefully considered the potential profits from spin-offs to movies, books, and even toys and games. There was an element of chance involved in income from product endorsements and personal appearances so they decided on a simple 50-50 split over the next decade. While there was clearly no potential in franchising, a carefully staged sequel was a distinct possibility.

For both partners the years of self-discipline and concentration paid off as they performed their carefully structured, but lonely, roles. As the drama unfolded and the tension grew they were continuously on edge and delighted with their success. Family, friends and colleagues reacted as foreseen, media attention gradually built during rehearsals and public interest grew with leaps and bounds at every step.

By the last act both knew they were in a certain win-win situation and with the pressure off both gave magnificent performances. In the final analysis everyone was happy. The joint endeavor had been an outstanding success by any standards. Their separate personal and financial futures were secure, nobody had been hurt, their profession had received enormous publicity, the media had sold more newspapers and filled lucrative air-time and an immense audience had enjoyed unparalleled excitement.

Everything had turned out perfectly. After a brief final hug the two skaters returned to the warmth of their rooms to prepare for the closing ceremonies of the Olympics.

Still Waters

SUE PIKE

Sue Pike is an Ottawa free-lance writer and editor now learning screenwriting. She credits her love of mysteries to the fact that her mother delayed her delivery until the conclusion of Alfred Hitchcock's classic "The Lady Vanishes". Still Waters is her first published crime story.

Lyle listened to the water lapping against the sides of the boat and the soft snicking sound of sunfish tasting and rejecting pollen floating on the surface of the lake. A few yards away a bass broke the surface and picked off a dragon fly that should have known better than to hover so close to these still waters. He wondered when it would be safe to suggest they head for shore and their own lunch. Getting the fire going and cleaning the fish always took longer than the clients expected. And Cooper Hetchlinger was a good deal more impatient than most.

Lyle rested his arms on the oars, trying not to make them squeak as they had done a few minutes ago. That had got Cooper's attention all right.

"Shut up, you jerk. Fish can hear that, you know."

Lyle knew. He figured he knew a lot more about the bass in this lake than Cooper did. He knew what spooked them and what didn't. And at the top of the list was Cooper's shouting and slamming his bait pail down on the floorboards. Next was his habit of flailing the water with that mangled frog of his.

"Take me over there. Next to that stump." Cooper indicated the direction with his shoulder, not taking his eyes off the spot where his line entered the water. "And this time don't get so close. I need room to cast. Gonna land this sucker right on top of the stump there, and then give a little pull like he's jumping off.''

As if those pathetic remains would fool any self-respecting bass. Lyle pulled on the oars to get Cooper into range. He felt a tightness in his right temple, a sure sign he was getting one of his headaches. He wished he could drop his own line in. Most clients invited him to fish with them, but never Cooper. It suited him fine to have Lyle resting his arms on the oars waiting for the next command.

Lyle watched a deerfly crawl down the side of Cooper's canvas hat and onto the reddened folds of fat of his neck. He held his breath, hoping it would survive long enough to insert the toxin that always caused a mean welt on Cooper's sensitive skin.

He moved his gaze to a cluster of tamaracks leaning down to the water. It had been like this between them for almost as long as Lyle could remember. They had spent their summers together on this lake as kids. Cooper arriving with his parents from Syracuse to spend two lazy months at their rambling white frame cottage with the Victorian gingerbread along the roof line and a huge verandah in front. Lyle living across the bay in the lockman's quarters above the storage building.

When Lyle's dad took over as lockmaster he moved his family into the old blockhouse up the hill towards the road. It was bigger all right, but it still didn't have electricity or indoor plumbing. It was pretty clear what Mrs. Hetchlinger thought of it. She asked him once how they managed in winter and he could still remember her drawing her thin shoulders up in a delicate shudder when he told her.

It wasn't any picnic plowing through waist-high snow in January to perch on a freezing privy. But the blockhouse had its compensations. Before Cooper had come to understand the difference in their social standing, the two boys had played Cowboys and Indians, shooting rifles whittled from basswood through the defense holes in the granite walls.

But Cooper had changed. Lyle remembered the summer they both turned fifteen. Cooper had shown up in June, surly and fat. He didn't swim at all that summer, preferring to hide his white corpulence under baggy jeans and sweat shirts even in ninety degree weather. When they were younger they used to gunnel-jump on an old cedar canoe they'd found under the bywash or throw themselves bellowing into the water from the wingwall of the lock. At night they would take turns luring bullheads into one another's nets with flashlights. But that was all over. Cooper still invited Lyle over to the Hetchlinger place occasionally, to hang around in his cabin playing cards or looking at dirty magazines he kept hidden under an old wind-up record player. He began making fun of Lyle that summer, his second-hand clothes, his haircut and most of all his accent.

The next year Lyle quit school and got a job as a fishing guide at the Lodge. He moved into the staff quarters and only saw Cooper a couple of times on his Sunday visits home. Cooper spent the summer at the cottage as usual and one July night he got Lyle's kid sister pregnant. Mr. Hetchlinger offered Lyle's dad five hundred dollars and the name of a special doctor. But Lyle's folks were good Catholics, so Colleen was sent to live with an aunt and uncle near Kingston. They found her bleeding to death in the barn one morning in September.

Lyle slapped a deerfly away from his ankle and longed for a breath of wind to stir the heavy air. Sun beat through the thin denim of his shirt and he knew the empty feeling in his stomach would soon turn to nausea.

He wished once more that he'd been able to convince Tom McInnis, the manager of the Lodge, to give the job to another guide this time. But Tom had been firm, not wanting to risk offending a long-standing customer. Tom never understood why Cooper always booked The Cedars, a damp, overgrown cabin that was a good fifteen minute hike from the dining hall.

Lyle knew why. So he could bring a girl back from the village and maybe slap her around a bit without anyone overhearing her protests. Or if he couldn't talk anyone into coming with him, just someplace private to drink.

Lyle pulled a plastic container of bug repellent out of his breast pocket and began to spread it on his neck, trying to massage away the tension that was building there as well. The oarlock squeaked again but before Cooper could draw breath to complain, Lyle pointed to his line.

"You want me to change your frog? That one's looking pretty beat up."

Cooper grunted and reeled in. Lyle knew he was relieved not to have to do the job himself but too proud to ask for help. He reached into the bucket and grabbed a fresh frog while Cooper swung the end of the pole over, forcing Lyle to grab at the sinker before the hook went into his face.

Cooper sucked up the rest of his beer, watching Lyle work the hook up through the frog's gullet and out the back of its head.

"Shit," he said, as the frog squealed. "I don't know how you can do that." He pulled his arm back and tossed the empty beer can, skipping it across the surface of the water.

Lyle rubbed the soreness around his eyes and thought about the four or five cans Cooper had lobbed into the lake already that morning. He fancied them bobbing along in a line behind the boat like Hansel and Gretel's trail of bread crumbs. Maybe he could bring the boat back later and collect them before they sank and ruined the bass breeding grounds. He eased the line over the side and looked across his shoulder trying to judge the pull needed to bring the boat within casting range of the stump again. Cooper opened another Bud.

The blockhouse had been built back in 1828 to defend that part of the Rideau Canal against the Americans who were threatening Britain's hold on Upper Canada after the War of 1812. But the invaders didn't come for many years and when they did it was in luxury yachts and bright clothes.

They began plying the Canal in earnest after World War II. Lyle used to help his dad crank open the gates that let the boats move up and down the lakes from Kingston to Ottawa.

Sometimes the Americans would get off their deck chairs to throw coins to Lyle, funny-looking dimes with an old man's head in raised relief. Sometimes they threw cans of meat onto the wingwall at Lyle's feet. His mother would be furious.

"Think we're poor Irish trash. Them and their fancy boats."

Since they were both poor and Irish, Lyle wasn't sure what the fuss was about. Not then anyway.

Cooper's attempts at getting the new frog to jump off the stump and into a bass involved much cursing and thrashing about.

"I told you not to get so close," he groused, as Lyle pulled up to shore to disentangle the frog from a hemlock branch.

"How am I supposed to cast that far," he complained, as his frog slapped the water several feet short of the target. And another empty Bud can hit the calm surface.

"How about we stop for lunch?" Lyle had been watching thunder heads piling up over the head of the lake. Even Cooper had to remember that bass never feed during a storm.

Cooper grunted and reeled in his line. He lurched to his feet and unzipped his L.L. Bean trousers. While he relieved himself off the side, Lyle put his weight against the other gunnel to keep the narrow boat from tipping.

Lyle started the outboard motor and was glad to see that the guides' shelter was empty. He didn't feel up to listening to fish stories. While he got the fire started and filleted the only bass Cooper had managed to land that day, Cooper sat at the picnic table drinking.

"Must be nice, eh? Getting to spend all summer in a boat. No worries, eh?" Cooper began imitating the local accent, exaggerating the long "eh?" at the end of each sentence and twisting vowels into a shape no one in the county would recognize. Lyle remembered how tired it had made him when they were younger.

"Well, I s'pose! Laze around all summer and then just set your trap line for winter. Wait for muskrats to stumble into it. Shoot a couple of deer and some ducks in the fall, eh?. No problem. Eh?"

Lyle stared at the grayish bass flesh. No problem. Only Joanie had got tired of waiting for him to get a normal life, as she called it. He'd come home from hunting one night four years ago to find she'd taken their two daughters and moved in with a guy who worked on the lines at Ontario Hydro. He'd gone to his first AA meeting that night and hadn't had a drop since, not that either Joanie or Cooper would notice.

"You should see the crap I have to put up with to make a buck." Cooper stretched out his legs and leaned back. "It got so bad this winter, I got sent on a stress management course. Taught me a lot about coping, eh?"

Lyle could feel Cooper's eyes on his back, trying to see how impressed he was.

"Mostly it means just getting rid of the things that are getting on your nerves." Cooper paused for another swig. "I had a girlfriend. Driving me nuts with her whining. I figured, who needs it? Gave her the old heave ho." He chuckled in remembrance of the event.

The tightness was all over his head now. Lyle did a couple of neck rolls while he checked the heat under the grate. He dipped the fillets into the plastic container of milk and egg and then the bag of coating that the Lodge had sent along. While the fish broiled, he set the salad and buttered rolls on the table beside Cooper's elbow. The staff had added plums and chocolate cake to the lunch basket but Lyle decided to ignore those, putting cups and a thermos of coffee on the table instead.

"You should try it, Lyle. Get rid of all those small annoyances that get you down." Cooper grinned and aimed a playful fist at Lyle's nose as he leaned over to set the table. "But then, I forget. You don't have any worries, do you buddy? You're the original still waters. Only I have my doubts about the running deep part." Cooper laughed.

Lyle put a bass fillet on each tin plate and set them on the table. Cooper eyed his plate with distaste and shoved it aside, reaching for another beer from the cooler that Lyle had carried up from the boat.

"Hey, forget lunch. I want to get myself a decent goddamn fish."
He lurched down the shore to where Lyle had pulled the boat up.

Lyle closed his eyes against the yellowness of the pre-storm light.
The leaves were turning with the gusts and the lake surface was stirring
in small eddies. He shoved a piece of fish in his mouth and bit off a hunk
of roll before pushing everything back into the basket. He poured the
thermos of coffee over the fire and checked that the site was tidy. The
coming storm would take care of any fire hazard.

Once in the boat, Cooper pointed to where he wanted to go and Lyle
rowed them around the point to Deadlock Bay. It was an isolated spot,
weedy and full of stumps, a valley drowned during the flooding of the
canal. The muck below the surface released bubbles of foul-smelling
marsh gas wherever Lyle's oar disturbed it. Most of his clients wouldn't
go near the place, realizing that even if they did manage to hook a bass
they could never land it among the roots and weeds under the lily pads.

Cooper directed them to the north end, trying to cast close to one
stump and then another. Nothing was working right and it was all Lyle's
fault.

"How many times do I have to spell it out, buddy." Cooper had
lost the country accent along with his temper. "Put this boat where I
tell you to put it or you are gonna be in deep shit."

Lyle struggled against the strengthening wind that threatened to
toss them up against the deadheads. Cooper cast his line and the hook
caught on a lily root. He tugged at the pole but the line refused to break.
The water was roiling up to the gunnels now and the first drops of rain
water fell on the boat.

"Get me over so I can unhook this line." Cooper was standing now,
thrashing the water with his pole.

Lyle moved both oars slightly and the wind caught and turned the
bow toward the offending lily pads. Cooper lost his balance and
dropped the pole over the side. He turned towards Lyle, the wind and
rain whipping his hair about, his face darkening with rage. Almost
without thought Lyle moved the oars again, this time in the opposite
direction.

Cooper pitched over the gunnels and into the murky water. He
surfaced with blackened weeds and algae clinging to his hair, sputtering
curses. The lily roots tangled around his trousers. He made a lunge for
the boat but his hands, heavy with muck, only managed to bunt it out
of range. The more he thrashed the more firmly the weeds and roots

knotted themselves around his thighs. He reached for the white lilies, pulling them under with his fat fists.

Lyle watched with interest, wondering when the anger in Cooper's face would finally turn to fear. When it appeared at last that Cooper understood, Lyle turned in the direction of the gathering storm and began to row towards shore. He let the rain and wind wash across his face and noticed that his headache had gone.

Lawn Sale

PETER ROBINSON

Peter Robinson, a transplanted Yorkshireman now living in the Beach area of Toronto, is the awardwinning author of the crime series featuring Inspector Alan Banks. Final Account the seventh Banks novel is scheduled for publication in the Fall of 1994.

When Frank walked through to the kitchen, glass crunched under his feet, and he sent knives, forks and spoons skittering across the linoleum. He turned on the light. Someone had broken in while he had been at the Legion. They had cut the wire screen and smashed the glass in the kitchen door. They must have emptied the drawers looking for silverware because the cutlery was all over the place.

Someone had also been in the front room. Whoever it was had knocked or pushed over the tailor's dummy and the little table beside his armchair where he kept his reading glasses, book and coffee mug.

Suddenly afraid in the case they were still in the house, Frank climbed on a stool to reach the high cupboard above the sink. There, at the back, where nobody would look beyond Joan's unused baking dishes, cake tins and cookie cutters shaped like hearts and lions, lay his old service revolver wrapped in an oily cloth. He had smuggled it back from the war and kept it all these years. Kept it loaded, too.

With the gun in his hand, he felt safer as he checked the rest of the house. Slowly, with all the lights on, he climbed the stairs. They had broken the padlock on Joan's room. Heart thumping, he turned on the light. When he saw the mess, he slumped against the wall.

They had emptied out all her dresser drawers, scattering underwear and trinkets all over the shiny pink coverlet on the bed. And it looked as if someone had swept off the lotions and perfumes from the dressing-table right onto the floor. One of the caps must have come loose, because he could smell Joan's sharp, musky perfume.

The lacquered jewellery case, the one he had bought her in Fort Myers with the ballet dancer that spun to the "Dance of the Sugar-Plum Fairy" when you opened it, lay silent and empty on the bed. Frank sat down, gun hanging between his legs. They'd taken all Joan's jewellery. Why? The stuff obviously wasn't valuable. Just trinkets, really. None of it could possibly be worth anything to them. They had even taken her wedding ring.

Frank remembered the day he bought it all those years ago: the fairground across the street from the small jeweller's; the air filled with the smells of candy floss and fried onions and the sounds of children laughing and squealing with delight. A little girl in a white frock with pink smocking had smiled at him as she passed by, one arm hugging a huge teddy bear and the other hand holding her mother's. How light his heart had been. Inside, the ring was inscribed, "FRANK AND JOAN. JULY 21, 1946. NO GREATER LOVE." The bastards. It could mean nothing to them.

Listlessly, he checked his own room. Drawers pulled out, socks and shorts scattered on the bedclothes. Nothing worth stealing except the spare change he kept on his bedside table. Sure enough, it was gone, the $3.37 he had piled neatly into columns of quarters, dimes, nickels and pennies last night.

They didn't seem to have got far in the spare room, where he kept his war mementos. Maybe they got disturbed, scared by a sound, before they could open the lock on the cabinet. Anyway, everything was intact: his medals; the antique silver cigarette-lighter that had never let him down; the bayonet; the Nazi armband; the tattered edition of Mein Kampf; the German dagger with the mother-of-pearl swastika inlaid in its handle.

Frank went back downstairs and considered what to do. He knew he should put the gun back in its hiding place and call the police. But that would mean intrusion, questions. He valued his privacy, and he knew that the neighbours thought he was a bit of an oddball. What would the police think of him, a man who kept the torso of a tailor's dummy in his living-room, along with yards of moth-eaten material and tissue-paper patterns? What if they found his gun?

No, he couldn't call the police; he couldn't have them trampling all over his house. They never caught burglars, anyway; everyone knew that. Weary, and still a little frightened, Frank nailed a piece of plywood over the broken glass, then carried his gun upstairs with him to bed.

***

The following morning was one of those light, airy days of early June, the kind that brings the whole city to The Beaches. The sky was robin's-egg blue, the sun shone like a pale yolk, and a light breeze blew off the lake to keep the temperature comfortable. In the gardens, apple and cherry blossoms still clung to the trees, and the tulips were in full bloom. It was a day for sprinklers, swimsuits, barbecues, bicycle rides, volley-ball and lawn sales.

Normally, Frank would have gone down to the boardwalk, about the only exercise he got these days. Today, however, a change had come over him; a shadow had crept into his life and chilled him to the bone, despite the fine weather. He felt a deep lassitude and malaise. So much so that he delayed getting out of bed.

Maybe it was the dream made him feel that way. Though perhaps it wasn't right to call it a dream when it was so close to something that had really happened. It recurred every few months, and he had come to accept it now, much as one accepts the chronic pain of an old wound, as a kind of cross to bear.   Separated from his unit once in rural France during World War Two, he had dragged himself out of a muddy stream, cigarettes tied up safe in army-issue condoms to keep them dry, and entered a forest. A few yards in, he had come face to face with a young German soldier, who looked as if he had also probably lost his comrades. They stared open-mouthed at each other for the split second before Frank, operating purely on survival instinct, aimed his revolver first and fired. The boy simply looked surprised and disappointed at the red patch that spread over his chest, then his face emptied of all expression for ever. Light-headed and numb, Frank moved on, looking for his unit.

It wasn't the first German he had killed, but it was the first he had looked in the eye. The incident haunted him all the way back to his unit, but a few hours later, he had convinced himself that he had done the right thing and put it behind him.

After the war, the memory surfaced from time to time in dreams. Details changed, of course. Each time the soldier had a different face, for example. Once, Frank even reached forward and put his finger into the bullet-hole. The soft, warm flesh felt like half-set jello. He was sure he had never touched it in real life.

Another time, the boy spoke to him. He spoke in English and Frank couldn't remember what he said, though he was sure it was a poem, and the words "I knew you in this dark" stuck in his mind. But Frank knew nothing of poetry.

This time, the bullet had gone straight through, leaving a clean circle the size of a ring, and Frank had seen a winter landscape, all flat white and grey, through the hole.

He still had the gun he had used that day. It was the same one he had got down from the high cupboard last night when he thought the burglars might still be in the house. It was the one he felt for now under the pillow beside him.

***

Had he got up that day? He couldn't remember. He sat propped up against pillows on his bed that night watching television as usual. He felt agitated, and whatever the figures on the screen were doing or saying didn't register. For some reason, he couldn't get the wedding ring out of his mind, the senselessness of its theft and the unimaginable value it had for him. He hadn't realized it fully until the ring was gone.

Then he thought he heard some noise outside. He turned the sound off with the remote and listened. Sure enough, he could hear voices. Beyond his back garden was a narrow laneway, then came the backs of the stores and low-rise apartment buildings on Queen Street. Sometimes in this warm weather, when everyone had their windows open, you could heard arguments, television programmes and loud music. These were real voices, Frank could tell. Television voices sounded different, too organized to be real. There were two of them, a woman's and a man's, hers getting louder.

"No, Daryl, it won't do!" he heard the woman shout. "Haven't I told you before it's wrong to steal? Haven't I brought you up to respect other people's property? Haven't I?"

Frank couldn't hear the muffled answer, no matter how much he strained. He dragged himself up from the bed and went to the window.

"So if Marvin Johnson stuck his finger in a fire, you'd do that as well, would you? Christ, give me a break. How stupid can you get?"

Another inaudible reply.

"Right. So how do you think they feel, eh? The people whose house you broke into. Come on. What did you do with it?"

Frank couldn't hear the reply, though he held his breath.

"Don't lie to me. What do think this is? It's a gold chain, isn't it? And what about these? Don't tell me you've suddenly started wearing earrings? I found these hidden in your room. You stole them, didn't you?"

Franks' heart knocked against his ribs. Joan had a gold chain and earrings, and they were among the items that had been stolen. But what about the ring? The ring?

"Shut-up!" the woman yelled. "I don't want to hear it. I want you to put together everything you stole and take it back or so help me I'll call the police. I don't care if you are my son. Do you understand me?"

There came another inaudible reply followed by a sharp smack, then the sound of a door slamming. After that Frank heard a sound he didn't recognize at first. A cat in the garden, maybe? Then he realized it was the woman crying.

About five of the apartments in the building had lights on at the back, and Frank hadn't been able to tell from which one the argument came. Now, though, he could see the silhouette of the woman with her head bowed and her hands held to her face. He knew who she was. He had seen both her and her son on the street.

***

Frank sat in the coffee shop across from the apartment building early the next morning and watched people come and go. The building was one of those old places with a heavy wood and glass door, so warped by heat and time that it wouldn't shut properly. He knew who he was looking for, all right. It was that peroxide blonde, the one who looked like a hooker.

At about eight-thirty, her son, the thief, came out. He had a spotty face, especially around the nose and mouth, and he obviously had a skinhead haircut, or a completely shaved head, under the baseball hat he wore the wrong way around. He also wore a shiny silver jacket with a stylized black eagle on the back under some red writing. Below his baggy trousers, the laces of his sneakers trailed loose. At the corner, he hooked up with a couple of similarly dressed kids and they shuffled off, shoving each other, spitting and generally glaring down at the sidewalk as they went.

At about ten o'clock, Frank had to move to the next coffee shop, a bit more upmarket, as he kept getting nasty looks from the owner. He ordered a cappuccino and a donut and sat by the window, watching.

At about a quarter to eleven, she came out, the boy's mother. She struggled with a trundle-buggy of laundry through the front door and set off down the street. Old though he was, Frank could still appreciate a good figure when he saw one. She wore a white tube-top, tight over her heavy breasts, revealing a flat tummy, and even tighter white shorts cut sharp and high over long, tanned thighs. But she wore too much make-up and he could see the dark roots in her hair. Common as muck, Joan would have said. A real tart, a piece of white trash. No wonder her kid was a burglar, a ring thief, a robber of memories, defiler of all things decent and wholesome.

He watched her totter down the street on her ridiculous high-heels and go into the laundromat. It took about half an hour for the wash cycle and about as long again to get things dry. That gave Frank an hour. He paid his bill, crossed the street and entered the apartment building.

***

He hadn't really formed a plan, even during the hours he had spent watching the building that morning. He knew from last night that the apartment was on the third floor at the back, right in the centre, which made it easy to find. The corridor smelled of soiled diapers and Pine-Sol. When he stood outside the door, he listened for a while. All he could hear was a baby crying on the next floor up and the bass boom of a stereo deep in the basement.

Frank had never broken the law in his life, and he was intelligent enough to recognize the irony of what he was about to do. But he was going to do it anyway, because the absence of the ring was beginning to make his life hell. Nothing else really mattered.

For three days he had waited for the boy to return Joan's jewellery, as his mother had told him to do. Three days of nail-biting memories: dreaming about the German soldier he had killed again; reliving Joan's long illness and death; watching again, as if it were yesterday, the woman he had loved and lived with for nearly forty years waste away in agony in front of his eyes. So thin did she become that one day the ring simply slipped off her finger onto the shiny pink quilt.

And now that he was on the brink of remembering the final horror, her death, the ring had assumed the potency of a talisman. He must have it back to keep his sanity, to keep the last memories at bay.

He had watched people on television open doors with credit cards, so he took out his seniors' discount card and tried to push it between the door and the lock. It wouldn't fit. He could get it part of the way in, then something blocked it; he waggled it back and forth, but still nothing happened. He cursed. This didn't happen on television. What was he going to do now? It looked as if he was destined to fail. He rested his head against the wood and tried to think.

"What the hell do you think you're doing?"

His heart jumped and he turned as quickly as he could.

"I said what do you think you're doing?"

It was her, the slut, standing there with her hands on her hips. It was disgusting, that bare midriff. He could see her bellybutton. He looked away.

"I'm going to call the police," she said.

"No, please." He found his voice. "Don't. I won't harm you."

She laughed. "You harm me!" she said. "That's a laugh. Now go on, get out of here before I really do call the police. Old man."

Frank had to admit, she certainly didn't look scared. "No, you don't understand," he said. There was nothing for it now but to trust her. "The robbery. I overheard. You see, it was my house your son broke into."

She stared at him for a moment, her expression slowly softening, turning sad. She was quite pretty, he thought, or she would be if she didn't wear so much lipstick, mascara and eye-shadow. She had a nice mouth, though her eyes looked a bit hard.

"You'd better come in, hadn't you?" she said, pushing past him and opening the door. "I came back for more quarters. Just as well I did, isn't it, or who knows what might have happened." She had a husky voice, probably from smoking too much.

The room was sparsely furnished, mostly from the Salvation Army or Goodwill, by the looks of it, but it was clean and the only unpleasant smell Frank noticed was stale tobacco. The woman pulled a packet of Rothman's from her bag, sat down on the wing of an armchair and lit up. She blew out a plume of smoke, crossed her legs and looked at Frank. "Sit down, it'll hold your weight," she said, nodding towards the threadbare armchair opposite her. He sat. "Now what do you want? Is it money?"

"I just want what's mine," Frank said. "Your son stole my wife's jewellery. It's very important to me, especially the wedding ring. I'd like it back."

She frowned. "Wedding ring? There wasn't no wedding ring."

"What?"

"I told you. There wasn't no wedding ring." Sighing, she got up and went into another room. She came back with a handful of jewellery. "That's all I found."

Frank looked through it. The only pieces he recognized were the gold chain and the pair of cheap earrings. The rest, he supposed, must have been stolen from another house. "I don't understand," he said. "What happened to the ring?"

"How should I know?" She stubbed her half-smoked cigarette out viciously. "Maybe he sold it already, or threw it away. Look, I gotta go before someone steals the laundry. That's all I need."

He grabbed her arm. "No, wait. Can I talk to him? Maybe he'll tell me. I have to find that ring. I'm sorry...I..." He let her go, and before he knew it, he was crying.

She rubbed her arm. "Oh, come on," she said. "There's no need for that. Shit. Listen, Daryl's a bit non-communicative these days. It's his age, just a phase he's going through. You know what teen-agers are like. Basically, he's a good kid, it's just...well, with his father gone...Look, I'll talk to him again, okay? I promise. But I don't want you coming round here bothering us no more, you understand? I know he's done wrong, and he'll pay for it. Just leave it to me, huh? Take the chain and the earrings for now. For Christ's sake, take it all."

"I only want the ring," Frank said. "He can keep the rest."

"I told you, I'll talk to him. I'll ask him about it. Okay? Here."

Frank looked up to see her thrusting a handful of tissues towards him at arm's length. Her eyes had softened a little but still remained wary. He took the tissues and rubbed his face. "I'm sorry," he said. "It's been such an ordeal. My wife died three years ago. Cancer. I keep a few of her things, for memories, you understand, and the ring's very important. I know it's sentimental of me, but we were happy all those years. I don't know how I've survived without her."

"Yeah, tell me about it," she said. "Ain't life a bitch. Look, I'm sorry, mister, really I am. But please, don't go to the police, okay? That's trouble I could do without right now. I promise I'll do what I can. All right? Give me your number. I'll call you."

Frank watched the broken cigarette still smouldering in the ashtray. He couldn't think of anything else to say. He nodded, gave the woman his telephone number and shuffled out of the apartment. Only when he found himself holding the revolver in his hand at home in the early evening did he realize he didn't even know the woman's name.

***

A day passed. Nothing. Another day. Nothing. Long gaps between the memories, when nothing seemed to be happening at all. Most of the time, Frank sat at his bedroom window, lights out, watching the apartment. He cleaned his gun. There were no more rows. Mostly the place was dark and empty at night.

At first, he thought they'd moved, but on the second night he saw the light come on at about midnight and glimpsed the boy cross by the window. Then it went dark again until about two, when he saw the woman. She must work in a bar or something, he thought. It figured. The next thing he knew it was morning and he couldn't remember why he had been sitting by the window all night. The sun was up, the birds were singing, and his joints were so stiff he could hardly stand up.

Still he heard nothing from the mother. He had been a fool to trust her.

After three days he decided to confront her again. Rather, he found himself walking into her building, for that was the way things seemed to be happening more and more these days. He could never remember the point at which he decided to do something; he just found himself doing it.

Halfway up the stairs to her apartment, he suddenly had no idea where he was or why he was there. He stopped, heart heavy and chest tight with panic. Then the memory flooded back in the image of the ring, burnished gold, bright as fire in his mind's eye, slightly tilted so he could read the inscription clearly: "NO GREATER LOVE." He walked on.

He hammered on the door so hard that people came out of other apartments to see what was going on, but nobody answered.

"My ring!" he shouted at the door. "I want my ring."

"Get out before I call the police," one of the neighbours said. Frank turned and glared. The frightened woman backed into her apartment and slammed the door. He felt the sweat bead on his wrinkled forehead and ran his hand over his sparse grey hair. Slowly, he walked away.

***

Finally his telephone rang. He snatched up the receiver. "Yes? Hello," he said.

"It's me." It was the woman's voice, husky and low. He heard her blow out smoke before she went on. "I heard you come over here again. You shouldn't've done that. Look, I've talked to Daryl and I'm sorry. He said he threw the ring away because it had writing on it and he didn't think he'd be able to sell it. I know how important it was to you but--"

"Where did he throw it?"

"He says he doesn't remember. Look, mister, give us a break, please. Things are tough enough as it is. He's not a real criminal, otherwise he'd've known he could sell it to someone who'd melt it down, wouldn't he? He won't do anything like that again, honest."

"That won't bring my ring back, will it?"

"I'm sorry. If I could bring it back, I would. What can I do? I'll save up. I'll give you some money." He heard her inhale the smoke again and blow it out, then he thought he heard her sniffle. "Look, maybe we can even come to some...arrangement...if you know what I mean. You must be lonely, aren't you? I saw the way you were looking at me when I found you outside my door. Just give Daryl a chance. Don't go to the police. Please, I'm beg--"

Frank slammed the phone down. If only he could think clearly. Things had gone too far. This whore and her evil offspring had conspired to ruin what little peace he had left in his life, his memories of Joan. What did they know about his marriage, about the happy years, the shock of Joan's illness and the agony of her death, the agony he suffered with her? How could a woman like that know how much the ring meant to him? She probably hadn't even tried to find it.

The next thing he knew, he was walking along the boardwalk. When he took stock of his surroundings and saw the ruffled blue of the lake and the tilted white sails of boats, heard the seagulls screech and the children play, he felt as if he were in one those jump-frame videos he had seen on television once, with no idea how he got from one frame to the next, and with seconds, minutes, hours missing in between.

***

It was dark. That much he knew. Dark and the boy was home. She was at work. He knew because he had followed her to the bar where she worked, watched her put on her apron and start serving drinks. He didn't know where he had been or what he done or dreamed all day, but now it was dark, the boy was home and the gun lay heavy and warm in his pocket.

The boy, Daryl, simply opened the door and let him in. Such arrogance. Such cockiness. Frank could hardly believe it. The music was deafening.

"Turn it off," he said.

Daryl shrugged and did so. "What do you want?" he asked. "My mother told me you've been pestering her. We should call the law on you. I'll bet you're one of those dirty old men, aren't you? Are you trying to get in my mother's pants? Or are you a pervert? Is it young boys you like?" He struck a parody of a sexy pose.

Out of the window, Frank could see the upstairs light he had left on in his house over the laneway. Daryl was smoking, his free hand slapping against his baggy khaki pants in time to some imaginary music. He wouldn't keep still, kept walking up and down the room. Frank just stood there, by the door.

"How old are you?" Frank asked.

"What's it to you, pervert?"

"Have you been taking drugs?"

"What if I have? What are you going to do about it?"

"Where's my ring?"

He curled his upper lip back and laughed. "Bottom of the lake. Or maybe in the garbage. I don't remember."

"Please," said Frank. "Where is it? It's all I have left of her."

"Tough shit. Get a life, old man."

"You don't understand."

Daryl stopped pacing and thrust his head towards Frank. The tendons in his neck stood out like cables. "Yes, I do. You think I'm a fucking retard, don't you, just like the teachers do? Well, fuck the lot of you. It was your wife's ring. It's all you've got to remember her by. Read my lips. I don't care."

Blinking back the tears, Frank stuck his hand in his pocket for the gun. He actually felt his hand tighten around the handle and his finger slip into the trigger-guard before he relaxed his grip and let go. At the time, he didn't know why he was doing it, but the next thing he knew he was walking down the stairs.

"And stay away from us!" he heard Daryl shout after him.

Out in the street, with no memory of going out the door, he found himself on the boardwalk again. It was dark and there was nobody else around except a man walking his dog. Frank went and sat out on the rocks. The lake stretched dark ahead of him, smudged white with moonlight. Water slopped around the rock at his feet and occasionally splashed over his ankles. He thought he could see lights over on the American side.

The next thing Frank knew he was at home and something like a thunderbolt cracked inside his head, filling it with light. It was all so clear now. It was time to let go. He laughed. So simple. From his window, he could see Daryl light another cigarette, hear the loud music. What did his feelings matter to Daryl or his mother? They didn't. And why should they? Nothing really mattered now, but at least he knew what he had to do. He had known the moment he got close enough to Daryl to see the tattoo of a swastika on his cheek below his left eye.

***

Even though it was dark, Frank managed to arrange the stuff on his lawn. He was thinking clearly now. His life had regained its sense of continuity. No more jump-frame reality. The memory he had tried so hard to deny had forced itself on him now the ring was gone, the talisman that had protected him for so long. It wasn't such a bad thing. In a way, he was free. It was all over.

It was a warm night. A raccoon snuffled around the neighbour's garbage. It stopped and looked at Frank with its calm, black-ringed eyes. He moved forward and stamped his foot on the sidewalk to make it go away. It simply stared at him until it was ready to go, then it waddled arrogantly along the street. Far in the distance, a car engine revved up. Other shapes detached themselves from the darkness and proved even more difficult to chase away than the raccoon, but Frank held his ground.

Carefully, he arranged the objects around him on the dark lawn. By the time he had finished, the sun was coming up, promising a perfect day for a lawn sale. Now that everything was neatly laid out, the memory was complete; he could keep nothing at bay.

What a death Joan's had been. She had spent ten years doing it, in and out of hospital, one useless operation after another, night after sleepless night of agony, despite the pills. He remembered now the times she had begged him to finish her, saying she would do it herself if she had the strength, if she could move without making the knives twist and cut up her insides.

And every time he let her down. He couldn't do it, and he didn't really know why. Surely if he really loved her, he told himself, he would have killed her to stop her suffering? But that argument didn't work. He knew that he did love her, but he still couldn't kill her.

Once he had stood over her for ten minutes holding a pillow in his hands, and he had felt her willing him to push it down over her face. Her tongue was swollen, her gums had receded and her teeth were falling out. Every time he smoothed her head with his hand, tufts of dry hair stuck to his palm.

But he had thrown the cushion aside and run out of the house. Why couldn't he do it? Because he couldn't imagine life without her, no matter how much pain and anguish she suffered to stay with him, no matter how little she now resembled the wife he had married? Perhaps. Selfishness? Certainly. Cowardice? Yes.

At last she had gone. Not with a quiet whisper like a candle flame snuffed out, not gently, but with convulsions and loud screams as if fishhooks had ripped a bloody path through her insides.

And he remembered her last look at him, the bulging eyes, the blood trickling from her nose and mouth. How could he forget that look? Through all the final agony, through the knowledge that the release of death was only seconds away, the hard glint of accusation in her eyes was unmistakable.

Frank wiped the tears from his stubbly cheeks and held the gun on his lap as the sun grew warmer and the city came to life around him. Soon he would find the courage to do to himself what he hadn't been able to do for the wife he loved, what he had only been able to do to some nameless German soldier who haunted his dreams. Soon.

By the time the tourists got here, all they would see was an old man asleep amid the detritus of his life: the torso of a tailor's dummy; yards of moth-eaten fabrics and folded patterns made of tissue paper; baking dishes; cake tins; cookie cutters shaped like hearts and lions; a silver cigarette-lighter; a Nazi armband; a tattered copy of Mein Kampf; medals; a bayonet; a German dagger with a mother-of-pearl swastika inlaid in its handle.

Death of a Dragon

ELIZA MOORHOUSE

*Eliza Moorhouse is a prolific short story writer living in Vernon, B.C.
Her first published crime fiction story appeared in* Cold Blood IV *and
featured a Hong Kong dealer in oriental artifacts with dubious prov-
enances.* Calvados *makes his second shady appearance here.*

The Hong Kong sun wandered across the carpet and paused at the
carved cherrywood bed, mercifully avoiding the old woman's face.
Hoarse and puffy-eyed, she was a formidable sight in the morning.
Thrusting the first cigarette of the day between swollen lips, she called
for the servant, Ana, to bring her breakfast tray.

Finishing the tea, toast and English marmalade to the last crumb, the
old dragon had one more cigarette then screamed for Ana to help her
dress.

"The grey dress today, madam?" Ana asked in amazement.

The grey dress and matching cape were the old woman's street
clothes, in new condition for she seldom bothered to dress but wandered
the streets in old slippers and shapeless black.

"Do as you're told! I'm going out. Important business."

The old dragon thrust the breakfast tray aside. "Take that away and
ring for the chauffeur at half past eight."

"Master would not like it, madam. I promised that you would stay
in the house until family leaves for Canada."

"I am not a prisoner! Do as you're told." She angrily dusted her
face with pearl powder and forced one more Double Happiness cigarette
from its thin package. There was no fear that Ana would run for help;
no one was about. The master of the house, her son, had gone at six as
usual in his Porsche, threading his way through the streets of Hong

Kong to his office in a high building in the Central District. And Ruby, her daughter-in-law, left promptly at seven a.m. for her antique and curio shop in the Penton Hotel, Kowloonside. The old chauffeur, Jim-Jan was no threat, for he usually slept until his bell rang. Lazy fool.

Ana produced the old woman's grey dress and cape, wiggling her stubby feet into loose carpet slippers. When Ana had gone, Tu opened a lacquer box and withdrew a bracelet. The old woman held it up to the light and doorways into yesterday opened softly. Between the shadows she saw her husband, Lung, dressed in his best cadre's blue wool suiting; felt again the mismatch of irony and tenderness. The bracelet had been his mother's and he had wanted her to have it on this special day - the seventh day of the first moon wherein all of China celebrated birthdays. The Manchu bracelet of gold filigree embraced two dragons, whose heads met in the centre to form eyes of emeralds. Her daughter-in-law, Ruby, asked about the bracelet periodically; indeed, she sometimes came upstairs to the old woman's room and opened the lacquer box without permission.

"When we get to Canada you will have a splendid room with a view of Stanley Park. And there will be no hanging about on the stairs or the streets in Vancouver, old one. Things will be different there. You must learn to live quietly behind doors, listen to music, watch television. Learn to read."

But Tu did not want to go to this city named Vancouver or this country Canada. She wanted to die here, in Hong Kong. First though she wanted to live a while longer; enjoy sunny afternoons of mah jongg in the park with friends, tea and laughter with old cronies in the evenings on the stairs, watch the cars and people go by, wander about in her old peasant clothes. She wanted no changes in her life.

And so she needed money so that she could run away. There was a large house in the New Territories where she could go. Her friends had talked about it; board and room was offered in exchange for working the land and she felt she would like that again; live as she had in her younger days. She could tend the ducks, they'd told her. Well, good, because she would not be carted around like an old sack of ginseng, leaking and spilling life-treasures into the earth.

The bracelet secure on her left arm, Tu left the house on Hennessy Road and climbed into the back of the limousine. They had only driven for about twenty minutes when she yelled: "Stop! Stop here!" Jim-Jan expertly parked alongside the crumbling vendor stands of Carpenter Road. If he had private thoughts about letting the old dragon free at the edge of the walled city, he gave no indication. Behind the vendor carts, in the shadow of the Hak Nam, one lone shop had opened for the day.

It was perfect. Her nosy daughter-in-law would never discover what she had done. It was far away from the glitz of Ruby's world! Over the noise of jets from nearby Kai Tak Airport, she yelled: "In about fifteen minutes."

The shop's door tinkled as she entered. For long minutes, no one came and her eyes wandered: a rosewood counter with glass cabinet underneath containing inferior goods, musty smell, a curtain leading to somewhere, spotted with grease. It began to move. "How can I help you, madam?"

Her gaze met the shrewd green eyes of the shopkeeper. Wizened and unclean, she sensed hostility beneath the extravagant politeness. Through the curtains came the simple, melodic flow of a zither. She felt displaced and fought a sense of alienation, but time was running out and she must grasp what frugal opportunities were available. Taking a deep breath, she removed the bracelet from her arm and handed it over the counter. "How much?"

The shopkeeper, holding the bracelet up to the light, allowed it to slip away and then return. "Lovely old emeralds. Manchu?"

She nodded.

"And old-quality gold. Hmmm." It was worth a great deal, much more than he had. What to do? "Leave it with me. I'll have it appraised for you, then we'll know its true value."

Complications. She frowned. Did one have jewelry praised? "No, I'll take it home with me and come back for this praising."

"I am most trustworthy."

She studied his close-together eyes, the wind and thunder angles of his face. "No. I'll take the bracelet home and return in two days. My chauffeur is waiting."

The shopkeeper returned the bracelet slowly, allowing the gold filigree to wander through his fingertips. Then he went to the front window and, rubbing a small portion clear, watched the old woman and her chauffeur drive off in a splendid limousine. He felt a terrible sense of loss. Something uniquely wonderful had come and gone. Money! He needed about a thousand American, or at the very least, five hundred. But who, where?

When outside shadows moved in, the Afghan withdrew a heavy, worn volume from behind the counter and allowed the pages to fall where they may: IT IS ADVANTAGEOUS TO DEVELOP SUP-PORTERS AT THIS TIME. He carefully restored the tome and sat pensively. Who did he know? Who, in all of Hong Kong's substrata could support him now? By the light of a candle, he consulted old lists of names, pages worn and brown with time. Then slowly, like a man coming out of the dark, he reached for the shop's key and went out to telephone.

Calvados pushed aside the fresh Shanghai lake crab and went to answer the phone. Seldom interrupted at supper time, he viewed the call with alarm. "Well? My supper sits waiting."

"Calvados? Grant Calvados? It's me, the Afghan."

Visions of the Turkish prison formed, overlain with the face of the Afghan, eyes and mouth out of sync...oh lord, how had the man found him. "Where did you get my phone number? It's unlisted."

"Had it for years. Remember? You gave it to me, something about those black pearls."

"Oh yes, quite right." Damn, a botched job. The Afghan had proven unreliable, as usual. "So, what is it this time?"

In a condescending tone, the Afghan told him about the bracelet. "Manchu and worth a fortune! She'll be satisfied with a small sum, maybe two thou American, but I don't have enough to even tempt the old witch."

Calvados hesitated. Dealings with the Afghan always backfired, yet he wanted badly to take a look at the bracelet. "All right, we'll meet. Mad Monkey Bar, ten this evening."

"My leg. I can't go out on the street. Sore leg."

He was lying, of course. No doubt in trouble again. Calvados imagined the shopkeeper's spicy face, lines ingrained with dirt, the eyes of a hundred echoes. He was a fool to get involved and, poised between the risk of acceptance and curiosity, at last agreed to drop into the Afghan's shop on the edge of the City of Darkness.

"With money!"

"Of course with money, fool!"

When Tu arrived once more at the shop of the Afghan, her appearance had altered. Gone was the finery of her previous visit; now she wore shapeless black and appeared to have wandered in from the street. The shopkeeper was obliged to produce a chair so that the old witch could sit and rest. Only then did she proffer the Manchu bracelet, the heads of the dragons meeting in the centre to form eyes of emeralds.

Suddenly there was an undefined presence - a change in the texture of the shadows and Tu stared at the man who had entered through the curtains, soft as snow in the dead of night. Soft dark beard, old pock marks, a continental air - lean and sharp like a cruel quicksilver wind. Like her daughter-in-law, he reminded her of winter.

"Ah friend," said the Afghan, "what do you think?"

Calvados accepted the bracelet. It reflected a prism of light, formed a pattern of loose gold coins against the wall. With a twist of one unruly eyebrow, he claimed the antiquity as his own. The Afghan must have no part of this unspeakably beautiful creation which, for some reason, was being exchanged for a paltry sum. Starting at five hundred American and working up to twelve hundred, (damn but the old woman was shrewd), Calvados at last closed the deal. They watched the ancient Chinese woman limp her way out of the shop and down the street. Calvados considered how easy it would be to strong-arm her when the Afghan interrupted his thoughts.

"We'll sell it at once and I'll claim only a half." The shopkeeper ignited a stubby candle which defined his face ghoulishly.

"A half? What? You said nothing about this when we met last night, and you've put up nothing!"

"A half. Finder's fee."

"Finder's fee be damned! I got you out of a predicament."

"Either half or the cops will be most interested in your phone number, from which they can get your address easy enough. Come, Calvados. Be reasonable. I'm being most generous in giving you half."

When Calvados crashed the money box into the shopkeeper's skull, it broke open and coins flooded the counter and floor. Even so, he could tell at a glance that the Afghan was dead. Then the evening developed as thrice before, with the elimination of fingerprints and every trace of his presence. And then, bending over to snuff the candle, his eyes found a worn photograph tacked to the wall - a sunny moment dissected from its sombre background; a young boy and an elderly woman in the traditional garb of Afghanistan peasants. And he remembered - the old Chinese woman. She could identify him. He tried to recall if the Afghan had used his name, but could not. Damnation, what to do. He gazed beyond the window onto the darkening streets.

Dressed casually in cotton slacks, sandals and an embroidered barong tagalog, Calvados jumped from the tram part way down Des Voeux Road, climbed a hundred or so stairs up a narrow pedestrian lane that led to Cat Street. For long hours, down the domino of days, he searched the streets for the old woman. He did not think she was a user of the pipe, yet obviously a wanderer and possibly a player of mah jongg. And while she might never divulge his description as the man in the Afghan's shop, the newspapers were asking for information. He could not chance a return to prison; life held so many delights:

He liked to walk among his treasures obliquely, posing choices: Should the spare elegance of the Ming be here, or there....should the yin and yang of the jade chess set be under the light...should the gold of the Manchu filigree bracelet lie uncoiled or be fastened to expose the dragon's heads?

On the fifth day of his hunt, at the hour of the dog, he found the old woman in a small park on Magazine Gap Road. He was looking down from the top of the peak out onto the harbour, when his eyes swept the picnic tables and penetrated a group of elderly Chinese women playing mah jongg. But by the time he came down from the peak, they had gone. Cursing his luck, he spent several days casing the park, to no avail.

And then one morning while inspecting the contents of a jade traders shop on Carnarvon Road in Kowloon, she brushed past like a ghostly wind from yesterday.

"Jo sun, my friend."

Startled, he dropped the Hong Kong Times. Bending to retrieve the newspaper gave him time for composure. "Do we know each other?" he asked innocently.

"Hai. Winter man who praised my Manchu bracelet."

He felt his life slip away; abandoned like a bad play. "How nice to see you again. Shall we go somewhere and have tea? My car is just around the corner."

"We shall walk." she announced decisively.

She wore the black, oily cloth of Cantonese coolie women and yet the Afghan had revealed that she had a chauffeur; contradictions that introduced speculation. They passed a couple of hotels, several shops, turned a corner and approached an open-air market. Hardly the place he would have chosen. They sat at a bench with bowls of tea and for a long while, said nothing. Finally she broke the silence with an astounding statement:

"Bracelet. Need it back now."

When she parted her palms, a cigarette dangled from her fingertips. "Um goy. When fields jade green with young rice, my husband give the bracelet to me. So it is recorded in our Book of Generations. He is dead but his spirit return and say, 'Oh Tu, where is Manchu bracelet?' And so you see, I must have once more."

Calvados studied her over the rim of his tea bowl. "I believe the shopkeeper sold it."

"Then get it back for me, winter man."

"I can try. How much are you willing to pay?"

She rolled up one sleeve and snapped an elastic band. "See? No money now. Gone to duck farm where I make new home."

"New home?"

"I am not going to this new country with my son and daughter- in-law. I stay here close to where I come from."

Calvados mentally wandered, like a wolf. She would soon be alone. "When are they going?"

"Six days from today."

Six days. Would he dare wait so long? "Surely you understand that you can't claim the bracelet as your own once you have sold it. You will need money, lots of it." He idly watched her, tried to read her thoughts. "Why don't you return to the Afghan's shop and find out who he sold it to?"

"The Afghan is dead."

Her statement sat on the air, malignant against the cries of the vendors. The old dragon had wisdom and strength and Calvados suspected she knew he possessed the bracelet and that he had killed the Afghan. The perception came together like a network of night-mares and confirmed all of his earlier fears. "Yet you got paid. A deal is a deal."

She refilled her tea bowl, spat onto the ground and drank noisily. Her third cigarette burned away in her fingertips. "We can bury in us wordless crimes, winter man."

Damnation! He stared around assessing the crowd, the possibilities for accidents. The bench they were sitting on, it could tip...suddenly she got up and walked away, through the open air market and out onto the street. A block behind, he trailed her all the way to the Star Ferry Terminal. Drifts of mist mingled with tropical scents as she disappeared into the second class entrance.

For several days he went nowhere, but hugged the walls of his home - the Emperor of Darkness Temple. He touched a taper to the candles after two days, the light mushrooming out of the dark, and prowled walls hung with fourteenth century scrolls. At darktime he opened the windows to insects and birds, allowing them the freedom of the temple hallways.

As he was about to retire, the FAX announced that a buyer would be stopping by and at midnight, Emir-al-Omer, Prince of Princes, rang the great bell and was admitted to the temple. Calvados descended to the entranceway and conducted his exalted guest to the House of Harmony, a showroom nestled behind secret panels, where they trod softly past the wonders of the ages.

"The ivory is most elegant." The Emir spoke with an Oxford-English accent. "And yet..." He paused before an ornamental green jade table screen from the Ch'ien Lung period then passed on, touching the Kuan Yin, Goddess of Mercy, on the forehead. Suddenly his white robe rippled to a halt as he spotted the Manchu bracelet, the gold filigree dragons shimmering in the half-light. Seeking permission, he lifted it to his arm and clasped it lovingly.

"The price is high," explained Calvados, fighting a sense of reluctance.

"No matter, I must have it, old chap."

To celebrate the deal, Calvados prepared Peking duck cooked five ways, the meal beginning and ending with fine dragon-well tea. A servant came to fetch the Emir at three in the morning and later, as he was drifting off to sleep, Calvados fancied he heard the roar of the Emir's private plane as it dipped in a salute over the cloud-enshrouded temple.

Six days had now passed and the old dragon's family would be departing for their new land. His role as predator would be reinstated, her role as victim no longer like an iridescent slick on water. He was relieved that the bracelet was not now in his possession, although he knew he would miss the emeralds, glowing like vigil lights in the semi-darkness. For a time he watched a cloud formation beyond the window, an old woman's head with watching eyes of striated grey. Witches, dragons. Peking duck. It all mingled in one hideous dream.

Determination his predominant emotion, Calvados hunted the streets of Hong Kong with renewed purpose and spotted a thought-provoking limousine while driving through Causeway Bay into the Wanchai District the following afternoon. Because the sun was playing on the car windows, he missed fine details but discerned a European woman driving with an elderly Chinese beside her, a man with a chauffeur's cap in the rear. Twice around the block and he was rewarded with a parking spot in front of the Golden Kat Bar with Muzak. As the limo cruised by, he got an excellent view of the occupants: the old dragon up front beside the driver, who was a severe looking white woman. Riding in the back was an elderly Chinese man, his chauffeur's cap askew.

The Golden Kat's muzak was out of order, the place stuffed with sailors on leave. Calvados edged into a seat at the rosewood bar and ordered a Guinness. Taking a long pull of his drink, he searched for answers. The old dragon's limo needed a wash, the woman driving hardly the chauffeur type. And staring out of the window, hunched up with dead eyes, the original chauffeur in repose.

Dead eyes. On the cross-harbour run, on buses, at festivals, in the Hak Nam. Everywhere. When last he visited his mother in the walled city, they'd gone to a den and passed the day chasing the dragon. Did the old chauffeur, who once drove for the family, now belong to the world of yen?

Calvados took the Carpenter Road approach into the Hak Nam, City of Darkness. His presence was immediately noted by the roof watchers, who signalled that he could pass on. Wearing rubber boots against the foulness of the narrow laneways and avoiding apertures, he nodded to old hags and clots of children, safely reached a doorway leading down watery steps to an opium den. Cots, stacked one above the other, were all occupied. The attendant was perhaps forty, wearing a grey smock and sunglasses. He had tiny pointed cat-like ears.

"An ex-chauffeur come here?" Calvados asked, handing the man an American five.

"Hai. Used to come Saturday, now every night. Employers leave for Canada and pension him off. Is named Jim-Jan."

"He get to keep the family limo?"

"Hai, but try to sell because can't buy gas."

"He here now?"

The smocked cat's hand made itself visible; Calvados parted with another five. Through the cloying half-light, he was led to the inert form of the ex-chauffeur, a screw of toilet paper, tinfoil and cardboard funnel lay beside him. Not even a decent pipe, thought Calvados absently.

"Somebody come for him? An elderly Chinese woman and a European woman, maybe?"

The den keeper consulted his Rolex watch. "Will be here in three hour."

"A long time to wait. Tung Tau Chuen side?"

The attendant shrugged. A heavy sweetness lay in pockets. To one not participating, the atmosphere was mortifying. For a while Calvados wandered amongst the peaceful forms, deriving a curious satisfaction. His own flirtation with the world of yen was one of choice, not of habit. Yet life was complex and harsh, and there were blank periods when he suspected that he, too, had succumbed. There were two women, side by side, obviously users of low-grade opium and he thrust the image of his mother aside, back into that subterranean cavern of iniquity.

He made his way out and stood in a narrow, filthy walkway that led through the labyrinth of horrors known as the Walled City. What appeared to be the plane from Saigon was on approach overhead, about to land at Kai Tak. Calvados searched the skyline for the rooftop gang, the 14K boys who controlled the many illegal drug operations within the city of darkness.

"You want missee white? Red chicken? Smokee?"

"Not today. Is Hank around? Got business with him."

A hand claimed an American five and before Calvados reached the crumbling vendor stands of Carpenter Road, a Chinese youth jumped from a tin hut and blocked his path.

"You want me?"

Colour, odour and sound ran together in the heat of the sun. The walled city was a melting pot. "Yes. Follow me and we'll talk."

"Talk? Want none with you, man." The kid, maybe about twenty, was dressed in designer jeans, gold chains and a silk shirt that vomited the odor of the dark city. He had a thin, concave face and a reflexive smile that didn't reach the eyes. "Don't shit me, man."

"Got a job for you. It'll pay well."

"You owe me for last time."

"So? I'll add that on." Damn but the kid had a memory like a hooker after her dough. The devil had been the kid's tutor and mentor and while Calvados could identify with such logic, seeing it in others repelled him.

"Okay. I take one more chance on you."

Calvados waited in the shadows for the old dragon, a sort of farewell to a woman who had lived with passion, who fought for her independence. Too bad she'd seen him in the Afghan's shop.

She came at last with her servant in tow, a middle-aged sour faced European woman in a cape. They parked the muddy limo and edged into the darkness bordering the craggy silhouette of the Hak Nam, the old woman stumbling a bit on tired feet.

And without thinking, without any reasoning at all, Calvados sprang from his car and ran after her. "Wait! I want to talk! Wait!"

Turning, she held a hand above her eyes and stared. "It's you, winter man."

"Yes. I - you don't want to go in there today. Not today."

She studied his physiognomy, stark against the light and shadow. ''So. The winter man has been plotting. Go and conduct your affairs while Tu expands her destiny.''

Calvados watched them enter the City of Darkness, the servant a nodular cape swaying on two skinny poles. It would be something thrown from a rooftop, most likely.

Damp with exhaustion, tasting the bitterness of regret, he drove away and parked near the sea. Far out, patched sails beat against the skyline. It was the first hour. He felt totally reduced; she had entered his sphere of awareness by her knowing, by her nobility and in a curious reversal of character, had become the champion.

Free, Has a Weapon

GREGOR ROBINSON

Gregor Robinson is a Toronto resident who combines two free-lance careers - writing and economics. His stories have appeared in such diverse publications as Alfred Hitchcock's Mystery Magazine, Ellery Queen's Mystery Magazine, Grain and Queens Quarterly. This is his third appearance in the Cold Blood series.

Three things happened at once: Toto leapt from the coat cupboard demanding his dinner, the stew boiled over, sending a flow of sludge lava-like down the side of the yellow pot, and Henry called out from the upstairs hall.

"Willa? Willa? Are you there?"

Mrs. Ivy put down the suet knife and wiped her hands on her apron. "Yes, yes -- of course I'm here." She was speaking as much to herself as to Toto. "Where on earth does he think I am?" She walked across the kitchen, Toto yipping at her heels. She opened the door to the back stairs and called up, "Yes, I'm here, Henry. I'll be right up."

Henry wanted his dinner. He liked an early dinner on Sundays. She heard him shuffling his walker back to the TV room. Behind her, the spilled stew sizzled and smoked on the element.

"Honestly!" said Mrs. Ivy. She walked carefully to the towel rack where the grease rags hung, gripping the counter as she went. She had only recently recovered from a fall herself, a broken ankle. "Honestly!"

Mrs. Ivy had been gently brought up; "honestly" was among the strongest of her expletives. In the large dark house on Bay Street where she had been raised (now a funeral home), her father had read from the bible every night before dinner. On Sundays, no activities were allowed other than rides to the country to visit aged relatives. "Sunday is a day for visiting shut-ins," her mother would say. (The gardener always drove on these outings. He was not a Methodist. Presumably the Almighty took a more indulgent view towards non-Methodists who broke the sabbath rule.) Blasphemy was a sin. As for profanity -- the famous four letter words -- when Mrs. Ivy was a girl, those were like a foreign language: they were simply not known.

A few months ago, a salesmen had phoned at dinner time. Would Mr. Ivy like the carpets cleaned? he had asked; they had a crew in the neighbourhood. No, Mrs. Ivy had explained. No--not today, thank you. And she couldn't talk just now, she was preparing dinner. Thank you, no.

"Fuck you, lady," said the man.

She had seen the word in print once or twice, in books and stories by modern lady novelists, books urged on her by Louise. And she had certainly heard it before, perhaps from one of the drunks who sometimes loitered in front of the church, she thought. Her mother had told her, "Never catch the eye of a drunk," and she never had, but still they sometimes muttered when you walked by. Where did these people come from? Somewhere east of Gage Street, she supposed. Mrs. Ivy had lived in Hamilton, Ontario all her born days (as she would put it), and in that time she had never been east of Gage Street.

There were also the deranged people, who occasionally wondered away from the Ontario Hospital and down one of the mountain access roads into the quiet leafy streets of southwest Hamilton. These ones were always muttering obscenities, that was for sure -- poor souls.

But this was the first time the word had ever been addressed to her. She was seventy-five years old. She phoned Louise and told her about it at once. Louise had laughed.

"Welcome to the nineties." Then she had said, "Really, Mother, it was partly your own fault. Always hang up on those people right away."

"I was only trying to be polite," said Mrs. Ivy. You should behave towards the postman exactly as you would towards the King of England. That was something her own mother had taught her.

Mrs. Ivy removed the stew from the element and wiped the stove. Then she returned to the pieces of fat on the cutting board. She liked the feel of the knife in her hand.

***

Soldiers being trained in close combat with unfixed bayonets are given the following advice: Always come at the enemy from underneath -- underhand. The very opposite of the popular image of the rushing dagger held high above the head. The fact of the matter is a blow from above has almost even odds of striking a rib and deflecting away; you can end up with a strained wrist or even a bad cut. Even a weak thrust from below will find its way into the soft flesh of the abdomen. A blow from above is easily deflected with a raised arm. A blow from below, on the other hand, is impossible to defend against in this way. And if you come from below, the enemy may not realize you are armed. He may not see the weapon until it is too late.

Henry must have told her this, years before.

He had won his Military Cross at Ortona, south of Rome, Christmas, 1944. Fighting house-to-house. Mouse-holing, it was called: you blew a hole in the roof and came down on the enemy from above.

Every fall Mrs. Ivy made suet cakes studded with seeds and corn with which to feed the birds through the following winter. She had been doing this since she was a girl. "If we feed the birds they will stay with us over the winter," her mother had said. And it was true, they did; now the cardinals were in the garden all year round, and she had read in the paper recently that even robins were beginning to stay. Mrs. Ivy was a devout reader of the newspaper. It gave her an outside view, and matters on which to comment to Henry and Toto.

The telephone rang. It was Louise. She called at least twice a week -- without fail on Sunday and often on Wednesday or Thursday. It was part of the pattern of Mrs. Ivy's life.

Louise was in the habit of giving her mother advice about Henry. "You've got to have your own life," Louise would say. "Get out more. Why don't you join Mrs. Ford's group -- take the bus to Toronto to go to the theatre."

"Who would cook Henry's dinner?"

"Let him get his own dinner for once," said Louise. "It won't kill him."

"It's my job to cook dinner," said Mrs. Ivy.

"Why."

"Well, after all, he worked all those years. Went to the war. And I don't mind, honestly. I enjoy cooking."

"Right -- he worked all those years," said Louise, like a shot, "then he retired. When do you get to retire? When do you get to stop doing the cleaning?"

"Maria does the cleaning -- twice a week she comes now. I only do the bed and the kitchen," said Mrs. Ivy.

"It's a rotten bargain, Mother."

But it was a bargain all the same. And Henry was a good husband. It was inconceivable that he would be unfaithful. When she made this point to Louise, she had to be rather diplomatic. Louise's husband Charles -- he refused to be called Charlie--had left, had an affair with one of the juniors at the law firm. Henry would never have done a thing like that. Charles helped around the house. But what good was helping with the cooking and the cleaning and changing the diapers if he was going to commit adultery? Mrs. Ivy was amazed that Louise could defend him. Charles was second-rate, that's all there was to it as far as Mrs. Ivy was concerned; unfortunately, it showed in her face every time she looked at him, rather straining relations.

What was less amazing to Mrs. Ivy was that Louise had taken Charles back, less than a year after they had separated. The junior lawyer had left him shortly after he had left Louise, as generally happens in these circumstances; even she could have told Louise that. Louise said, "It was a mid-life crisis. He was afraid of death."

Afraid of death? Charles was forty-four years old and in perfect health. What on earth did he have to be afraid about?

When Louise took Charles back, Mrs. Ivy had wanted to say to her, "There, you see how complicated it is?" What she had said instead was, "How are you explaining it to the children?"

"I am telling them that Charles and I have made a choice -- that this is what we have decided to do."

Choice? Chose to take Charles back? What kind of a choice was that? Mrs. Ivy did not believe this for a moment. She believed that Louise took Charles back because she was trapped, enmeshed in this tangle of love and fear and duty the same as she and Henry were, the same as everyone else. She wanted to tell Louise that the possibility of choice -- even the making of very tiny choices -- diminished as the years passed. Instead she had said, "I see."

There was a pause. Mrs. Ivy's "I sees" were filled with meaning.

Then Louise had said, "At least he's not gay." She had gone on to explain once again how this had happened to one of her friends -- the husband leaving for another fellow -- "coming out" as the phrase went.

Louise said, "Have you heard from Jonathan lately?"

Jonathan was Mrs. Ivy's second child. He had moved to Vancouver. Mrs. Ivy was not a fool. She understood that when she criticized

Louise -- the way she was bringing up her children, this matter of Charles -- even obliquely, Louise often turned the conversation towards Jonathan. She believed Louise did this almost unconsciously, and she saw in this way of saying things indirectly something of herself, and how alike she and her daughter were. Still, why did it have to be this way, she wondered, always two conversations going on at once, the one out loud and the silent one underneath? Wouldn't it be lovely if, just once, people could say what they really meant, instead of all this shilly-shallying around.

Mrs. Ivy had not known there was such a thing as homosexuality until she was middle-aged, and when she found out, the idea quite astonished her. Of course there were ladies who lived together -- her own aunt was such a lady; what fine old family in Wentworth County did not have a maiden aunt? And there were confirmed bachelors, old Mr. Harris at the end of the street, for example. But did they actually do anything with persons of the same sex -- try to act like man and woman? She could not begin to imagine what went on.

Mrs. Ivy was on excellent terms with Jonathan; the matter was never discussed. But she gathered from Louise that he was living with another man, a free-lance designer of cowboy boots. Incredible how a person can make a living nowadays. Jonathan was an architect. He was thirty-seven. Rather old to be having a roommate, Mrs. Ivy knew.

"I know I shouldn't say this, dear," said Mrs. Ivy, "and I know there's supposed to be nothing wrong with it, really, but, well, I don't think you should mention this to your father. You know, about Jonathan."

"I never would. He may be difficult -- a jerk to you sometimes -- but he's my father."

Mrs. Ivy carried the tray with the two dishes of stew upstairs to the library. Henry was watching the TV and reading a book at the same time. She put her dinner on a low table in front of the chesterfield. She put Henry's bowl on the table beside his whisky. That was the way Henry liked things done. Just so. It was true, what Louise said: he was difficult. One thing she rather disliked was the way he asked for things. His lunch for example. "I think I'll have some cold beef," or "Willa, I'll have the rarebit on toast." Never, "May I please have some of last night's beef?" or "I love that rarebit you make. Could we have some of that? If it's too much trouble, don't bother -- I'll boil an egg."

Henry had never said anything like that. He had never boiled an egg in his life.

Tonight, when he had finished both his stew and his drink, he said, "I think I'll have some of those berries."

"But I asked you before dinner. You said didn't want any berries."

He turned to look at her, his mouth half open.

"I can't keep going up and down those stairs to get you berries. I'm an old woman!" she was almost shouting. She felt her cheeks burning, feverish. She had not spoken to Henry like that since Jonathan was a boy.

Mrs. Ivy was rinsing the plates for the dishwasher when the police came. They rang the front doorbell, and then they banged the knocker as well. She hurried to answer; she did not want Henry to waken. "Masterpiece Theatre" had come on and she knew he would probably be sound asleep. He had trouble sleeping in the early hours of morning. "Masterpiece Theatre" was the only peace he had. Mrs. Ivy too, for that matter.

One of the policemen held a clipboard. The grouchy-looking one to Mrs. Ivy's way of thinking.

"Mrs. Ivy, is it?" he asked.

"Yes," said Mrs. Ivy.

"And there's a Mr. Ivy?"

"He's asleep."

"No need to wake him," said the other, the nice young man. "We are advising people, keep your doors locked -- fellow has escaped from the brow." (That is what everyone now called the Ontario Hospital on the mountain. When Mrs. Ivy was a girl, it had been called the booby hatch.)

"Mind if we check your garage, the potting shed?"

"Go right ahead," said Mrs. Ivy.

She asked the other one, "Who has escaped? Is he dangerous?"

"Well, not one of the, you know, regular inmates," said the polite policeman.

"Not a lunatic, you mean," said Mrs. Ivy. "That's a relief."

"He's a murderer," said the other policeman, the plain speaking one. "Was up there for a psychiatric examination."

"The cook from the Connaught Hotel?" said Mrs. Ivy. It was a celebrated case, being tried in front of Judge Morrison. The man had strangled his wife.

"That's the one. He's free. Has a weapon."

"A weapon?"

"I'm sure you don't need to worry," said the nice one, looking askance at his partner. "He won't get far. You just keep your door locked."

He turned and looked up the driveway, past the garage. There were rutted lanes behind all those houses, from the days when people had coach houses and back entrances. Now those lanes were thick with weeds and nettles.

As a rule Mrs. Ivy tidied as she cooked and then went over everything again immediately after dinner. She looked at the stew pot with the vile stains on the sides, at the remaining greasy plates and the bone-handled knives which had to be washed by hand but which Henry insisted on using because they had belonged to his mother.

Never start a job you can't finish.

If a thing's worth doing, it's worth doing right.

So many rules.

She called upstairs. "Henry? Henry?" He had definitely fallen asleep. Her outburst must not have been as bad as she thought. She would do the strawberries anyway, have some by herself with a little cream. She carried the colander with the berries from the refrigerator over to the sink. In he window she could see her reflection and, beyond, the last of the dead leaves of the maple tree.

My seventy-fifth October, she thought. The house where she had been raised was three blocks from where she stood.

She would have liked to travel more. But Henry did not like travel, never had since the war. He had promised to take her to Taormina but he never had.

"Don't you ever resent it, Mother?" Louise had once asked. Mrs. Ivy had not answered. If you don't have anything nice to say, don't say anything at all.

When Willa had first met Henry he was an articling student and an officer in the reserve, the militia they were called. The Royal Hamilton Light Infantry, trained for close combat. There was a photograph of him somewhere, taken on some dry foreign plain. In Sicily, perhaps, the summer of 1943. He was standing in front of a jeep, squinting a little, in the bright Mediterranean sun. The Expeditionary forces has just landed; he was a dagger pointed at the heart of Europe. He was over there fighting for his country, so that people like Charles and his friends might grow up to have their mid-life crises and turn into homosexuals in peace.

How dashing he looked in that photograph; the trim moustache, the curl of the lip -- almost insolent.

She smiled. Foolish woman. Foolish woman to be thinking thoughts like that of Henry. Henry, upstairs asleep beside his walker.

An immense crashing and clatter at the side door, the door to the sun porch where she and Henry sometimes had breakfast. She thought: the cook from the Connaught Hotel. Was the porch door locked? Mrs. Ivy dropped the colander in the sink and limped into the pantry. She picked up the telephone. The line was dead. Can it be? thought Mrs. Ivy. She had seen this situation many times on television.

The banging at the side door stopped. Mrs. Ivy heard him walk from the wooden porch. She saw his shadow now at the back door, beyond the dim yellow light.

As fast as she could, Mrs. Ivy hobbled through the back hall to the side door; she wanted to make sure it was locked. She looked through the window onto the porch.

"Toto!"

There was no blood, mercifully. The police told her later that the dog had been kicked once in the head, the blow had shattered the skull. But he was dead. That was clear at once. Quite dead.

Mrs. Ivy returned through the kitchen. She picked up the suet knife as she walked by the counter. It was smaller than the big knife but larger than the paring knife, and more solid, with a sharp end. The handle was moulded to fit snugly in the hand.

She could see a shape in the window of the back door, closer now. Then the sound of splintering glass.

Mrs. Ivy reached for the door knob. Her hands were blood red from the pulp of the berries. She flipped up the catch and yanked the door open.

He was large, soft, flabby -- rather like Charles, in fact. He looked surprised, as no doubt he was. His hands, long-fingered and incongruously delicate, Mrs. Ivy noticed, still gripped the garden shears with which he had smashed the window, so that he lurched forward when she yanked open the door and now stood only about eighteen inches from her. He was dressed in light blue, like those pyjama things doctors wear at the hospital. His breath was rank. These details Mrs. Ivy took in in an instant, as though there had been a flash of lightning.

Physiologically, the signs of rage and fear are virtually the same. The hair stands on end. The eyes open wide so that you are able to see better. The heart beats faster -- more blood for the brain, muscles and heart. The skin goes pale. The muscles tighten -- this is noticeable even in the face -- ready for action. Mrs. Ivy had gone quite pale: that is what he would have seen.

He made a slight movement, as though he would push by her.

There he was: big, soft, shambly, ugly, demanding, stupid, selfish -- oh, how selfish!

Movement upstairs. Henry was awake. He called out.

"Willa?" His voice was weak. He was a poor old man with a bad heart, a bad leg and an enormous fear of death. "Willa? Are you there?"

In the distance, there was noise. From somewhere down the lane and through the shrubbery at the back of the garden, a light shining through. No doubt the police.

The intruder raised the garden shears over his head, ready to strike.

"Not like that," said Mrs. Ivy. "Like this."

She brought the suet knife up from the folds of her skirt and buried it in his gut.

Ash Wednesday

MAUREEN JENNINGS

Maureen Jennings has strong Toronto ties. She has had two mystery plays produced there, is presently working on a historical mystery novel set in the city and lives there with a husband and a dog called Watson.

A tentative Spring warmth had dropped over the city and desperate for sunshine and natural light, I decided to walk home from the glass tower where I worked. I was waiting at the intersection of Bloor and Yonge for the light to change and if the signal had been green and not red I would never have seen the brooch. A young street vendor had set up her tray of jewelry near the curb and the late afternoon sun glittered on the silver piece pinned to the silk-lined lid. My stomach squeezed tight and my mouth was suddenly dry.

"Excuse me, where did you get that?"

She looked at me, startled. "Huh? Wha -?

"There! The brooch with the turquoise enamel cat's head. Where'd you get it?"

The girl regarded me warily. "I bought it."

"From where?"

"What's it to you, lady?"

I tried to soften my voice. "Sorry. It's just that I recognize it. It belongs to my sister."

The girl assessed me. She was young, with a close-cropped head of spiky pink hair. A row of steel rings climbed along the rim of her ear and one had wandered into her nose.

"How'd you know it's hers? There must be dozens like it."

"No, I made it myself. If you look on the back, you'll see my initials. L.P."

She unfastened the brooch from the tray and held it close to her face in a short-sighted way. "Yeah. I see them."

"Please tell me where you got it. It's very important."

She glanced at me curiously and shrugged. "From a church rummage sale."

"Where?"

"The big one downtown."

"You mean the cathedral?"

"I guess so."

"Catholic or Protestant?"

"The one with a Father. What's that, Catholic?"

"Yes. When was this?"

"Couple of days ago."

"Can I have the brooch?"

She grinned slightly, showing discoloured, chipped front teeth. "You can buy it. Ten dollars, no tax."

I paid her, took the pin and hurried across the road to a corner telephone booth.

To my relief, Steve was at home. I explained what had just happened.

"What do you think?" I asked.

"About what?"

"Pauline was wearing the brooch when I last saw her. How could it end up in some church bazaar if she left for Mexico first thing next morning?"

"She probably dropped it. Somebody picked it up and gave it to the church. Simple."

"I'm worried, Steve."

"How so?"

"It's not like her. Not to tell me. Or write or anything."

"You said she did write."

"Not really. She sent roses but the note came from the florist here in Toronto. They said the order was made over the phone."

He yelped. "You checked?"

"Why not? I thought they might have an address where I could get in touch with her."

He blew the air out of his nose in a loud sigh. "Give the girl a break, Lynne. She went away so she could work things out, quote, unquote, and that's what she's doing. She'll be back when she's good and ready."

"I don't know why she hasn't contacted me. It's been two months already."

"Oh snap out of it. She'll forgive you. She always does."

"Forgive me for what?"

"For whatever you did to aggravate her that night." His voice was sharp. "Were you talking about me?"

"You should be so lucky."

Outside the phone booth, a young woman walked by, her cherry-red raincoat gleaming from the recent shower.

"Steve, do you think it's possible she didn't really leave? Maybe she's still in town and just not contacting us."

"No way."

"How can you be so sure?"

"I wasn't planning to tell you this but, ..." he let out an exaggeratedly patient sigh.

"... Yes?"

"I spoke to her yesterday. She called me from some godforsaken pueblo on the west coast."

"What! How is she?"

"Fine. A touch of Montezuma's revenge but nothing serious."

"When is she coming back?"

"Who knows? She says she likes it there. She's working on a Mexican portfolio."

"Did she say anything about me?"

"Fraid not, little sister-in-law. We had other things to talk about."

The mockery in his voice entered like a sliver under my skin. He whistled on the other end of the line. "Hey, you still there? Are you miffed that she called me and not you?"

"Of course not. You're her husband aren't you? Sort of anyway." See how you like that dig, I thought. "I'm just glad she's all right. Anyway, I still want to know how this brooch ended up at the church."

"Hell, what's it matter?"

"It matters to me. It was a special gift for Pauline. I'm going to talk to the priest at the cathedral."

"Jeez, woman, will you chill out!"

"See you."

I would have liked to slam the phone in his ear but with Steve my anger was always a defeat.

I stepped out of the phone booth and started to search the steady stream of rush hour traffic for an available taxi.

Why had Pauline married the guy? She was a stunner. Could have had her pick of a dozen men. Unfortunately, she had zilch confidence and she always settled for some jerk who ended up misusing her. Like Steve. I'd tried to talk to her several times but it was useless. She just got mad and accused me of being
jealous.

I caught the eye of a cruising taxi-cab driver who cheerfully braved the wrath of the rushing cars and pulled over for me. I asked him to take me to the cathedral and he quickly shoved his way back into the traffic.

Steve moved into Pauline's apartment a scant six weeks after they met. He didn't have any money. Claimed he was an actor. The only thing he'd done that I knew of, was a voice-over commercial for Molson. He spent a lot of time lying around the apartment watching videos. Said it was educational. They weren't the kind of movies I'd want to learn from.

It was Christmas Eve when Pauline sat me down at the kitchen table and told me they'd got married. Quietly, at City Hall. She could see how shocked I was and she took my hand. It was Steve's idea really and it had all happened fast. She'd wanted to tell me but he preferred not to. I gritted my teeth at that. "It won't make any difference to you and me," she said. But of course it had. Not just the getting married but Steve being in the picture the way he was.

The taxi-cab driver was staring at me over his shoulder and I realized he'd said something.

"Sorry...what...?"

"Why so serious? It's Spring. What's a matter? Love problems? Forget him. Life's too short."

I shook my head and to my relief he turned his attention back to his driving.

The last time I'd seen Pauline was a cold, snow-thickened night in February, when we'd had our traditional, pre-Lenten pancakes at the Golden Griddle. Unfortunately, we'd had a huge row. About Steve. She stomped out of the restaurant into the winter darkness leaving me squirming at the table.

The next morning, I went over to the studio apartment she rented on Adelaide street. Pauline is a talented photographer and has done very well. She gets lots of business in the entertainment world. That's how she'd met Steve.

I pushed on the bell, trying to keep a grip on my nerves, not sure how she'd be with me. I had to ring a couple of times before Steve opened the door. His blond hair was tousled and his forehead was smudged and dirty. He looked as if he'd been crying.

"What's up?" I asked.

"Pauline's gone off to Mexico."

"What!"

He lowered his head into his chest so that I could hardly hear him. "When she came home last night, she was real weird. She wouldn't even talk to me. Not a word. She must have left early this morning while I was asleep. I woke up just now to the phone. She's at the airport. Says she's got to get away, think things over. Jeez! She wouldn't even say what she meant."

He rubbed at his eyes like a child. His hand was shaking and I noticed a couple of long scratches along the back.

"Do you want me to take Cassy?"

"What?"

I pointed at the scratches. "Shall I take the cat to my place?"

Cassandra was a pure-bred blue Abyssinian with a long lineage and a short temper. It was her silhouette that I used on the brooch. From the beginning Cassy made it clear, she didn't like Steve. She was the only one who wasn't deceived for a minute by those boyish good looks. I was surprised Pauline had left her in his care.

Distractedly, he nodded. "I'll bring her over tonight. Anyway, I'd better go. Today of all days, I have a big audition."

"Congratulations." I barely managed to keep the sarcasm out of my voice. Perhaps this time, he'd get to say more than, 'he scores!' However, he seemed genuinely shaken, the usual sexy come-ons weren't in evidence.

Three days after that, a huge bouquet of roses arrived at my apartment with a note.

"Hi Lynne. Don't worry about me. Had to do it this way. I'll write soon. Love, Pauline."

I was relieved by the friendly tone but so far I still hadn't got a letter.

With a few more soul-cheering words, the taxi driver deposited me at the corner of Church and King street where the city is showing the wear and tear of time. The Catholic cathedral occupies an entire block and the gothic spires soar above shabby row houses, pawnshops and the moraine of another era.

I went through an open gate in the black, wrought iron fence that encloses the church, and entered through the side door into a small foyer.

To my right was a life-sized statue of the crucified Jesus on his mother's lap. In front was a bank of red glass jars which contained the votive candles. Most of them were lit and they threw off a surprising amount of heat. The smell of melting candle wax mingled with that of hyacinths. A clay pot of fresh flowers was at the Virgin's feet. Underneath like a nether note, was the heavy perfume of incense. Old familiar feelings began to stir within me. The painful mixture of anxiety and yearning that I remembered so well from my childhood.

I walked forward into the main area of the church. Even though we'd lived in Toronto since I was ten, I'd never been inside the Cathedral before. Dad had always taken us to the unpretentious new church two blocks from the house.

It was quiet, the thick stone walls blocking out the noise of the traffic. Statues, ornate windows, elaborate carvings, all vied for attention but the place seemed deserted except for one elderly woman leaning her head against the back of the pew in front of her. Praying or asleep, I couldn't tell.

A door opened to my left and a tall, bespectacled man in a black cassock came hurrying out. He set off down the aisle. I intercepted him.

"May I speak to you, Father?"

A look of weariness passed across his face. "Actually, my office hours are finished."

"Oh no. I don't mean confession."

He pulled up his sleeve and glanced quickly at his watch. "I have a dinner engagement..."

"Please, Father, it's most important." In a gush, I told him my story, handing him the brooch. He studied it for a moment, smiling.

"Lovely piece of work. I do so like cats. Wonderful creatures, aren't they?"

I agreed. "Do you recognize it?"

"Indeed I do. Somebody dropped it by the communion rail. I put up a notice but nobody claimed it." He pushed at his glasses. "At the end of every winter, I gather up all the lost items and put them in the church Spring bazaar. The proceeds are used for special projects."

"Do you remember when it was you found the brooch?"

"As a matter of fact, I do. It was about two months ago. On Ash Wednesday."

"Are you sure!"

"Perfectly sure. I always record the date and time when articles are found."

The dryness had never really left my mouth and as I absorbed what he had said, it got worse. My heart was starting to race.

"Father, if you found the brooch at the altar, does that mean the person was taking communion?"

"Yes, I suppose it does."

"My sister is hard to miss." I hesitated not sure how relevant this was to a priest. "Medium height, lots of dark, curly hair. Big brown eyes."

He shook his head. "As you can imagine, a lot of people use the church. Tourists and so on."

He handed the pin back to me and smiled, a professional smile that didn't quite reach his eyes. "I really must go. Don't worry. I'm sure your sister will come back when she's ready."

"But I haven't heard from her. We are very close. I don't understand why she hasn't contacted me."

He was already edging away from me but I moved with him.

"She's sort of dramatic. Wears a red cloak and one of those black toreador kind of hats."

"No, I don't..." He turned.

"Father, please!... One more thing. She has a small discoloration on her forehead. Here, by the eyebrow. Looks like a smudge of dust. People are always pointing it out to her."

He hesitated in his retreat. "Hmm. That does seem to ring a bell." Then, he clicked his fingers. "I do remember her. I have to put a touch of ash on the penitent's forehead and for a moment I thought she had already been up. Yes, yes. I recall her vividly now. She was at the eight o'clock morning mass."

"Eight o'clock? Are you sure?"

I was beginning to sound like my own echo. An expression of irritation flitted across his face.

"Yes, I am sure about that also. I had a severe head cold that day and it was the only Mass I celebrated."

Once again, he checked his watch. "There is probably a logical explanation for her silence. You say she had quarrelled with her husband. People in distress often do unpredictable things."

"Yes... Thank you for your help, Father."

"Good-bye then." Lifting the skirt of his cassock, he hurried away.

I glanced around the church. The elderly woman had left and the place seemed completely empty. The silence was soothing and for a moment I was tempted to kneel in one of the oak pews. I sat down instead on the hard wooden bench and stared at the stained-glass window which glowed in patches of cobalt blue and amber above the altar.

I wanted to tell myself that nothing made sense but that wasn't so. I was trying to deny what I'd known in my heart for two months.

That February morning, I'd gone to the apartment about nine-thirty. Steve said Pauline had just called from the airport but that was impossible. She wouldn't have had time to get there if she was at eight o'clock mass. And the priest was positive it was her. He had marked her forehead with palm ash ...

"thou art dust and unto dust thou shalt return."

Had she lied to Steve to give herself a space to escape into? I saw him at the door again, pushing his blond hair from his tear-streaked face.

And I faced the truth.

Someone slipped into the pew directly behind me. The kneeler creaked.

"Piety looks good on you, Lynne," Steve said. "You should have been a nun...No, don't turn around and don't shout. We're in a church don't forget."

There was the bitter taste of bile in my mouth. It was from hatred not fear.

"You've killed her haven't you?"

I was half aware that we were speaking quietly in a parody of reverence. The vast church was swallowing our voices.

He exhaled violently. "I didn't mean to. She fell. You shouldn't have interfered, Lynne. I know it was your fault she decided to leave me. On your head be it."

"What have you done with her?"

"She's at your cottage."

"You know you won't get away with it."

"I don't see why not. People go missing all the time. I'll tell everybody you've gone to Mexico to visit your sister."

I wasn't referring to myself but he chose to misunderstand.

Half of my mind was wondering if the priest would hear me if I screamed, the other half was attuned to Steve as if my nerves were hairs that could pick up every shift in the air waves. I wanted to buy time, every moment maintaining my life.

"You followed her to the church didn't you? When she went to Mass."

"Not followed, came with. We even knelt together at the altar rail."

"I know. When I saw you, you still had the ashes on your forehead."

"How observant of you little sister-in-law. I thought Pauline might see how repentant I was but it was a wasted effort wasn't it? She'd made up her mind to leave me." His voice dropped so I almost didn't hear him. "I couldn't stand that, you see."

Then he shifted, leaning over the back of the pew, pressing against my shoulder. He pushed a gun so close to my face I could smell the cold metal. His knuckles were white around the gun barrel and he was shaking. That didn't offer me much solace. He didn't need to have a good aim from that distance.

"In case you're wondering, it's real."

"Heck, Steve, I thought you'd stolen it from a movie set. Like PSYCHO, for instance."

He shoved the gun barrel so hard against my ear, I gasped.

"Very witty. Too bad you didn't get beauty instead of brains." He poked me again just as hard, but this time I didn't make a sound. "Come on."

"Where?"

"Let's say we're going to take a trip into the country."

He yanked me to my feet and half-dragged, half-pushed me out of the pew. At the aisle, he put his left arm tightly around my waist, lover-like, while the right pressed the gun against my side. He stank of sweat and fear.

We headed for the entrance, through the foyer where Mary grieved for her dead Son.

"Wait! At least let me light a candle."

He jerked me forward but I resisted.

"Please, Steve. We were brought up as Catholics. The church meant a lot to Pauline."

I didn't give him time to protest but wrenched myself out of his encircling arm and stepped towards the rows of softly flickering candles. I knew I had only a moment to act.

In one motion, I grabbed one of the glass jars from the rack, swung around and flung the hot, liquid wax into his face.

He screamed, dropping the gun as he clawed at his skin. I pushed him violently to the ground and ran for my life.

***

Spring had shifted into summer and the church was cool after the heat of the afternoon. I pulled back the heavy curtain of the confessional box and slipped inside. I had phoned ahead and Father Mahoney was waiting for me. I could just make out his profile through the grid. I knelt down.

"Forgive me, Father for I have sinned..."

I stopped, the air in the booth was stifling, with a sour edge that was from my own breath.

"I have sinned terribly before God ... I am responsible for my sister's death."

"In what way? Her husband has confessed."

"He killed her because she said she was leaving him."

"That was her decision surely?"

"No. I forced her into it..." My words were tumbling out. I had no ownership of them anymore. "When we met that Tuesday night, she didn't look good. It had been happening for a while. She was usually so full of life. But she was being systematically quieted down, by Steve..." I leaned my head against the grille, pushing my forehead hard against the wood. "I tried to talk to her. Tried to make her see what he was really like but she wouldn't listen. She never could give up being the big sister who knows better. She was making me angry. ...So I told her...I said Steve was playing around. That he was unfaithful. Had been before and after they got married."

"Was it true?"

"Oh yes. But she didn't believe me. She got angry back. She got up to leave...Oh Father, don't you see, I had to convince her....For her own sake. There was nothing else to do..."

"Yes?"

"I told her I was the one...That Steve had betrayed her with me."

I stared through the screen at the priest's bowed head. He hesitated.

"You must make an act of contrition for telling such a lie."

"No, Father, no. That's not it. Dear God, that's not it. I must beg forgiveness because what I said was true."

One Bad Apple

MEL D. AMES

Mel Ames is a prolific, and talented, writer of short stories who lives in the Okanagan Valley of B.C. His book The Ogopogo Affair offers fact and fiction about the famed "monster" alleged to dwell in the depths of Lake Okanagan.

The morning sun had not yet risen over Grizzly Hills when Jake D'Amato walked across the concrete working slab at the Okanagan Fruit Shippers Cooperative, to where his fork-lift sat impassively waiting. It was a promising mid-March morning in the lush rural environs of Oyama, a little piece of paradise in the northerly stretch of British Columbia's Okanagan Valley; a gift from God, the locals were fond of telling, to keep the tourists flowing and the apples growing.

Jake was not impressed.

He had been doing this same job for well-nigh seven years; a wearisome, mindless task. But it paid well. Union rates, with incremental raises and a 'don't bust your butt' mandate. Jake was not one to look a gratuitous jackass in the heehaw.

They'd be packing out McIntosh today, he noticed. Not that he cared a lick one way or the other. On this job, one bin of apples came on pretty much the same as the next.

The Mac bins were already lined up for him, stacked six high, twenty deep, fresh out of CA Storage*, red and green skins of the apples glistening with condensation. The bins were of heavy plywood, roughly four feet square and about two and a half feet high; each one with the capacity to hold almost half a ton of apples.

*Controlled Atmosphere: system for pronlonging the shelf-life of rew fruit by replacing oxygen with carbon dioxide and/or hydrogen in a cold, sealed environment.

Jake looked at his watch. With luck, he had time for a quick drag before old Fats started up the Grader. He made a cigarette as he studied on the waiting stockpile of fruit, his thoughts drifting off (with some complacency) to his own small orchard; about four acres of semi-dwarf trees on a five acre parcel. He and his wife, and his three pre-teen kids, worked the orchard themselves and sold the fruit off at roadside where his land abutted the highway. They took in twice what the Packing House would have paid, and, to sweeten the pot even further, it was cash in hand, without having to wait the better part of a year for the money.

He chuckled wryly. Just because he worked for the Packing House, didn't mean he had to ship to them. It was a sentiment widely shared by more than he.

"Okay, Jake." It was the gravelly voice of Floyd Millerman, the Operations Manager, disaffectionally known as 'Fats' when the big man was out of earshot. "Let's get the lead out, eh?"

Jake nipped out his cigarette as the rumbling of the huge grader suddenly reverberated across the slab. He fired up the fork-lift and headed for the row of bins. The specially designed forks gripped the first bin at the sides and lifted it cleanly from the stack. He swung the fork-lift back in a graceful arc, lining up the suspended bin with the dip tank, a large steel reservoir of recycling water, just inside the opening to the long, high, hanger-like room that housed the Grader.

He maneuvered the bin above the tank and lowered it gently into the water, then paused to make sure the apples that floated to the surface were being fed off to the grader as they should.

But as the apples began bobbing up, he saw another, long murky object push up among them, floating low and sinister in the water. He slid off the fork-lift and climbed quickly to the upper lip of the tank to get a better look.

"Hey, Fats," he yelled; then again, louder, to cover his slip of tongue, " -- uh, Floyd

"What? What?"

"We got one bad apple in here, Floyd, and it ain't going to take kindly to being waxed, polished, and gave off to some teacher --"

Jake D'Amato's five acres reposed peacefully on the western slope of Oyama's northerly approach. It was orchard country by and large, with the odd farm on the upper hills running a few head of Herefords, feedlots mostly, a second income to the picayune rewards of growing fruit. There were the inevitable tourist inducements along the highway and a scattering of secondary light industry on the valley floor, proliferating out from the neighboring town of Winfield; but the Packing House was the undisputed core of the small rural community.

It was a scant five minute ride in the Chevy pickup from the Packing House to the gate of Jake's orchard. A weathered sign, the lettering branded into a slab of sun-bleached fir, read, The Sunny Five, alluding, one was sure, to not just the five fruitful acres, but to the five resident bourgeois who had made them so.

Jake always felt a tingle of pride as he drove up to the low, ranch-style house that he had built and populated himself. There was a fenced lawn in front, studded with clusters of ornamental shrubs, and off to one side, a small corral and a cedar-planked stable that gave roof and romp to half a dozen saddle horses and their tack. In back was a implement-shed-cum-hay-barn, with a cold storage adjunct that could cool down fifty bins of fruit to 34 Fahrenheit in less time than it took to pick it.

This time of year it stood quiet and empty. "What in hell you doin' here?"

Jake's father-in-law emerged from the back door of the house as he got out of the truck.

"I live here," Jake said.

He looked at the older man standing loose-limbed on the back stoop with on-going wonder and deep affection, emotions he ordinarily reserved for his wife and kids. He really did look like some kind of scarecrow, Jake thought. You had to get to know Figaro Fagan to like him, and only then if the feeling was mutual. He was a tall man, six-three and counting, with wide knotty shoulders that V'd up and out from hips so frugal they had a time hanging on to his jeans. His hands and feet were too big for the most of him, and they grew off his ends like they'd been dog-eared by the Almighty, still pondering on how to finish up a Fagan.

"They shut down for the day," Jake said, "sent everybody home." Then, after a deliberate pause, "Lonnie Sykes turned up."

"That a fact? Well. When was it he lit out? Last October?"

"Bout then."

"So -- where'd he say he'd been?"

"He didn't say." Jake steered his father-in-law back into the house. "He wasn't up to it."

"Why's that?"

"He turned up in the dip tank -- dead."

Marcy was in the kitchen putting lunch together when the two men came in.

"I heard," she said to Jake. "How'd he die?" Marcy had her father's laid-back calculating ways, but happily she favored her late mother for her dark beauty.

"Someone caved in his skull with a two-by-four. It was in the bin with him. Must have happened last Fall, sometime. He's been cooling his buns in CA ever since."

"Who found him?" Fagan asked.

"I did. I was floating out the first bin of Macs when he come levitatin' up with the apples. Old Fats shut it all down soon as he seen him and called in the Mounties. Sykes didn't look all that bad, mind, for someone being dead nigh on six months. I guess it was CA, keeping him fresh along with the apples. When I finally got away, seemed like there was enough law out there, lights flashing, guns bristling, to put down the next French-Canadian revolution."

"The next one?" Marcy asked cautiously. "Yeah -- but it 'pends who you talk to," her father said sourly. "Was a time when I was a boy, we all knew who owned this damn country. Nowadays --"

"Now, Pa, don't start on that."

"She's right, Fig," Jake cut in, "you got bigger things to worry on now."

"Do tell."

"That bin Lonnie Sykes came floating up out of, Fig, was carrying your number, 1051. The police was asking, how come?"

"Oh? And what'd you tell 'em?"

"I told them a man'd have to be chawing on wet barley to try hiding a body in his own bin. But old Fats, he kept on about how you been having a set-to with the Co-op, 'specially with Fielding and Millerman and all. And then he said they was getting set to dump you, end of March, to cancel Your contract with the O.F.S.C. Fats told them you knew what was coming and you weren't too chipper about it, neither."

"So how in hell they 'spect me t'feel? Bein' accused of sellin' off part of my crop, illegal like? Even hintin' I been unloading it through your Fruit Stand --"

"You have."

"That ain't the point, damn it. It's a free country, and a body's got a right to make an honest livin' best way he can. 'Sides, they don't have a speck o' proof."

"They don't need no proof, and you know it. They can pull your pin anytime they got a notion."

"Ain't their job to go pullin' pins, Jake. It's the Board of Direct'rs, dooly 'lected from 'mongst the growers themselves, it's them what's got the last say."

"Come o-o-on, Fig, you know as well as I do, that Board is no more than a rubber stamp for the mercenaries they had to hire on to run the place, because they don't have a clue on how to run it themselves. Sad to say, there ain't a mite o' moxie twixt the lot of them."

"But, Jake, you name me one grower who ain't doin' the same damn thing they're accusin' me of."

"Can't. Most everybody's into it. Still, you better figure on the law coming out to ask questions. Best mind your temper, and don't give them no further cause to tie you in with Lonnie Sykes."

"Next thing," Marcy said, "they'll be coming after you, Jake, for siding with Pa. I'd hate to lose that extra money."

"Don't fret on it, Marcy. To get to me, they'd have to butt horns with the Union. And that don't seem likely."

"I wouldn't count on it." Fagan shook his clumsy great head. "There's trouble brewin' down there at the Packin' House, and it's got nothin' to do with me sellin' off a little fruit. The way I see it, Jake, it ain't but a matter of time b'fore a few bad apples gets sorted out from the barrel -- foist by their own regard."

Marcy sighed ruefully. "Hoist, Pa," she said, "hoist by their own petard

"Whatever."

* * *

The Fagan place was on the Valley's eastern slope, across the isthmus between Wood Lake and Kalamalka, a colorful fifty acre quilt of old standard trees and newly planted blocks of semi-dwarfs. In a bad year, he'd harvest a thousand bins, and as much again when the Big Guy in the sky was smiling down on him. From the old turn-of-the-century house on the high ground of the orchard, Fagan looked west across the valley to Ellison Ridge, and, when he had a mind to, he could see clear into the pastoral verges of The Sunny Five, nestled in against the highway.

Fagan liked Jake D'Amato, he was a good man. Marcy, he thought, had married well. And while he missed his only daughter, he did not mind living alone.

Priscilla (Prissy), Fagan's wife of thirty-seven years, had died of some obscure womanly ailment within a week of his sixty-second birthday. One year later, Marcy had flown the nest to marry Jake, and now, at seventy-five, Figaro Fagan had become somewhat inured to living without a daily dose of domesticity. He'd put a door on the stairwell to the second floor and attic, to conserve heat, mostly, but as well, to narrow the house down to his current needs.

Twice a week, Ellie Becker, a somewhat plain, yellow-haired young woman of sturdy German stock, came in to clean the one-floor living area and to service Fagan's natural needs. He was not an attractive man, Fagan, except perhaps in a rough-hewn and endearingly ugly kind of way, at least so thought Ellie; but she soon found him to have a libido that she could swear was fed by an army of tapeworms, putting to shame all other would-be Lotharios she'd ever had occasion to cradle, regardless of age.

Ellie was there waiting for him when he arrived home, shortly after lunch.

"I was hoping you'd get back," she said as he crossed the yard to the back door.

"Why? Got y'rself an itch, have y'u?" He patted her firm round bottom. "You weren't supposed t'come until t'morrow." He chuckled salaciously. "No pun 'tended."

Ellie blushed. "You're a dirty old man," she scolded, "you should be locked up."

Fagan slipped an arm around her waist, herding her back into the house. "They'll be coming back," she told him.

"Coming back? Who?"

"The police. They were here looking for you."

"Shit! They say what they wanted?"

"Yeh -- you."

He looked at her blankly, then over her shoulder through the open door. A blue police car was winding its way up the long driveway toward the house. Fagan went out to meet it.

"You Figaro Fagan?"

Fagan towered over the young officer. He nodded. "What d'you want?"

"Just a few questions, Mr. Fagan. May we come in?"

"Out here'll do."

The officer glanced back at his female partner, shrugged. "Lonnie Sykes turned up at the Packing House this morning," he said.

"So I heard."

"Dead."

"Heard that, too."

"In one of your bins."

"Don't own no bins."

"This, Mr. Fagan, was a O.F.S.C. bin, and it had your tag on it. 1051, right?"

"Wrong." Fagan straightened up to his full, considerable height. "Now you hear me, Mr. Policeman ---

"Constable Shepherd."

"Uh-huh -- well, there's a couple dozen people down there to the Packin' House, prob'ly more, and a couple hundred growers crawlin' over these here hills, and any mother's son of them could've switched tags on as many bins as they'd a mind to. So I'll tell y'u this just once. I don't know nothin' 'bout y'ur Lonnie Sykes. I don't know nothin' 'bout y'ur bloody bin. And I don't know sweet Saint Shit 'bout no bin tag. So put y'ur tight liddle ass in gear, young fella, tell y'ur lady friend there t'do the same, and get the hell off my prope'ty."

With Jake D'Amato's cautionary words, Best mind your temper ringing guiltily in his ears, Figaro Fagan turned on his heel and stomped back into the house.

* * *

"I tell you, Staff, he's a certified flake," Constable Shepherd said. "He's as tall, and as ugly, and as mean, as -- as Frankenstein's Monster. I wouldn't go out to that place at night without an after-life guarantee, signed, sealed and delivered by the Almighty, himself."

"Don't you think you're overreacting?" Staff-Sergeant Gary Goetze said dryly. "Figaro Fagan is a farmer. He works fifty acres of apples. Not much time after that for spooking up the neighborhood."

Shepherd regarded his superior officer with dubious conviction. When he stopped to think about it, Staff Goetze (or, Ghost, as he was known to his peers), was not exactly a knight in shining armor, himself. The epithet, Ghost, suited him well. His sallow complexion was sufficiently death-like to have him body-bagged and buried *in articulo mortis* the moment he chanced to stop moving. In fact, Shepherd mused, with an involuntary chuckle, put Fagan and Ghost together, with a few local rubes as extras, and you'd have yourself a bona fide B-run horror flick -- Ghostman Meets Frankenstein

"You find something amusing?" Ghost asked, his pallid features drawn tight in a no-nonsense frown.

"Uh, no -- no, Staff. Not at all. Just a nervous habit. No offense, sir."

Ghost treated the young constable to a hard curious look. "Write up your report and leave it with the Watch Commander, then report back to General Duty."

"Yes, sir."

"And, Constable ---

"Sir?"

"You ought to take something for that nervous habit. People could get the impression that what you're saying isn't what you're thinking."

Shepherd left the office feeling like he'd just been a party to a private Seance.

* * *

When Ghost drove out to the old Fagan place, late that same afternoon, the sun was just about to sink from sight behind the thickly conifered humps of Ellison Ridge. There was little warmth left in the dying day.

Fagan and Jake D'Amato sat hugging a cup of coffee on the wrap-around porch of the old house. They were silently watching Ghost's gray, unmarked Plymouth maneuver the long driveway, up through the orchard. They saw the tall, gray-faced man emerge from the car. He wore jacket and jeans of faded denim and a khaki-colored Tilley hat that looked tired and threadbare.

"I know that man," Jake said quietly. "Yeah. He was one of them Mounties at the Packing House this morning."

Fagan knitted his bushy brows. "Don't look like no Mountie I ever seen."

"Trust me," Jake said.

Ghost approached the porch. "Evening." Fagan and Jake nodded their heads.

"I'm Staff-Sergeant Goetze, from the Kelowna Detachment, R.C.M.P. He shrugged self-consciously. "They call me, Ghost."

"Don't wonder at it." Fagan gave birth to a grimace that, given time, might have grown up to be a grin. There was something about this gray man he liked. "Come and set."

"Coffee?" Jake asked, taking his cue from his father-in-law.

"Thank you," Ghost replied. "You're Jake D'Amato, as I recall -- - and you, you'd be Figaro Fagan, right?"

"Never met nobody yet who'd willingly lay claim to that name but me,'' Fagan told him, reaching back to pull up another chair. "Come by it honest enough, though.''

Ghost tried for a grin, but the end result wasn't much better than Fagan's smile. "Sounds like there's a story there," Ghost said. "I'd like to hear it.''

Jake had left the porch long enough to fetch a pot of coffee and another cup. "There's a story there all right," he said, "and Fig don't need his arm wrung to tell it.''

Fagan took a deep breath. "Name of Fagan goes back a long ways,'' he began reminiscently, "a proud name, proudly worn. But it seems that back in Old Blighty in 18-and-38, a man name of Dickens gave it an ugly bent. Folks lived with it, even so, until about seventy-five years ago. That's when my sainted mother was fixin' to name me, and she got the notion to lighten it up a bit. She come to thinkin' that Mozart's happy-go-lucky Figaro might help to balance out Dickens' felonious old Fagan but she couldn't a knowed, o'course, how the Almighty was having hisself a trial just piecin' me together.''

"There's more," Jake cut in. "When my wife, Marcy, was born, Fig and Prissy (Fig's late wife). decided to carry on with the name-game. They called her Marcellina, after the flirty duenna in Mozart's opera, Nozze di Figaro. Marcellina was soon shortened to Marcy. And Marcy, bless her heart, went to the edge of make-believe with our own three cherubs, naming each one after a character from the same comic opera: bartolo, who is now Bart; Basilio, who is Basil; and Susanna, Sue. And she didn't even have the name Fagan (any longer) as an excuse. We picked up the opera on a Video, and the kids love watching their namesakes perform, in Italian.''

"That's quite a story," Ghost said with feeling, "You've got yourself a proud and loving family, Figaro Fagan.''

"I do that,'' Fagan agreed, "but you didn't come all this way to hear us palaver-on about our kin.''

"True enough.'' Ghost took a sip of coffee. "What I came for, I guess, was to hear you tell me you did not kill Lonnie Sykes. And the, with any luck, who did.''

"Well, to the first of it, Ghost, I can say, straightout, I didn't kill nobody. It's no secret they was gettin' set to give me the heave-ho from the Co-op, but that ain't no reason for me to kill anyone, Lonnie Sykes least of all. I barely knew the man. B'sides, what would I need with a two-by-four when I got me these?'' Fagan held up hands the size of well-worn catcher's mitts.

"You make a point," Ghost grinned.

"As for who did kill him, " Fagan went on, "I can only spec'late, same as you. But with all there's going on down there at the Co-op, you oughten need to look no further than those who got their fingers in the till. Lonnie Sykes was the one who kept the books. Sec'tary-Treasure, they called him. So maybe he was mixed up in some fancy figurin', eh? Your guess is good as mine. But think on this, Ghost, soon as Sykes was out a the way, they got a Garth Dextter in to take his place; and for what it's worth, Dextter's a brother-in-law to the Gen'ral Manager, Allan Fielding. And then there's old Fats Millerman to 'tend with. I was you, I'd be lookin' to the money. That's the key. They all been suckin' on the same sow, understand? And no one's willin' to settle for the hind tit. Leastwise, that's the way I see it."

"I don't doubt there's something in what you say, Figaro, and you can count on me to get to the bottom of it. But, tell me, if they do kick you out of the O.F.S.C., how do you plan to move your fruit?"

"No big deal, Ghost. I been tryin' to talk Jake into mergin' his Sunny Five with my place. We could move more'n half the total crop through his Fruit Stand on the highway, 'specially with the help of Marcy and the kids. The rest would go to an Independent House in the Cold Stream, SKYLINE FARMS, just north of Vernon."

"Sounds great," Ghost enthused.

"Tell that to Jake," Fagan said, "he just can't seem to let go of that damn job at the Co-op. Never get rich workin' for someone else."

Ghost looked at Jake.

Jake shrugged. "I'm thinkin' on it."

"I promise you, boy," Fagan said evenly, "we go in together, me and you, and by Fall, we'll come out smelling like a nose."

"A rose, Fig," Jake said dryly, "smelling like a rose

"Whatever."

* * *

When Jake D'Amato stepped onto the concrete slab at the Packing House the following morning, there was a new man sitting on his fork-lift. He was about to cross over to find out what was going on, when he spotted Fats Millerman coming toward him. The fat man walked with a painful waddle, looking as though someone had just spiked his Preparation H with a debilitating drop of Compound W.

"Best see Gertie at the front desk, Jake. She's making up your time."

"My time? Christ, Floyd, what gives?"

"I got orders to let you go."

"The hell, you say. I got seven years seniority here. You can't hire on a new man over me."

"Just did."

"Union won't stand for it, Floyd. I'll grieve it."

"You do that. Meanwhile," a nasty little chuckle gurgled up from his gut, "don't call us, we'll call you."

Jake was livid. Fig had said this would happen, Union or no Union. Fats was too sure of himself; they had already made some kind of case with the Union. Hitting back at Fig Fagan, what else? And Jake had little doubt that any attempt to grieve it would be a waste of time and dignity. Well, so be it. But if he was about to get the ax, he had a hatchet of his own to bury.

"Tell you what, Fat-ass ---

"Name's Floyd."

"Yeah, right -- Floyd Fat-ass. I been waiting to tell you this for seven long years. You just about the dumbest, ugliest, foul-smelling sonofabitch I ever had the bad luck to work for, ever, and you can go back and tell those two other bastard-born buddies of yours, Fielding and Dextter ---"

"Why don't you tell them? You got the mouth, D'Amato, especially with big Fig at your elbow. Whyn't you get smart? Go collect your time and get the hell out of here."

Jake had always been in awe of the unholy fear that Figaro Fagan could stir in the hearts of other men. Even now, at the advanced age of seventy-five, there were precious few, if any, who would care to run afoul of the big man.

"Don't be buffaloed by the bullshit, Fat-ass. I fight my own battles. And anytime you get to thinking different, you come calling."

At that moment, Jake spotted a police car pulling into the parking lot, and turning his back on Millerman, he headed toward it. He could see an attractive young policewoman behind the wheel, then as he drew near, Ghost's familiar countenance rose above the roof on the other side of the car. The gray Mountie was in uniform.

"Morning, Jake."

"They canned me," Jake said without ceremony.

"Mmmm." Ghost raised a dusty eyebrow. "Figaro said they would, didn't he? But I thought the Union ---

"They must have got through to the local rep, Ghost. Bought him off, I suspect."

"That wouldn't be easy."

"No. But every man's got his price, they say." "Not every man, Jake. But, look, it could be all for the best. Figaro's offered you a promising future on that big orchard of his. I imagine it'll be yours and Marcy's anyway, sooner or later." He paused thoughtfully. "Figaro got any other kin?"

Jake nodded. "A son, about my age. He's off somewhere seeing the world. Fig hears from him, time to time."

Ghost lit a cigarette. It had been a genuine surprise to Jake to see how readily Fig had taken to this unordinary man. It was a rare thing; yet, in some weird way, the two men were much alike.

"I doubt I'll get a chance to smoke inside," Ghost lamented, inhaling deeply, "best get a lungful while I can."

"Can anyone join this cancer cough-in?" the young policewoman quipped, taking the cigarette from Ghost's mouth to tuck it tightly in her own. She smiled at Jake, extending a dragon's-breath of smoke and a firm hand. "I'm Gini Stark."

"Ma'am," Jake acknowledged, and to Ghost he said, "Can I ask why you're here?"

"I'm here on Figaro's prompting, much as anything," Ghost told him candidly. "A man's been murdered, Jake, and I'm looking for answers."

"You really picking up on what Fig was saying?"

"Why not?" Ghost reclaimed his cigarette. "We've got to start somewhere."

Jake was suddenly aware that this man knew what he was about. "Glad to have you on our side, Ghost. You, too, Miss. If there's anything me and Fig can do -- "Thanks, Jake, I'll let you know." He glanced at his watch, then, as two more patrol cars swung onto the parking lot, he stomped out his cigarette. But before he moved away, he turned to Jake with a quick, playful shake of his head. "That Figaro of yours, Jake, he's got to be something else, eh?"

Jake laughed, and feeling strangely good inside, he turned and headed for the front office to pick up his last cheque.

Allan Fielding was seated behind his desk when Ghost and Gini Stark were ushered into his office. He was a tall, angular, soft-bodied man, with a florid complexion and a matched set of bulgy, pale-blue eyes. A desktop nameplate told all who cared to know, he was General Manager.

"Mr. Fielding." Ghost's voice was as gray and colorless as his pallid persona.

Fielding looked up irritably. "I thought we went through this routine yesterday, officer."

"We did."

"And?"

"We're going through it again, today."

"Bloody nuisance," Fielding muttered. "I've got work to do."

"Yes, as do we all. And, I strongly suspect, Lonnie Sykes would be only too glad to have some work to do, as well, but seeing that he is obviously not up to it, I've decided to fill in for him. A bit of, Maintièns Le Droit.* you might say."

"What are you talking about?"

"A man is dead, Mr. Fielding. Someone took a swing at his head with a hunk of lumber, then cooled him down for a few months in CA Storage. We want two simple answers: who and why Sorry for the inconvenience."

"So what do you expect to find here, in my office?"

"A motive would do nicely. And if you don't mind, sir, I'd like your new Secretary-Treasurer to join us."

"I do mind, damn it."

Ghost turned to Stark. "Get him."

"Okay, okay." Fielding punched numbers on his telephone. "Send Dextter in," he said, then, a moment later, "Well, for Chrissakes, Gertie, go find him."

The two Mounties sat stolidly silent until Garth Dextter arrived, nursing a cup of coffee with both hands. He was a thin, pasty-looking man, wearing glasses with thick owlish lenses set in tortoiseshell frames.

"I could use one of those," Ghost said, nodding at Dextter's cup of coffee.

Fielding went back to the phone with a surly sigh. "Three coffees," he said, and after a short pause, he added an emphatic "NO" then treated Ghost to a sullen smirk. "No doughnuts."

"I hate doughnuts," Gini Stark said brightly. Fielding leveled contentious eyes on Ghost. "Let's get on with it."

The gray Mountie waved an ashen hand toward his attractive partner. "Gentlemen," he said, "I would like you to meet Constable Gini Stark -- "

* The R.C.M.P. motto: Maintain The Right

Gini stood and took a perfunctory bow.

"Constable Stark is into computers," Ghost continued. "She

began her early civilian career as what was then known, derogatorily, as a Computer Hack. Fortunately, when she joined the Force, she mended her errant ways, and she is now reverently referred to as a Computer Whiz, but lacking, I might add, none of her former skills.''

He paused to weigh the weight of his words; a heavy silence. ''And so,'' he pressed on, ''in view of the Constable's acute (if unseemly) expertise, I have assigned her the task of ''peeking in,'' shall we say, to the Computer Systems of the O.F.S.C., with special emphasis on coded memory banks and secured files ---''

''What?'' Dextter's sickly features colored angrily. ''Those records are private and confidential. You have no right messing about with them.''

Ghost drew a folded document from his pocket. ''Here is our authorization, gentlemen, to execute Search and Seizure these premises. It encompasses all financial records, account books, and component computer systems relevant to our quest. And I am obliged to inform you,'' he consulted his watch, ''yes, your remote terminals in Winfield and Vernon, have also been seized and held inoperable, simultaneous with our presence here, as well as other random terminals throughout this complex. And they will remain so, until Constable Clark deems it prudent to release them. Are there any questions?''

''This is outrageous,'' Fielding sputtered.

''That is not a question, sir.''

Three cups of coffee arrived just as Gini Stark rose to leave the office. ''I'll find my own,'' she said in parting. Ghost collared a coffee and escorted Dextter down to the accountant's office. Fielding went bursting out into the main front office to confront his startled staff. Uniformed policemen seemed to be everywhere.

''Well, get busy, damn it.'' Fielding barked at his stunned employees, ''We've got a shipment to fill. We're a day late now!'' But the bemused men and women continued to mill about like a flock of headless chickens. They had become so dependent on the computer, they seemed to have forgotten how to function without it.

Floyd Millerman appeared suddenly, shoving his way into the front office from the Grader room. The grader had just been shut down. ''What in hell's going on?''

Jake D'Amato, having been handed his cheque just prior to Gini pulling the plug on the main terminal, grinned at his former boss. ''Why don't you grieve it to God, Fats? I've got a hunch you're going to need all the help you can get.''

* * *

Marcy took the cheque from Jake with pursed lips, her liquid brown eyes reflecting her concern. "I had a feeling this would happen."

"It could be worse, Marcy. Fig's been pestering me to go in with him, but I've kept on putting him off. Maybe now's the time to make the move. He's not getting any younger, and I know he'd welcome the help."

"Pa likes you, Jake."

"Yeah, I know. And the feeling's mutual. It's like that gray-faced Mountie, Ghost, said to me this morning: "That Figaro Fagan of yours", he says, "he's got to be something else. eh?"

"What a strange name," Marcy said, "Ghost. Has he found out who killed Lonnie Sykes?"

"Not yet. But he took over the Packing House this morning; just walked in pretty as you please and shut it all down. Mounties were everywhere. For a fact, Marcy, if Louis Riel had a had as many men down to the Red River in 18-and-69, we'd all be talkin' pidgin French and thinkin' it was the last word in utterin'."

"You're beginning to sound like Pa."

Jake laughed. "Where do you think that came from? But you know what, Marcy? All of a sudden, I feel kind of free; like a born-again rattler that's just wiggled out of an itchy old skin. Getting fired from the Co-op could be the best thing that ever happened to us."

"But what about Pa? Do they still think he killed Lonnie Sykes?"

" Ghost don't think so, and that counts for a lot. Had it been anyone else but Fig, Marcy, that Mountie would of done his job last night, and took him in then and there. 'Figaro,' he says to your Pa, 'are you going to stick around until I get this all sorted out?' Fig says, 'Yep,' and they shook hands on it, and that was that. You don't see that no more, Marcy. Ghost and your Pa; they're two of a kind."

"Uh-huh." Marcy pulled her husband's head down into kissing range. "And Jake makes three."

* * *

After an hour of almost comic confusion, Allan Fielding reluctantly conceded defeat and sent his staff home early, for the second day in a row. "This is a travesty," he complained to Ghost. "There should be some form of compensation to the Packing House for loss of production."

"Write your M.P.," Ghost suggested. He and Dextter were deep into reams of computer printouts and bills of lading.

"I still don't know what you're looking for," Dextter fretted. "There's nothing there but numbers."

"And as long as they keep adding up, you have nothing to worry about. Besides, " Ghost added affably, "it's just routine."

"You call this routine?" Fielding blustered. "All these men rifling through our files? It's more like an invasion."

Floyd Millerman lumbered into the office. "I'm on my way," he said. "No point me hanging around --"

"Uh-uh," Ghost interjected quietly. "I would like you three gentlemen to remain in the building until we're through. It shouldn't be too long."

Fielding jerked his head at the two men. "We'll be in my office," he told Ghost. "I've kept Gertie on at the front desk. She'll get you anything you need."

"You might tell her I could use a coffee," Ghost said. "Make that two." Gini Stark came into the office as the others withdrew. She was wearing an uncharacteristic frown. When she felt they were well enough alone, she said, "It's not going as smoothly as I'd hoped."

"What's wrong?"

"I don't know. Everything seems to be pretty much on the up-and-up, and yet ---

"Somethings bugging you."

"Yeh. Something. I can feel it. I can smell it. But I can't find it"

Gertie arrived then with two coffees, cream and sugar. She was a small, dark-haired woman with a quick efficiency and an abiding smile. "If you want seconds," she said cheerily, "dial ought, ought, one."

"Thank you." Ghost smiled after her. "Now there's a happy soul."

Gini responded with a long pondering look. "How much time do I have?"

"Like one minute to now. I had a hell of a time getting these men, Gini, and I can't hang onto them much longer. There are a lot of routine patrols going unpatrolled this very moment. The S&S warrants cost me every I.O.U. I ever had in the Sheriff's Office. And if I go back with nothing to show, I'll be walking around with a bad case of kick-ass -- and you know how catching that can be."

Gini shifted her vulnerable buns. "Do I ever."

"But let's not get negative, Gini. We'll give it one more try, okay?"

"Okay. It's as though it's there in front of me all the time, Ghost,"
Gini mused, "staring me right in the face, almost like it was daring me
to find it."

"Like The Purloined Letter

"The what?"

"It's from a detective story, Gini, by Edgar Allan Poe, about a
document, a letter, which remained successfully hidden throughout an
exhaustive search by the police. It had been "hidden" in full view of
those who were searching for it, and, thusly, totally ignored. The point
I'm making ---"

"I know the point you're making, damn it. And that has to be the
answer. I've been searching for coded data in secured memory banks,
when all the time ---"

A moment later, Ghost looked up from doctoring a cup of coffee,
alert to the sudden sound of silence. Gini was gone.

"Fancy that," he reflected aloud with a knowing chuckle. "Edgar
Allan, still showing us how it's done, away along here in 19-and-93."

* * *

It took Constable Gini Stark less than forty minutes to come up with her
own version of The Purloined Letter. She sent Gertie off in search of
Ghost, with instructions for him to join her at the main terminal of the
computer.

He loomed up behind her, moments later, like a gray cloud before
a storm. "'Look," she said.

Ghost looked. He saw a sheet of data displayed on the computer's
visual screen. It seemed to be weighted heavily toward the left margin.

"So?"

"Gini worked the keyboard. Another sheet of data, this one
weighted predominantly toward the right, eerily superimposed itself
upon the first.

"So? again."

Without responding, Gini manipulated the keys one more time. A
narrow, vertical, graph-like column of figures flashed onto the visual.
It appeared to dove-tail precisely, to right and left, merging with the
other data, becoming at once, without overlap or disruption, one
complete and comprehensive document.

"There's your evidence," Gini said. "There is a system of secret
coding using the first nine letters of each data sheet, but they must be
resurrected in sequence, otherwise The Purloined Letter remains hidden. Now that we have it, the sequence, the rest should be fairly simple.

The computer itself, when programmed, will eke out and assemble all other data that has been stored piecemeal in this manner.''

"Good work, Gini.''

"Notice, too, Ghost, that each separate frame of data has credibility within itself, but it is not until the three frames are brought into final juxtaposition that the true character of the document is revealed.''

"Ah-hah,'' Ghost exclaimed, with a rare show of emotion, "we now have the second set of books we've been looking for, and if I recall rightly from going through those bills of lading, some of the companies listed here are spurious. See how the names in the original data, upon being merged, have taken on an entirely new entity?''

"Dummy companies?''

"More than likely. A way of siphoning off funds, I suspect.''

"Want me to keep digging?''

"Need you ask? I want all the dirt you can find, Gini. Just pretend you're rewriting the Book of Revelations, according to the gospel of the unholy Ghost, namely me. And I want printouts of everything.''

Gini Stark addressed the computer keyboard with renewed enthusiasm, as well as a profound sense of relief. Kick-ass time could now be postponed, if not totally abolished.

* * *

Figaro Fagan pulled into the driveway of The Sunny Five just at suppertime. Marcy traded grins with Jake; her father's timing was not all that unusual.

"He should be hungry,'' Jake said drolly, "he's been entertaining Ellie Becker all afternoon.''

"Jake!'' Marcy darted a glance at the three children, already at the table. Bart, twelve, the eldest, turned his head away with a titter. The other two were oblivious. "She's doing for him,'' Marcy stammered, "Pa's got to get himself cleaned out every once in a while.'' She turned back to rattle the pots and pans on the stove, regretting at once her choice of words.

Jake gave Bart a manly wink. "There's plenty to eat,'' he said to Marcy's back, "and the kids love their grandpa.''

Figaro Fagan suddenly filled the doorway. "Hope I'm not intrudin','' he said, then, "oh, lookee here, now. I guess I caught you folks just at supper.'' His feigned surprise fooled no one.

Marcy could not repress a smile. "Sit yourself down, Pa. You're just in time.''

Jake said, "You going to buy that new truck you been looking at, Fig, over at Terry's?"

"Not a chance," Figaro said, bibbing up. The kids got a kick out of seeing their grandfather tuck a napkin into his shirtfront. "I found out," Figaro said conspiratorially, "the damn thing runs on profane."

"Propane, Grandpa," Mark said kindly, "It runs on propane."

"Whatever."

"If it ran on profane," Jake said, "one thing's for sure, Fig, you'd get good mileage."

Everybody laughed, including Grandpa. Sue, eight, going on nine, laughed because everyone else was laughing. Basil, eleven, always that one frustrating year behind his big brother, was not about to reveal his ignorance.

"They fired me, Fig." Jake's curtly spoken words stalked across the supper table like four pallbearers at a wedding.

Fagan shrugged his heavy shoulders. "Good," he said. "Now we can set ourselves down an' talk turkey, me and you." He seemed barely able to contain an undercurrent of excitement. "You been holdin' that job up as a s'cuse for too long, Jake, pr'tendin' bein' on y'ur own was the manful thing to do." He held up his hand to silence Jake's attempt to speak. "You jus' let me have my say, now."

Fagan wiped his mouth on the back of a thick wrist, then dried the wrist on his napkin. "I'm glad we're all here," he said solemnly, "B'cause I want to remind y'u all that I'm gettin' on, and I don't want to work that hard no more. Time for me to step aside an' let someones else take over the realm --"

When Marcy opened her mouth to correct him, he stopped her with a quick, "Whatever."

"Don't think I'm doin' you any favors," he said to Jake. "As I see it, it'll be me what comes off best. Anyhow, b'fore you start gettin' all huffed up --"

"When do we start?" Jake said.

"Huh?"

"I been trying to tell you, Fig, I'm all for it. I can see the sense of it now. Have you got all your winter pruning done yet?"

"Uh, yeh. Had me some Aye-rabs workin' on it."

"Great. Then I'll be over first thing tomorrow morning. We can settle out the details over coffee."

Figaro Fagan's face was a study in contrasts; a late afternoon sun emerging slowly from a pall of clouds. He smiled a typical Fagan smile. And little Sue looked up endearingly into his happily contorted features.

"Can I help, too, Grandpa?"

After the meal, Jake and Figaro settled for the brisk mid-March air on the sundeck, warming their hands and their friendship with cups of hot coffee. They could see down onto the 'tween-lakes' isthmus where the Packing House sprawled against Wood Lake like a cancerous red wart. The old loading deck was visible where the rail line snaked along beside the lake, but the parking lot was hidden from view by a cluster of towering willows.

"Wonder if Ghost is still down there to the Packin' House, harrassin' the brass?"

"Dunno." Jake blew the rising steam from his cup. "Can't see the parking lot from here."

"Y'u know, Jake, I got a serious stake in this thing. I'd be in the pokey right now, t'weren't for Ghost."

"You want to go down and see what's going on?"

"Yeh, I do. Be better'n sittin' here wonderin' on it." They took their cups inside. "We'll be back directly," Jake told Marcy. "We're just going down to the slab to see what's going on, if anything."

"Don't you go letting loose on no more trouble, Pa," Marcy cautioned. "You got a mean streak in you not everybody knows of."

"I ever lay a hand on you, Marcy?"

"Not but gentle, Pa. But I ain't the one trying to tie you in to no killing, neither."

Fagan walked away, leaving his daughter standing stubborn, arms akimbo. "Ain't life a travail?" he muttered softly.

Most of the police cars had gone from the parking lot when Jake and Fagan coasted into an empty slot.

"Can't be more than half a dozen Mounties left on the property," Jake surmised aloud, "but Fielding's car is still here, Dextter's, Millerman's, and that yellow Volkswagen belongs to Gertie. The Dodge pickup must be Night Security."

As they approached the building, they could hear angry voices coming from the open door to the main office. A young Mountie moved up to block the entrance, but a level gray voice from within gave them clearance. "It's okay, O'Hara, let them in. They've got a stake in this mess."

To Jake and Fagan, Ghost said, "We're just wrapping things up here."

"You are like hell," Fielding fumed, his face the color of a split-stone peach. "I want to put through a call to my attorney."

"Be my guest," Ghost replied pleasantly, "but you might have him meet us down at HQ. We'll be leaving here momentarily." He turned to Gini Stark. "Have you phoned for the van?"

"Yes, sir. A good ten minutes ago."

"Right. Now shut down the computer and seal it. O'Hara and Smith will be baby-sitting it overnight. And, Gini, gather up these printouts, we'll be taking them in as evidence."

"Evidence?" Dextter squeaked. "That material is nothing but a gross manipulation of the computer, by this person .-- He wagged a finger at Gini Stark. "It proves nothing."

"It's not proof I'm after, Mr. Dextter, not primarily, although there's enough here to see you all in prison for a lengthy stretch. What I'm after, sir, is motive."

"Motive?" Dextter turned another shade of pale.

"Motive to murder," Ghost said quietly.

Fielding, still on the telephone, pointed an accusing finger at Fagan. "There's the man who killed Lonnie Sykes," he said vehemently, "he's the one with the motive. Why aren't you arresting him?"

Fagan snarled like a chained pitbull. "Cool it, Fig," Jake said with a gentle nudge.

Dextter tugged at Ghost's sleeve. "What's murder got to do with anything? Lonnie Sykes was dead long before I even came to work here."

"You'll have your say in court, Mr. Dextter."

"But -- " The man suddenly looked emotionally fragmented. He glanced nervously from Fielding to the fat grader boss, Millerman, who was moving slowly toward the group huddled around the computer. "I won't accept any talk of murder," he whined. "That was not part of the deal --"

Millerman glowered. "Shut up, you bloody fool."

Dextter stayed close to Ghost. It was obvious to most itself out. "Okay," the owly-eyed accountant whined at his elbow, "I was in on the scam. I'll admit that. But murder -- "

Millerman drew his arm back to deliver a blow at Dextter that would have sent him reeling into the dark side of midnight. Fagan reacted instinctively. He extended one long arm to trap the fat man's balled fist in the palm of his own over-sized, God-given mitt, looking much like he was smoothly fielding a line drive to third base. But instead of throwing the ball back, he held onto it. He closed his fingers and squeezed.

Jake winced at the sickening sound of joints and ligaments snapping, clearly audible, even over Millerman's obstreperous roar of pain. Ghost seemed to hesitate a moment or two, for no apparently good reason, before asking Fagan politely to desist.

"It just ain't neighborly," Fagan complained with wide innocent eyes, "not allowin' a man t'say his piece." He looked down on Millerman who was cradling his injured hand in the palm of his other, moaning like a freshly nipped bull.

"Went and hurt y'urself, did y'u?"

* * *

Looking like a fat green-and-yellow caterpillar, Fagan's old John Deere 1120 diesel came inching down the row between the high overhanging trees. It was a bright and sunny Saturday morning and Ghost, watching the tractor creep toward him, felt that his day-off had every promise of being well spent.

Marcy sat the tractor like a homespun Madonna, while fanning out behind, on foot, Fagan, Jake and the three children seemed to be walking in circles. It looked, to Ghost, much like a scene from the fanciful old classic, Midsummer Night's Dream, as each member of the family, pail in hand, went weaving around the big trees, tossing out looping white plumes of 34-0-0 fertilizer, and all the while seeming to maintain some manner of order and purpose. When the weird cortège reached the spot where Ghost was standing, all activity abruptly stopped and the entire Fagan clan gathered around the gray Mountie.

Ghost, wearing his faded denims and his threadbare Tilley hat, looked more like an itinerant in pursuit of work, than a long-tenured member of the R.C.M.P. He was introduced first to Marcy, then to the children, all of whom gleefully recounted the operatic origins of their names, as well as their current, more trendy diminutives. They took to Ghost at once, it seemed, and the hard-nosed Mountie experienced an unfamiliar but welcome sense of affinity. There was an ironic comfort, too, in knowing that the children were already well inured of a family presence that was less than beautiful (but nonetheless loved) and that his own somewhat grim corporeal facade might also be as easily taken in stride.

"Y'u come t'tell me the way of it?" Fagan asked.

Ghost had been watching one elephant's-ear-hand make a cigarette without the help of its twin. The big man grinned as he moistened the paper with his tongue, smoothed it, them handed it to Ghost before beginning another.

Ghost accepted the sad looking object gingerly. "Thanks," he said, "and, yes, you can now forget the whole inbroglio

"Easy for you t'say."

"The Lonnie Sykes thing, Grandpa," Bart said obligingly. Jake shrugged his eyebrows, as clearly miffed as Fagan to have had to have the word interpreted.

"You'll likely have to testify," Ghost continued, "but that's still a few months off. I'll be taking a statement from you in the interim--"

"In the meantime," Bart ventured absently.

"Hold y'r tongue, boy," Fagan scolded, " 'nough's enough. We ain't a bunch of ignore-namuses, y'u know."

Bart opened his mouth to claim the brass ring, then thought better of it.

"Dextter was obviously the weak link in the chain," Ghost went on, "so we went after him first. He was so terrified of a possible murder charge, he admitted readily to being part of the embezzling scam. He produced a complete second-set-of-books (with Gini Stark at his elbow) that were totally incriminating -- - but, oddly, he will be the only one of the three to be charged under the evidence that he, himself, provided."

"What?" Fagan almost dropped his cigarette, a miserable clone to the one he had given Ghost. "What about those other two, Fielding and Millerman --"

"Yes. They, too, have been charged," Ghost said, "but not with embezzlement, with murder. Actually, Dextter knew all along who killed Lonnie Sykes, but his testimony would have been shaky in court, to say the least, because he was not an eye witness. Still, we managed to sweat enough information out of him to break Millerman, the next weakest link. Old Fats finally took a plea to murder; he'll be our key witness in putting Fielding away for twenty-five years."

"Then it was Fielding who actually did it?" Jake asked.

"Yes. He and Millerman, on some pretext or another, took Lonnie Sykes down to a CA Storage room that had not yet been sealed. It was after hours, and Millerman had sent the nightman off to a local greasy-spoon for some fast food. Fielding was the one who swung the two-by-four, but Millerman helped get the body into a bin and covered up with apples before their gofer got back. And, by the way, Figaro, they thought it was a masterful move when they labeled the bin with your tag."

"Those that sin shall reap the ill wind at the Devil's due," Fagan recited with a straight face, as though truly waxing philosophical.

Bart stood in wide-eyed silence. "I wouldn't touch that with a ten-foot pole," he muttered finally.

Ghost had been toying cautiously with Fagan's hand-made cigarette; now, he cupped his hands, lit it, and almost coughed up his breakfast. "What have you got in here?" he gasped, eyes watering, cheeks burning, "skunk weed?"

Fagan laughed, pointing a ponderous finger. "At least I fin'lly got y'u t'show a little color."

The others tittered, politely.

"But, why, Ghost?" Marcy asked when calm again prevailed. "Why did they kill him?"

"Because he wouldn't go along with their scam, Marcy. He just didn't want any part of embezzling the Co-op. He was an honest man; but by then, he also knew too much."

"Fielding, eh? Well, well." Fagan shook his big ugly head. "No s'prise to me, though. I had that man tagged all along as one sad apple --"

"BAD, GRANDPA," his three grandchildren sang out loud and clear in gleeful unison, "ONE BAD APPLE."

Figaro Fagan's eyes sparkled, as though he harbored an abiding secret he was not about to share with anyone.

"Whatever."

An Eye for an Eye

NANCY KILPATRICK

Nancy Kilpatrick has published 65 fantasy/horror stories and 3 novels including a vampire/mystery Near Death. Her first published short crime story won the 1992 Arthur Ellis Award from the Crime Writers of Canada. She lives in Toronto.

Alexander Mifflin was stabbing my mother as my brother Bill and I walked in the back door. I dropped the Eaton's shopping bags I carried and screamed. Last-minute gifts tumbled into the pools of bloody mince meat. Mifflin turned. He and Bill fought. Bill outweighed him; he had wrestled at college. I rushed to my mother's blood-soaked body. The knife was lodged in her eye and, desperate, I yanked it out. Mother died in my arms seconds before Bill brought her killer to the ground. Before I could dial 911. Before she could say goodbye.

I know what you're thinking, the same thing the media is saying-- I'm a psychopath. What makes me believe I have the right to be judge, jury and executioner? Your silly questions have nothing to do with me. I have that right by virtue of the fact that I have fought to stay alive in the face of shattering despair. You know yourself, it's survival of the fittest. You've thought that, even if you can't bring yourself to admit such a politically incorrect idea. I was a woman with a mission. Mission accomplished. If you'll hear me out, I know you'll understand.

Four years after my mother's death I came to the conclusion that murder is not so terrible. We all die anyway so what's it matter when or how. That might seem a jaded statement, but you know in your heart you've thought the same thing. We all have. It follows then that if one murderer can get off virtually scot free, why not another? Why not me?

I used to believe in divine justice. Then I grew up. For a while I had faith in our man-made justice system. When that failed, when jurisprudence let a guilty man walk away with his freedom and my mother's blood on his hands, I grew up some more.

Who would avenge my mother? Who would stop that madman from repeating his crime against humanity? No one. No one but me.

Let me start closer to the beginning, the easiest place to try to make sense of me and my 'crime', although there's no sense to his senseless crime.

The evidence was tangible, not circumstantial: Alexander Mifflin, a thirty-five-year-old Caucasian male broke into our North Vancouver home on Christmas Eve, ostensibly to steal anything of value. My mother was preparing mince meat pies for the holiday dinner the next day. The lights were out in the rest of the house--apparently she had been working in the kitchen and when the sun set turned on only one light. He surprised her there. She fought him--she was a large, strongly built woman of Scandinavian ancestry who did not give herself over easily to being intimidated. No one would have ever called her a coward. Neither is her daughter.

It was apparent they struggled. Chairs were overturned, the floor was a sea of mince meat. A paring knife lay on the table, to trim crusts, but he reached to the white ash knife rack and pulled out a Henckel with a six inch blade. Mother always loved good knives and had the blades honed by the man with the knife-sharpening cart who came by weekly. The coroner commented on the sharpness of the blade, because the twenty-eight stab wounds were, for the most part, clean. There were seven in her chest, two in her stomach, one in her left leg. The knife penetrated her diaphragm. She was left-handed and that side received the worst treatment. But the majority of the stab wounds were to her back, puncturing both lungs, one kidney, and, because the blade was so long, her heart. The most gruesome sight was to her left eye, where I found the knife lodged. The blade had pierced her brain. As I withdrew it, pale matter seeped from the wound. I can still see the tissue, like wood pulp.

I lived in a state of numbed grief. At the funeral I couldn't cry. Later, when we sold the house, before I left for college, as Bill and I sorted through my mother's belongings and I asked for her knives, he stopped and advised me, "Connie, try to forget what happened and get on with your life." But how could I forget?

No fourteen year old should have to experience what I did. Unless you've seen death close up, you cannot know how shocking it is. When the body seems to sigh. When the light fades blue lace crystal eyes to flat dull agates. When a kind of gas--maybe it was her spirit--wafts from the open mouth and ascends, rippling the air. My mother was gone. Her murderer would pay.

But he did not pay. Four years passed before Alexander Mifflin came to trial. I waited patiently through the delays, the motions and counter motions. He opted for judge only, no jury, knowing that ordinary people would find his acts against my mother incomprehensible. Still, through my frozen grief, I had faith.

But he'd had a bad childhood, a therapist testified, and had paid in advance. A minister assured the court that Mifflin attended church, helped out in the community, would be missed. He was a father, out of work, with a lovely wife and children to support. Not a crazed dope fiend, but a decent man, just desperate, said his brother. A police officer reported he'd been a suspect in several crimes and charged with burglary once before, but those charges had been dropped for lack of evidence. The court ruled that information inadmissible. Mifflin testified he did not recall reaching for the knife. He did not realize he stabbed my mother. Twenty-eight times. When I pulled the knife from my mother's brain, effectively I destroyed his fingerprints.

All throughout the trial I felt nothing, just stared at Mifflin, memorizing how he looked, his mannerisms, and finally his cursory testimony. The entire process had been like mining a vein that turned out to be corrupted. And the further along we traveled, the worse it got. The delays only helped his case. And the deals. Not murder one for Mr. Mifflin, who pleaded guilty, but manslaughter. Twenty years. He had already served four, he would be eligible for parole after another six.

The system failed me. But I vowed not to fail my mother.

How do you kill a murderer? It's not as easy as one might think. It takes a lot of planning. Alexander Mifflin was paranoid--he assumed everyone had an intent as evil as his own. I understand paranoia. I've lived with it since that Christmas Eve. I have not felt safe since because there are other Alexander Mifflins in the world and you never know when they will invade the privacy of your home and take control of your life and stab you or a loved one to death. You understand that, I know. You read the news. You have the same fears.

During those years of growing up without her, when I needed my mother most, I developed a plan. The day he entered that penitentiary as a convicted prisoner, legally I changed my name. I earned a BA, and then a master's in Social Work. All the while I was doing time too, waiting for Mifflin.

In anticipation of his release, I changed my hair color, even the color of my eyes--I needed contact lenses anyway, and blue to green was not much of a stretch. The business suit and crisp haircut that had become my disguise were a far cry from the sweater and skirt and shoulder length hair he would remember.

With my excellent grades at university, I could have taken a job anywhere, but I wanted to work for the province, in correctional services. Normally the so-called easy cases--like Mifflin--are the plums and newbes are assigned the junk no one else wants. I told my supervisor I needed extra work and begged for Mifflin's case--I wanted to research a case with a good prospect for rehab. She was happy to get rid of an extra file folder.

That Thursday morning of his release--Thor's Day--I phoned his wife and told her not to bother taking the six hundred kilometer bus ride to the prison. "I'll get him," I assured her. I left a message with the warden's office with instructions for Mifflin to meet me at the gate; I would drive him home. It was partially true--I did meet him at the gate.

The day was overcast, I remember, with steely clouds hanging low over the British Columbia mountains, determined to imprison the sun. The day suited my mood. It's inappropriate to feel jolly when a life is about to be extinguished. Even I know that.

I watched him walk out of the prison a free man. Mifflin reeked of guilt. But his guilt would not bring back my mother, and I wasn't about to forgive him. He would not make it home to his lovely wife and three children. He would not resume his good works in the community. He wouldn't make it past the parking lot.

Mifflin hadn't seen me in six years--since the case finally came to trial. My testimony had been brief. Over that week as the travesty of justice unfolded, he faced front and didn't look at me, although my eyes were drawn to him like iron filings to a magnet. I will never forget his left profile.

He looked the same, although his muscles were more developed--presumably from working out in the prison gym--and his cheeks more gaunt.

"Mr. Mifflin," I said, removing my glove and extending a hand. I wanted to feel the skin of this killer, the flesh that held the knife that had ended my mother's life. Is the flesh of a killer different from normal flesh? Would I feel the slippery blood of my mother that had seeped into his pores ten years before, blood that could never be washed away?

He shook my hand. His grip was not as firm nor as cool as I'd anticipated, but mine made up for it. He looked at me skeptically. "Shelagh McNeil," I said, "your new case worker."

Mifflin ran a hand through his greying hair; his brown eyes reflected confusion--he didn't know what to do with me. Maybe it was hard for him to be in the presence of a woman without a weapon of destruction.

"I have a car," I said. "This way."

I slid behind the wheel of the tan Datsun and he got in on the passenger side. I sat without turning the key, staring at his left profile.

He fidgeted, punched his thigh in nervousness, looked out the window. "Mind if I smoke?" he asked, pulling out a pack of Rothmans.

"Yes I do," I said.

He slid the pack back inside his jacket submissively. The silence was getting to him.

Finally he turned. "Do you need my address?"

"I know your address."

He scratched his head. "Can we get going? My wife's waiting. Christmas, you know. The kids and all."

"I know everything I need to know about you, Mr. Mifflin. All but one thing."

He waited, expectant.

"How did you feel as you murdered Mrs. Brautigam."

"How did I feel?" Now he was really uncomfortable. "Look, I talked to a shrink about all this, inside." He shifted and turned away from me. "Can't we talk about this later?"

"That's not possible, Mr. Mifflin."

He turned back. His eyes narrowed. He struggled to make a connection but there wasn't enough left of the girl who had watched her mother die. And it wasn't just the physical changes. I was no longer vulnerable, but he was.

He put his hand on the door handle. "Look, I'll catch the bus."

"The last bus is gone," I told him, "and I believe your parole stipulates that you are required to meet certain conditions, including working with your social worker. I simply want to know how you felt, that's all. When you stabbed Mrs. Brautigam twenty-eight times, and her blood gushed out, splattering you with red gore, and her screams filled your ears. And her son and daughter watched their mother die. How did you feel?"

He turned away. In a small voice he said, "I don't remember."

"I need to know how it feels," I said, slipping a hand into my briefcase, "because I don't remember feelings either." I hit the automatic door lock.

His head snapped back.

I used both hands to plunge the knife into his left eye. I had sharpened the Henckel daily after the police returned it. Most of the six inches slid in as easily as if it were pie dough I was cutting. I felt the finely-honed steel pass the eyeball and enter the pale brain tissue.

His hands had clamped around my wrists; I couldn't tell if he was trying to pull the blade out or helping me push it in as far as it would go, but I held tight.

Mifflin went rigid. He stared at me for a moment, his face creased with uncomprehending horror, his pierced brain struggled to make the awful connection. His hand clutched the handle and he yanked the blade out. Blood spurted into my face, across the windshield, over his brand new prison-release shirt. He was shocked. Before he could react, I grabbed the knife and stabbed him twenty-seven more times, counting aloud. He didn't struggle, like my mother. He did not possess her character. The same character her daughter possesses.

The media would be surprised to know how passionate I felt as I stabbed him. My feelings, the first after so many years, were surely different from whatever Mifflin must have felt as he murdered my mother, although I'll never be certain. Pressure lifted from my heart when I pierced his. My mind cleared of thoughts as blood and brain tissue gushed from his mutilated left eye. His body cooled and I defrosted. I watched his life dwindle much as I had watched my mother's life fade, and now I feel released. Finally I've reached the end of the corrupted vein and moved beyond that constricting tunnel into a world of complete and utter freedom. I have arrived back where I began, into a state of innocence. Justice has been accomplished. Don't you agree?

Many questions have been asked about me, but I have questions of my own and I hope you'll consider them calmly and rationally now that you've heard how it was. Do I deserve a worse fate than Mr. Mifflin's? Is my crime more heinous than his? I'm charged with murder one. The papers say I'll get life in prison unless I plead insanity, but I can't do that. He killed my mother. I killed him. What act could be more rational? An eye for an eye. Isn't that the purest form of justice? You decide.

PRINTED BY THE WORKERS OF
IMPRIMERIE D'ÉDITION MARQUIS
IN SEPTEMBER 1994
MONTMAGNY (QUÉBEC)